"So much has happened since then, for both of us...since you left."

But Brig had pulled her off the path into the shelter of the big sycamore tree by the front porch. Surprised by his movement and her own lack of resistance, Molly gazed at him, trying to read his expression. In the soft glow of light from the living room, she could barely make out his eyes, so dark and...dear. The years hadn't changed that.

"We were finished long ago," she said to save herself. "There's nothing—"

"There's *something*," he insisted. "Ever since Indiana at least."

Molly couldn't deny that. "But those were a few days out of time," she murmured. "I can't go back—"

The rest was never said. As Molly stood there, unmoving, he grasped her shoulders to draw her closer, and then Brig's mouth was touching hers.

Dear Reader,

I love a good reunion story! I always have.

It's not as if, in my "real" life, I'm still pining for the one that got away. The only guy I do remember who twisted me into knots years ago came nowhere near being Mr. Right for Me. In other words, I don't yearn for another reality, for what might have been. I like my life just the way it is.

Still. There's something about first love revisited—in fiction anyway—that always gets to me and touches my heart. That relationship history intensifies both conflict and emotion.

In this book Molly and Brig were engaged once and headed for the altar, but their wedding never happened. Since then Molly has had other losses in her life; she's not taking any more chances. Besides, some things never change, and for her Brig is one of them. In his military career he is still all about risk. He's a true daredevil whose life is filled with danger. Just what Molly doesn't need.

But, well, you know that old saying about the best-laid plans. In spite of the years and the distance between them, neither of my characters has forgotten the other. When romance knocks at the door once again, Molly and Brig must face their long-unresolved feelings for each other after all. Add an adorable baby to the mix and even more second chances begin to seem at least possible.

And yet having all Molly's dreams come true at last won't be easy for her or for Brig. They have some difficult choices to make. First, they both must learn to let go of the past—including loss—before they can find their own happily ever after.

I hope you enjoy their roller-coaster ride in these pages as much as I enjoyed writing it.

Happy reading!

Best,
Leigh

HARLEQUIN HEARTWARMING

Leigh Riker

If I Loved You

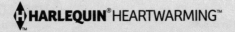
HARLEQUIN® HEARTWARMING™

Recycling programs
for this product may
not exist in your area.

ISBN-13: 978-0-373-36684-2

IF I LOVED YOU

HARLEQUIN®

Printed in U.S.A.

www.Harlequin.com

LEIGH RIKER

like many readers and writers, grew up with her nose in a book, and to this day she can't imagine a better way to spend time than to curl up with a good romance novel– unless it is to write one! When not at home on her small Southern mountain, the Ohio native and award-winning author likes to travel with her husband, the model hero (of course) for her stories. With added inspiration from her mischievous Maine coon cat always perched on her desk, she is at work on a new novel.

To the memory of
Virginia Helen Riker,
the best mother-in-law ever…
Somewhere out there, I know you're still dancing

CHAPTER ONE

"HOW DO WOMEN ever manage?"

Brig Collier had no clue. In the past twenty-four hours, through seven and a half time zones, he had seen females nowhere near his size juggle crying infants, fussy toddlers and screaming five-year-olds without breaking a sweat. He figured it had something to do with different elbow joints and pelvic structure.

Even getting out of a cab was a major ordeal. Worse, now he was talking to himself. After fumbling for his wallet, his brain fogged from travel, he paid the fare, then heaved himself from the taxi's rear seat into the pouring rain.

He reached back in for the overstuffed diaper bag and, finally, for the baby. He lifted her out of the mandatory car seat she'd been sitting in, but Laila just didn't fit in the crook of his arm. One tiny leg insisted on poking out from her blanket. Poor kid.

Brig felt like a total failure. Never mind his

expertise with the black-ops stuff that was his bread and butter. He was still trying to deal with the shock of becoming all too suddenly a stand-in father.

He waited while the driver unloaded their bags from the trunk. One for him, three for Laila. By the time she reached kindergarten, they'd probably be traveling with a U-Haul.

The cabbie couldn't hide his smirk. "Good luck, mister." He probably had a dozen kids and could handle six at a time. As he pulled away in his cab, he called out the window, "The first one's always the hardest."

Brig frowned. Could it be more obvious that he didn't know what he was doing? He *always* knew what he was doing. His life depended on it…and so, unfortunately, did the lives of others. As if he needed that reminder, now he had Laila, and Brig meant to do right by her.

He gazed around, but for one jet-lagged second he couldn't remember where he was. Oh, yeah, not in Wardak province, Afghanistan. No bullets whizzed past his head here. This was Liberty Courthouse. Small-town America in the heartland of Ohio.

His heartbeat settled. He was looking

straight at his parents' neat suburban house, the safe place he needed for Laila.

The baby whimpered. Cold water dripped from Brig's hair, making him shiver. And he realized he was standing in the rain like a turkey with its mouth open. Laila was getting wet, too. Brig hurried up the walk to the modest house he'd once called home.

It looked…empty?

Alarm flashed through him. How could that be? After he leaned on the doorbell a third time, he realized no one must be inside.

Brig hadn't been here in a while. He had no door key to the house.

What to do?

Laila would have to have a bottle soon, dry clothes, a clean diaper.

Other than his absent parents, he had no relatives in town. His friends had moved away. As for the neighbors…he'd burned that bridge long ago, especially with *her*.

Nonetheless, the next minute he was picking a path across the sodden lawn anyway with Laila in his arms. He'd left her car seat and most of their luggage on his parents' doorstep to lighten his load, but the insistent memory of a brown-haired girl with laughing green eyes weighed him down at every step. *Molly.* He'd be lucky if she didn't kick him across the street.

The very picture of a desperate man, he carried Laila up the sidewalk to Molly's house. She probably no longer lived here, either. But no doubt her dad still did, except the man would likely greet him with a shotgun.

Brig climbed the steps, one foot slipping on a wet slate tile. Startled, he lost his balance, nearly tossing Laila and him into the rain-flattened peony bushes that flanked the porch.

He grabbed the railing to steady himself at the same time a blast of noise from inside the house assaulted his eardrums. A party? Not in his honor, for sure.

Maybe he shouldn't have come back to Liberty.

But he had to consider Laila's welfare now, not that of the men under his command. Not his own.

MOLLY DIDN'T BELIEVE in bad omens. As if there were any other kind, including the rain that now slashed the windows. She was already running late, and even the red-and-white banner stretched over the dining room archway didn't bring her usual smile. The party guests in the living room, ranging in age from six months to sixty years, had begun arriving early, well before midday—had she put the wrong time on the invitations?—and most of them seemed to be talking at once. Every minute or two, the doorbell rang again.

Normally Molly loved parties. At least, she had loved them when there was something to celebrate with that special someone. Now, in the midst of her annual Valentine's Day bash, she was merely going through the motions for other people.

What else could go wrong?

Maybe the romantic holiday itself had unsettled her.

February was no longer her favorite month, and except for her dad, Molly had loved only two other men in her life. The first she'd rather not think about. The second, sadly, was gone, too.

Determined not to slide further into a slump, she turned to finish with the decorations, hoping no one would notice her disorganization. She should have stayed up later last night, but then, she hadn't expected the horde to get here this soon. She stuck another heart-shaped decal on the back of a dining room chair. And gave thanks for the blessings she still had.

Her friends. Her family. Her widowed father. Thomas—also known as Pop—was already in his element, riding small children on his knee, telling corny jokes to the teenagers, ignoring his diet to drink a beer or two with the men. Molly wouldn't spoil his fun.

The family—most of all Pop, who still mourned her mother—relied on her. She was great at holding them together, and proud of it. If this was her fate in life now, instead of a house full of babies to care for and a husband to love, so be it. Molly didn't expect to find love again. Her family and her day care center, Little Darlings, had to be enough.

And they would be. Molly already needed to expand the center. If all her current plans went well, she could take in more children, hire more assistants to improve her already good teacher-to-student ratio and enhance her program.

Still, she couldn't shake this stubborn foreboding, her feeling that something was about to happen that would change her life again.

And as if someone had just been cued, the doorbell chimed once more.

In a last attempt to alter her mood, she

dabbed one remaining shiny red heart decal at the corner of her mouth, like a beauty mark. Then she shoved the now-decorated chairs back under the table and went to greet her newest guest, determined to enjoy herself if it killed her.

But when she plowed through the crowded living room and opened the front door, her smile vanished. Molly froze. She knew exactly why she had felt such foreboding.

In the doorway stood a tall, all-too-familiar man. His piercing blue eyes met her gaze of recognition, equally shocked.

Molly's heart tripped on itself as too many memories flooded her mind. She tried to focus on his rain-dampened hair, dark and sleek against his head, but his gaze kept drawing hers back. She had to admit he was still the most attractive man she'd ever seen.

Molly exchanged a glance with her sister, who stood on the other side of the living room, a party hat in one hand. Ann lifted her eyebrows, and Molly stifled the urge to flee. She was no longer a naive twenty-two-year-old. He might still be handsome, but at thirty and a widow, she was immune, she reassured herself. Why let his abrupt reappearance shake her?

Yet the bluish circles of fatigue under those eyes threatened to undo her. If only she could hide behind the red heart pasted at the corner of her mouth, cool the heat that rose in her face. The last person she'd expected to see was the man she had once loved to distraction, the man who hadn't wanted to make that final commitment to Molly on their wedding day. Brigham Collier. Her ex-fiancé, the first terrible loss in her life, had come back.

Holding a baby!

THE PARTY WENT downhill from there. After Brig walked in, Molly was definitely not in a festive mood. The good thing was, nobody noticed except Pop, whose back went rigid with disapproval as soon as he spied Brig. Apparently he hadn't forgotten, either, what had happened eight years ago.

"Look at this adorable baby," one of Molly's cousins cooed, crossing the room with her arms outstretched. "Take off that soaked trench coat and give this poor child to me."

Looking disoriented, Brig didn't move except to relinquish the baby. Like Molly, he seemed numb. He was an only child, and his smaller family never had get-togethers of such utter chaos. Then, too, he wasn't a homebody like Molly, who had never been out of Ohio. No. Brig had left Liberty Courthouse right after he'd run out on her. To this day, according to his worried mother, he preferred flying around the world, getting in and out of trouble on behalf of some quasimilitary outfit no one was supposed to know about. Trying to get himself killed.

Brig was all about risk.

Molly, who had suffered enough loss, hated the very thought of risk.

For years, she reminded herself, she and Brig had literally been worlds apart. The last she'd heard, he was somewhere in Afghanistan.

If he expected her to welcome him warmly, he had some nerve. She peered behind him but didn't see a wife, which didn't mean he didn't have one somewhere. Before she had all her defenses in place, Brig walked right toward her, his gaze as piercing as a laser.

His deep voice sent an unwanted shiver down her spine.

"Hey, Molly." He bent as though to kiss her cheek, but Molly stepped back to avoid contact. Seeming to sense her rejection, Brig glanced away. "I didn't know you'd be here," he said. "Or that you'd still be putting on this show every year. Sorry to burst in—"

"No, really, it's a party. The more, the merrier." She pasted a smile on her face but folded her arms across her chest. "Actually, I haven't been here," she went on, "but things change…life changes…and now I'm back."

Apparently so was he. But why? And for how long?

Not that it mattered to Molly.

"My parents weren't exactly expecting us," he said, then explained about new locks and the key he didn't have. "Do you know where they are?"

She hesitated. "No, but since your dad retired, they come and go all the time." Unlike Thomas, Molly thought, who stayed home way too much. She paused again, wishing Pop had other interests besides the house and, above all, Molly. "We invited them to the party. I thought they were coming, but maybe they made other plans."

Brig frowned. "Do you or Thomas have the new key to their house?"

"I'm afraid not."

Last summer Molly had watered the Colliers' garden while they were on vacation, but that hadn't involved her going inside.

She risked a peek at the baby in her cousin's arms and felt a familiar, deep ache. Surely Brig's parents would have spread the word about their first grandchild. If that had been Molly's baby, Pop would have trumpeted the news.

As for Brig, she hadn't heard a word about any wedding, either.

"I didn't know you were married," she murmured, unable to stop herself.

"Me? In my line of work? No, I'm not." He shifted, looking uncomfortable at the reminder that he'd once left Molly. Across the living room the baby, who was being passed around and admired, began to cry. Brig quickly retrieved the tiny bundle and picked up a bulky diaper bag. "Long story," he said with a harried glance toward the kitchen. "I'll tell you later. She's hungry. I need to fix her a bottle. May I—?"

"Follow me," Molly said with a sinking feeling.

She didn't usually turn away from people. Right now that meant Brig.

And, to Molly's utter dismay, a tiny, helpless infant she couldn't bear to even look at full-on.

BRIG STOOD IN the kitchen doorway, the diaper bag weighing down one shoulder and Laila fussing in his arms. Two laughing teenagers sat at the table, and Brig watched them swipe red frosting from a lopsided cake.

"Stop that, you two," Molly said, but her tone was laced with affection. "I'm no gourmet chef, and you're not helping my cake appear any better." She smiled. "My cousins," she told Brig. "Second cousins."

Crooked or not, the cake made Brig's mouth water. The whole room smelled of comfort foods: fried chicken, baked beans laced with brown sugar and onions, and, if Brig wasn't mistaken, his favorite macaroni and cheese.

Red heart decals—the same kind Molly wore on her face—skipped gaily across the kitchen chairs, and in the dining room on his way through, a green balloon had bounced from the ceiling on his head.

He didn't belong here. This was like all those birthday parties he'd gone to as a kid but had never felt part of. As though he'd forgotten to bring a present. With a father in the military, he and his parents had lived all over, and making friends became harder and harder as Brig grew older. It was the only life he knew and one reason he'd followed in his father's and grandfather's footsteps. Now, after hearing Dari and Pashto being spoken every day in Afghanistan, even the cadence of English sounded foreign to him. Brig kept losing words in what was being said.

Molly, on the other hand, fit right in. She handed the boy and girl a bowl of potato salad and a relish tray from the fridge. "Set these in the dining room, please."

When the giggling pair vanished, she waved Brig toward a chair.

"Sit. You look like you need to."

Brig put down the diaper bag but stayed on his feet, gently rocking Laila in his arms. His head ached.

All he wanted was sleep. All Molly wanted, he guessed, was to avoid him. She hadn't taken one real good look at the baby, either, and like a cat, Molly maintained a deliberate space between herself and him. Obviously, she hadn't forgiven him for breaking their engagement years ago. Not that she should. Not that he expected her to.

At the same time he couldn't seem to stop staring at her. The instant he'd seen her, his memories and his guilt had overwhelmed him. His gaze traveled now from her blunt-cut brown hair—shorter than he remembered—to her trim sweater, her fitted jeans and her feet in scarlet socks. But the red heart by her mouth was what kept his eyes riveted. Thick honey seemed to flow through him. *And what kind of jerk am I?* Molly, with her warmth and openness, had always deserved more.

"Do you have formula?" she asked, still keeping her distance.

It took Brig forever to find a can in the overloaded bag, a clean plastic liner for the bottle and one fresh nipple. Juggling Laila, he managed to put the whole contraption together. Then, Molly eyeing him with obvious suspicion as he walked past her, he opened the microwave and stuck it inside. One minute should do it. He hoped.

Right behind him, Molly almost stepped on his heel.

"You can't warm a baby's milk in there."

"Why not?"

"The bottle might feel cool to the touch, but the milk could be too hot in spots and burn a baby's mouth and throat." With an efficiency he could only admire, she took the bottle to the sink and held it under the water. When she seemed satisfied with the temperature, Molly thrust the bottle at Brig. "Shake some on your inner wrist before you give it to her—to make sure."

He sat down at the table, tried to nestle Laila into a good position, then watched her latch on to the nipple. He could hear the party noise swell from the living room, and the teenagers in the dining room were still giggling. When he glanced up, Molly was all but tapping her foot at his incompetence.

He knew she adored children, but how did she know about babies?

Brig guessed it was time to explain what he was doing with one. Or try to.

"This is Laila," he began. "She's two months old." He smiled down at the baby's intent expression as she drank, her dark eyes fixed on his face. He cleared his throat. "She isn't mine, in case you're wondering…." He trailed off, reluctant to call up the painful memories.

Molly waited for him to go on.

After a long moment Brig tried again. "I was on duty overseas. Hush-hush stuff, flying under the radar, the kind of thing we always do." It was one reason he'd left Molly. He hadn't wanted to worry about her worrying about him. At least, that was what he'd told himself then. "Long story short, Laila's dad was one of my men, one of the team. Sean… fell in love there with a local woman."

"And they had Laila," Molly guessed.

Brig nodded, still gazing down at the baby. Her tiny hand closed around his little finger, and his heart melted, which happened about ten times a day.

"They had Laila," he echoed, his tone husky. "Then, while she was still in the hospital with her mother after the birth, a bunch of insurgents hit the place. *Boom.* In the bombing, Laila's mom died instantly." He paused. "Her name was Zada. You know what that means?"

"No."

"The lucky one. But that day she wasn't so lucky…and Sean lived just long enough to make sure Laila was okay."

Molly's eyes had softened. "This must be hard to talk about. You don't have to go on, Brig."

Why was he surprised at her words? Molly had always been sensitive to other people. Once, she'd even been sensitive to him. Now he swallowed the pain that sometimes threatened to consume him. His anger over Sean and Zada was easier to feel and just as hard to forget.

"But I ask you, Molly—what kind of thing was that? A man goes to see his wife, his new daughter, the happiest kind of day for a young couple in love—a family for the first time—and he ends up dead. They do," he added.

Molly seemed to be holding her breath. "What about the baby? How did Laila survive that ghastly explosion?"

"The nurses claimed they wanted to give Sean and Zada some time together. They took the baby back to the nursery at the other end of the building minutes before the device went off. She didn't get a scratch, which is a miracle in itself. I spent the past two months entangled in red tape before I got permission to bring Laila to the States."

Molly's gaze brightened, as if a light had been turned on. "Your friend…asked *you* to keep her. If anything happened to him."

Brig nodded again. "We all make wills," he said, "before we deploy. Kind of a downer, wouldn't you say? But necessary when you think about it. I'm officially Laila's guardian now. Not the best choice of 'parent' for her in my opinion, but, yes, I promised Sean. Who would have guessed that he and Zada would both…that Laila…" How was Brig going to care for the little girl, though? She could stay with his folks when he was in the field, as they'd already agreed, but that arrangement would be temporary, and now he had to find them first.

Molly briefly touched his arm. "You've had a really bad time."

"Not just me," he said, wanting to change the subject before he totally fell apart. "I'm sorry about your husband. Mom told me."

There was another long silence while Molly appeared to gather herself, and Brig wondered if she felt as uneasy talking about this as he had about Sean and Zada.

"Thank you," she said at last, her voice husky. "Andrew was a great guy."

And I wasn't. She had a point, even unspoken. Brig couldn't fault her for not wanting to dredge up her sorrow. But still he went on.

"I remember Andrew Darling from school," Brig said, "but I didn't know him very well. He was a couple of years ahead of me. Two, I think. He always seemed quiet, but he was friendly. A serious kind of guy."

"He had this laugh, though," she said. "It always surprised me—when he wasn't the type for surprises. We were a lot alike, really, I guess. He was so steady, settled…"

Not like me.

The next words almost stuck in his throat. "Were you happy, Molly?"

He needed to hear her say yes, so he wouldn't continue to feel guilty for leaving. Yet he dreaded hearing her say just that.

"We were," she said at last, "but not nearly long enough. While we were together, yes, we were happy. Can we stop talking about this now?"

She fell silent, as if lost in her memories, and Brig knew again that the topic would have been better left alone. Like Sean and Zada. Still, this was his and Molly's starting point. A crazy sort of catching up.

In the next second Brig stiffened. Warmth had spread through his sleeve. But not from the touch of Molly's hand, which had dropped from his arm. He held out Laila and saw a widening stain on the fabric.

"She's wet," Molly noted with that little frown he remembered so well. "When was her diaper changed?"

Already feeling guilty, Brig checked his watch. "About five hours ago."

"Five *hours?*"

"On the hard floor in the customs area at JFK while we waited for our bags. I never had time between planes to buy more diapers, and at Frankfurt we ran low. I've been rationing Laila's changes."

Molly's soft eyes had turned steely, and her face appeared pale under the festive red heart stuck to her face.

Both he and the baby must look like dirty laundry, wrinkled and thrown together. Now they were both damp and not getting any drier. To Brig, that meant he was losing his grip on the situation—which had happened the first time Laila had screamed on the military cargo plane out of Bagram airfield near Kabul.

"Overseas," he said, "a local woman took care of Laila while I took care of business. Guess I'm not doing so well now."

Molly raised an eyebrow. Her expression challenged every one of his insecurities.

"You can use the spare room upstairs to change her."

Brig could hear the doubt in her tone, and his male pride kicked in. Their brief rapport— if it had even been that—was over. And here he'd thought he and Molly were doing okay as long as they avoided any mention of his betrayal of her.

"You think I can't change a diaper?" he asked icily.

That was pretty close to the truth.

Not waiting for her answer, he took Laila, the half-finished bottle, and stalked out of the room.

"WONDERFUL," MOLLY MUTTERED. "Why not just give a lecture or four or five to a man who's already half dead on his feet?"

And clearly hurting. The loss of his teammate and the orphaned child had shaken Brig. Just as Brig's questions about Andrew and Molly's marriage had shaken her.

She had noted the weary slump of his broad shoulders, and how he held the baby to him like a security blanket.

But Molly pushed aside the observations. There was a party going on, and for the next few hours she had to play hostess. With the rain still falling, she supervised the younger children's game of indoor tag. She refereed a fight over a TV basketball game. Pop should have known better than to get involved. She comforted her teenage cousin's angst and soothed toddler tears.

She taught four-year-old Ernie Barlow how to play pin the tail on the donkey—or, rather, on a SpongeBob SquarePants poster—then pretended not to see how her sister, Ann, ignored Ernie's dad, a new local sheriff's deputy who seemed to have a thing for her.

And Molly tried not to notice that Brig never came back downstairs to eat or to show off the baby.

By evening, when the festivities wound down, the house resembled a giant trash basket filled with broken toys and exploded balloons. As her guests prepared to leave, every child under the age of five was crying—a sure sign in Molly's experience of too much stimulation and total but happy exhaustion. For everyone but Molly, the party had been a huge success.

After all the guests left, she hurried upstairs. She found Brig in the spare room, where her offer to heat a late supper for him died on her lips. Brig lay sprawled on the double bed, sound asleep. Clearly he was down for the count. His face told her nothing, which was probably what he wanted after Molly's earlier criticism. Lying beside him, with Brig's arm over her like an anchor, the baby stared wide-eyed at the overhead light, flinching each time thunder rumbled in the night sky.

Now at last Molly gave in to the urge churning inside her during the party and slipped to her knees next to the bed. Brig must have dozed off in the midst of dressing Laila for the night. Her right arm was in one sleeve of an aquamarine sleeper, the other, still bare, waved in the air. Half the snaps on the sleeper were undone.

"You giving your old man a hard time?" Molly whispered.

At the sound of her voice, Laila turned her head as if searching for her. Molly reached out, brushing Brig's arm without meaning to, and quickly touched the baby's silky hair. Laila's gaze, dark as a midnight sea, met hers.

Molly's breath caught. She was a beautiful baby, another victim of the senseless violence that had taken both her parents. "Oh, sweetie," Molly murmured.

Blinking, she eased Brig's arm aside and heard him grunt in his sleep. She could hardly wake him and make them leave. Where would they go? A glance out the window told her Brig's parents were still gone. Not a single light glowed in the house next door. She tucked Laila into her sleeper, then snapped the garment all the way. The little girl's skin felt like velvet, and she smelled, as only a baby could, of sheer innocence. A baby like the one Molly had always yearned for, and lost.

Children were the best, yet the hardest, part of her job. She got to spend so much time with them, yet they were other people's, not her own.

On impulse she peeled the red heart from her face and leaned closer to stick it on Laila's chest, then nuzzled the infant's small belly.

And, against every instinct to protect her heart, Molly fell in love.

Like the rain that pounded against the windows and the thunder that still grumbled overhead, the feeling seemed to Molly another omen.

CHAPTER TWO

BRIG AWOKE THE next morning fully clothed
with no memory of having gone to bed—and
no knowledge of where he was. Disoriented,
he checked his watch, then made a quick cal-
culation. It was six-thirty in the evening in
Kabul, but eleven in the morning was late
enough here. He'd overslept.

For another moment, he lay yawning in the
sun-splattered bedroom—then recognition
dawned. Ah, right. He was in Molly's house.
Almost immediately, he heard a snuffle. Brig
shot upright and spotted the baby nearby in a
portable crib. Laila! Some guardian he made.

"Hungry, cupcake?"

He tucked in the shirt he'd worn all night,
fighting a growing sense of parental neglect,
and picked up the baby, who was swaddled
in a pastel-striped receiving blanket that
smelled of fresh air. He didn't recognize it
as one he'd crammed into their suitcases,
which he assumed were still on the porch

next door. Molly must have donated the wrap. Wearing yesterday's socks, he carried Laila downstairs. She needed more milk, and Brig needed coffee.

At the bottom of the steps in the front hall, as if running into an ambush, he met Molly's father. Thomas Walker turned from the door with the newspaper in hand. He didn't smile, and Brig remembered his stiff manner at the party. He imagined that Molly, not her dad, had let him stay the night—as if they'd had an option once he'd fallen asleep, one hundred ninety pounds of deadweight.

"The Reds are in trouble," Thomas said, reading the headline on page one.

For a second Brig thought the Russians were stirring up trouble again.

The older man gave a snort of disgust. "Barely into spring training and already headed for the bottom of the standings. Would you believe? Just traded their best pitcher for some rookie." He glanced out the front door's side window. "Look at that," he muttered.

Again, Brig missed the connection. "What?"

"Nosy woman across the street. Every time I get the paper, she's peering out." Without missing a beat, he said, "Doesn't look to me

like your folks are home yet. Didn't see anyone next door. You get any rest, Brigham?"

Brig nodded his head. "Passed out as soon
as I got horizontal." He still felt drained
and his eyes were grainy, but his stomach
growled. Or was that Laila's tummy? And
where had his parents gone, if not out for the
evening?

"Molly said you never ate dinner."

"Wasn't hungry." And where was she now?
"My stomach's off schedule, still in central
Asia."

"Well, there's coffee in the kitchen."

But Thomas sounded begrudging.

Brig shifted Laila from one arm to the
other. Dark haired, dark eyed and oblivious
to the undercurrents between the two men,
she sucked on a fist.

As if he couldn't help himself, Thomas
studied her. And Brig studied him. Molly's
dad was still a solid-looking man. Retirement
had added a slight paunch to Thomas's stomach, but even so, except for his brown hair
with touches of gray at his temples, he didn't
look his age.

Thomas gestured at Laila. "Baby sleep
okay?"

"I never heard her," Brig confessed,

knowing that wouldn't win him any points. "Thanks for finding her a crib."

"Molly keeps one here," he said in what sounded like a wistful tone. A condemnation of Brig for leaving Molly practically at the altar?

A dozen questions ran through his brain, but he didn't ask them. They were for Molly to answer, although maybe he had no right to ask. After the loss of her husband, she should find another man and have the family she'd always wanted, the family she and Brig had planned until he'd thrown a wrench into things and hightailed it out of Liberty.

Better for her, he had tried to think.

And if he'd stayed…he wouldn't have Laila now.

"And Molly must have dressed the baby for bed," he said.

Thomas eyed him like a bug he wanted to squash.

"Must have."

Which meant she'd seen Brig asleep, lying down on the job. He glanced toward the kitchen. Inhaled the lingering smells of bacon and toast, and that freshly brewed coffee.

"Molly's not here," Thomas said. "You can fix yourself anything you like. She was up at six cleaning the mess from yesterday, made me breakfast, then took her second cup of coffee to the office." Thomas waved toward the backyard.

Office?

Thomas's casual statement told Brig just how little he knew of Molly these days. All he remembered seeing was an old carriage barn at the rear of the property. His mother, the neat freak, had complained it was an eyesore.

Laila squirmed in his arms and Brig's shaky parental confidence took another nosedive. Mano a mano with Thomas, he'd nearly forgotten his original mission in coming downstairs.

"I'd better grab some of that coffee, then get going. I heated the last of Laila's formula yesterday. Hope I can find the same brand in Liberty. Fast." If he bought the wrong stuff or used whole milk instead of the prepared infant kind and the baby got sick, Molly would likely be on him in a second. And how had Laila made it through the night without waking him to feed her?

Thomas took another, longer look at the baby. For an instant Brig was sure he saw yearning cross the older man's face.

"Molly went to the corner store for you last

night. She fed the baby around eight, at midnight and four, and again this morning. She left another bottle ready on the stove."

Wow. Surprised by the information, Brig didn't know whether to feel guilty because Laila must have kept Molly up most of the night, grateful that she'd let him sleep or relieved that she'd done both. Actually, he felt all three.

"Thanks," Brig said, which seemed inadequate.

"Don't thank me." Thomas had turned away and was taking his newspaper into the living room. End of discussion, or so Brig thought. But Thomas wasn't finished. "Oh. Molly said to tell you her sheriff friend brought your bags and the baby seat from next door before he left the party."

Then, as if his feelings had built like a volcano set to erupt, he spun around again.

"I'm not going to ask why you're here, Brigham. I guess this baby is answer enough. For now." Thomas pointed the rolled-up paper at him. "But don't think I've forgotten what happened between you and Molly. She and Ann are the best daughters I could ever have, and Molly's had enough grief in her life. I swear, if you hurt her—"

"I don't intend to hurt her."

"—like you did before, you'll answer to me."

Brig had no reply. He'd been a "father" himself for a short time and he was still all thumbs at the job, but, like Thomas with Molly, he knew he would protect her to the death from any threat.

To Thomas, Brig must represent six feet plus of threat.

Brig headed for the kitchen, duly warned.

He would need more caffeine than usual to get through the day in this close-knit family, which he understood even less than he did taking care of Laila. Far less than he might the workings of the Taliban.

But before Brig exited the room, he got in the last word.

"I'll work on finding a key to Mom and Dad's house. Move Laila next door as soon as I can. That would be best for you—and for Molly."

MONDAY WAS NOT Molly's favorite day of the week at Little Darlings, or anywhere else, and sometime between last Friday and this morning she had lost her equilibrium.

Oh, who are you kidding, Molly? She knew exactly when.

Around her, toy trucks clashed, the laughter of children shrilled and someone pounded on a drum. She couldn't term the noise unusual, yet her jangled nerves wanted her to shout surrender. Today her day care center's proximity to Pop's house seemed way too close. That was, way too close to Brig.

She hadn't been herself since she'd spied him yesterday standing in the doorway with Laila, like a broken dream come back to haunt her.

No, make that a nightmare.

At least the rain had finally stopped last night. The clouds had disappeared as if someone had rolled up a rug, and by midnight the sky had been full of stars. Holding Laila, feeding her while Brig slept, Molly had watched the weather improve even as a storm still roiled inside her.

Fortunately, for the rest of the day, she wouldn't have another chance to dwell on the situation. Which was a good thing, because without half trying, she could summon the image of Brig's lean, fit body and handsome, serious face.

Too bad for her, but he looked better than

ever. Any remnants of boyishness in his face were now gone. In their place was an uncompromising set of male features with interesting planes and angles.

It wasn't every day that an old love walked back into her life, and when she added Laila to the picture, Molly felt shaken anew. Better to keep her mind on business.

At the end of the afternoon, many of "her" children had left by the time Jeff Barlow, little Ernie's dad, arrived dressed in his tan sheriff's deputy uniform. At the same time, her sister, Ann, who helped with the babies in the nursery, reached the front door from outside after walking baby Ashley Jones and her mother out to their car. Under a darkening sky, she stopped cold.

Her expression told Molly that her sister's timing couldn't have been worse for her. The distinct chill in the air didn't just come from the freezing wind.

Molly bit back a sigh. Jeff was one of her favorite people, and she wished her sister would stop giving him the cold shoulder.

As if he hadn't noticed Ann's frostiness, Jeff held the door open for her, but Ann took care not to brush against him as she came inside. She hurried down the hall with just a murmured "Thank you."

Jeff raised an eyebrow at Molly. "Hello to her, too," he said.

"I don't know what gets into her," Molly said, hoping to soothe his feelings.

But of course she did.

He looked glum. "I called twice last week to ask her out. Once, for dinner, and then to see a romantic comedy playing in town—don't most women enjoy a good chick flick?—but she said no. Both times." He paused. "Not that I've been dating enough to be up on what a woman might like."

Molly had heard about Jeff's bitter divorce. Clearly he was wounded. But when he and Ann had started dating a few months ago, Molly had hoped that their relationship would take root and grow, and that Ann could be happy again, as well. Then, all at once, to Molly's dismay, Ann had pulled back like a turtle withdrawing into its shell.

"I know she wanted to see that movie," Molly said without thinking.

"Yeah," he mumbled. "Just not with me."

She eyed him sympathetically. Jeff was just the latest example of romance gone awry in her sister's life. Ann didn't date often or, when she did, for very long. Molly had no idea what—if anything—she should do about that.

"Ann's a good-looking woman," Jeff added, "and she can be very funny when she lets her hair down. We like the same kind of books, Mexican food, sunsets... I don't understand what happened. I thought we had clicked," he went on. "I mean, she seemed to enjoy the one dinner we had together. We found a lot to talk about. And we went hiking one weekend with my son—"

"Daddy! Guess what I made?"

As if on cue, Jeff's four-year-old son, his spitting image, raced up to them, his mop of sandy hair flopping into his blue eyes. He thrust a green construction-paper triangle studded with spiral pasta dyed a fluorescent pink into Jeff's face.

"Whoa, buddy." Jeff dodged the pointed artwork that threatened to put out an eye and gathered Ernie up with a grin. A blob of glue dripped onto Jeff's clean uniform. "This is one great-looking..." He scrambled for a word.

"You know. It's a tree!"

"Ah." Jeff shot Molly an amused glance. "Ernie, I've never seen a better one."

Ernie beamed. "I did it all by myself."

Jeff's plain-to-see love for his son caused Molly's throat to tighten. Her Andrew would also have made a good dad, and Ernie was like the child they'd never had.

"Molly, do you like it, too?" the little boy asked.

She ruffled his hair. "I love it. Your father is an excellent judge of art."

Smiling, Molly walked them to the outer doors. A couple of homeward-bound little stragglers ran past them, scuffling and laughing. Benjamin Crandall, a pint-size troublemaker of late, made sure to knock against Ernie on his way. But Molly focused on her more pressing problem. As she said goodbye to each child and parent, she could sense the tension still radiating from Jeff's broadshouldered body.

Her smile faded. He was a nice man. A decent man. A solid man.

And it wasn't as if men like Jeff Barlow grew on trees, including pink ones like Ernie's collage.

"I'll talk to Ann," she said, following Jeff's glance toward the nursery.

"I don't know that you should, Molly. But is it—" he nodded toward his small son

"—you know. Because if that's her problem—" His voice had hardened in Ernie's defense.

"I'll talk to her," Molly repeated.

As if she was an expert on romantic relationships.

Jeff didn't wave goodbye when they left, but Ernie gave Molly an exuberant flip of one chubby hand. He was the most lovable four-year-old at the center.

Once Jeff had buckled Ernie into his car seat in the back of the cruiser and pulled out of the lot, Molly took off for the playroom adjacent to the nursery.

She organized paint cups in the art cupboard for the next day. Within a moment, Ann appeared.

"Don't say a word," she warned. "I don't need the big-sister act."

Molly faced her, intent on speaking her mind anyway. "I can't believe how you treated Jeff. I'm disappointed in you."

Ann tossed honey-brown bangs out of her eyes. They were a rich hazel, their mother's color. "Maybe I just like being an old maid."

"Don't be smart. There are no old maids these days." Molly tried to lighten the mood. "Not since Aunt Tilly went to her heavenly reward still 'intact,' as she always said, at the age of ninety." They shared a weak smile before Molly went on. "You're only twenty-seven, Ann. You can't seriously want to be alone for the rest of your life."

"Why not? You are."

Ouch. The words echoed in the silence.

"I'm sorry," Ann murmured. "That was an awful thing to say. But I should never have gone out with him, and the sooner Jeff Barlow realizes I'm not interested, the better. With Ernie here at the center, I can hardly avoid him."

Molly's eyes still stung from Ann's earlier words. "You sure try."

"Yes, and my new best friend is caller ID."

The throwaway tone didn't sit well with Molly. She bustled around the room, gathering stray blocks, stacking them and trying to wrestle the remnants of her own fresh pain into some sort of order.

She didn't have a choice about being alone, but in Molly's view, Ann was throwing away her potential for happiness with both hands—if not with the sheriff, then with someone else.

Molly shut the cupboard doors for the night and turned to find Ann with tears in her eyes. And Molly's shoulders sagged. "Is it because of Ernie?" she asked, echoing Jeff's earlier concern. "He's a great little kid."

Ann sniffed. "I know."

"And I know you like children. You're wonderful with the babies here. You like them so much you just had to carry Melissa Jones's diaper bag to the car so you could spend one more minute today with her little Ashley."

As if caught committing some terrible crime, Ann flushed.

"Well, you are good," Molly said. "Would I have hired you if not?"

Ann rolled her eyes. "You hired me because you were shorthanded, and I had my degree in education and no other job."

Which was only part of the reason. Yes, Molly had needed to fill that staff position, but was she simply enabling her sister to avoid dealing with the long-ago tragedy that had changed her life?

For years Ann had not only kept to herself, but she refused to go more than a mile or two from home. Her apartment was just blocks away from Little Darlings, and every day she walked to work. Ann owned a car, which she maintained, and for which she renewed her registration and driver's license. But she never got behind the wheel. She hadn't driven once since the accident.

Just as Molly rarely drove past the house she and Andrew had shared in Cincinnati's Hyde Park neighborhood—and always told herself it was out of her way now. She'd been living with Pop since shortly after Andrew died.

Molly softened her tone. "I also hired you because I love you," she said. "And to keep you close," she added with a teasing grin, "so you can take over when Pop gets to be too much for me. In the meantime…I honestly thought you and Jeff were going somewhere. Why not give him—"

"A chance?"

"If it doesn't work out, you can move on."

"Like you?" Ann asked.

Another barb for Molly.

"That's enough," Molly said, barely holding her temper in check.

"Or maybe I'm wrong." Ann hesitated, frowning. "Maybe I'm not the only one here with man trouble. I've talked to Dad. What is Brigham Collier doing in the house?"

"Waiting for his parents," Molly said.

The image crossed her mind again before she could stop it. Brig, his dark hair tousled, his blue eyes unable to hide his exhaustion. Brig all but asleep on his feet, holding Laila in his arms.

"Really? Waiting? That's all?" Ann said. "You're sure?"

Molly looked away. She could feel her cheeks coloring. "I'm sure."

Ann was no fan of Brig's, she knew. From the moment he'd canceled his wedding to Molly and Ann had returned her bridesmaid's dress to the store, she'd kept him at the top of her personal blacklist. Molly reminded herself that she and Ann were sisters. How could she blame Ann for caring about her?

"You don't have to worry," she said, hating that she was justifying herself. "You won't have to pick up the pieces again. And may I point out that Jeff Barlow is a very different guy?"

"Oh, no, you don't," Ann said, turning toward the door.

"Just something for you to think about," Molly murmured, but Ann was gone, leaving her alone with her unhappy awareness of her sister's increasingly isolated existence. Like Pop. Then she thought of herself.

Hadn't she learned *her* lesson years ago? Brig wouldn't stay long in Liberty Court-

house now, either. Well, she had no intention
of letting him into her life again. Even if he
did have the most adorable baby on earth.

CHAPTER THREE

Hey, Collier. Trip go okay? How's the little lady? The guys already miss her. Bet your mom and dad like her, too, huh? Off to find some bad guys. H.

BRIG READ THE email again from his team-mate, but his smile didn't last. His thoughts were elsewhere. He had meant what he told Thomas. He had no intention of hurting Molly.

At her kitchen table he punched another number into his cell phone. And frowned. After his earlier run-in with Thomas, he'd double-checked next door again, but Thomas had been right. Still no one was home. His parents' mobile number kept telling him they were unavailable and sending his calls to voice mail. Their landline didn't help, either. Right next door, behind a lock he couldn't access, their answering machine announced their voice mail was full.

Many of those messages were probably from him. He hung up one last time. Molly was home and in the kitchen before he could get out of her way.

"It's freezing out again." She bustled around the kitchen, taking off her coat, shaking out her wind-whipped hair. "Where's Laila?"

"Still napping. I hope. I'll see in a minute." He closed his phone, determined to clear the air. "Molly, I didn't mean to crash on you like that yesterday. Thanks," he said, "for giving us a room last night. And feeding Laila for me. You've been more than generous, considering…" Then he couldn't find the words he really needed to say.

"What?"

"Well, you know. For one thing…" He looked past her toward the dining room, the front door. "My running off like that years ago—as if I couldn't get away fast enough."

"You did appear to be in a hurry." She attempted a smile, but it didn't come. "Of course, watching a hometown girl walk down the aisle in a long white dress can't be as exciting as trying to save the world."

Brig felt as if she'd punched him in the stomach. Her tone was blithe—deliberately so?—but she made him sound petty. He deserved that, too.

Molly pushed up her sleeves and started to fix dinner. His gaze tracked her movements as she took hamburger from the fridge, a package of buns from the bread box. She flipped on a burner, formed patties from the meat, slapped them into a skillet. Who knew a woman's efficiency in the kitchen could be a turn-on?

"Well," she said, just as he had, "now we've gotten that off our chests…"

"Have we? Molly. I didn't want to leave you then. I just wanted—"

"To leave," she finished for him. "No, let's not go there. That's all water under the bridge," she said, "and we're not kids, Brig. Eight years is way too long for me to hold a grudge. But last night, I admit, I was a little— a lot—shocked to see you."

"And Laila, certainly."

"And Laila," she agreed. "I doubt Pop's very keen on having you here, but—"

"No, he's not. He already warned me not to make another mistake."

She quirked an eyebrow, then opened the pantry door. Brig studied her slim figure and the way she fit her jeans, but with Thomas's words in mind, he knew he had no business ogling Molly.

"Your dad's a hard case," he said to distract himself. "Kind of like my dad. So I'm used to that. When I was a kid and my father was still on active duty, he could be a real force to contend with." He paused. "But then, so was I."

"No wonder Pop and Joe are friends as well as neighbors."

"Yeah, and a good thing Dad's mellowed over the years."

Have you? But Molly didn't pose the question.

Brig looked down at the cell phone in his hand. "Sorry to still be sticking around. I've tried all day to reach my parents." He could have kicked himself. "This is my own fault. The last time I spoke to them, I told them not to phone me again. Communications are never the best over there, and I was busy making arrangements to bring Laila to the States. I said my next call would be to let them know when we'd arrive."

"So your coming back wasn't a surprise."

"No, but too bad I couldn't give them a firm date. I don't know who else to call now," he said. "Another locksmith just told me he can't open the door to a house that isn't mine. No surprise there."

"Oh, dear."

"Yeah, I knew better than to ask. It was a desperate move on my part." Another one, he thought, and stood. He could have picked the old lock—one of his many warrior skills— but the new dead bolt was a more difficult obstacle. So was the alarm system, assuming his father had remembered to set it.

Molly emerged from the pantry. "I wish I could think of someone…"

"Don't worry. As soon as Laila wakes from her nap, I'll phone for a cab and we'll be out of your hair." And Thomas's. He flipped open the phone again. "I'm sure we can get a hotel room for tonight. My folks are bound to turn up soon."

That sounded pathetic even to Brig, and deepened his frown.

"And miss seeing them when they pull in the drive?" Molly hesitated a bit too long, then said, as if she'd surprised herself, "I've forgotten my manners. You have the perfect vantage point from here to see when they get home."

The warm air in the cozy kitchen carried the aroma of seared beef, and Brig's mouth watered. Or was it the sight of Molly's green eyes dark with concern?

She'd always been pretty, but at thirty she had an inner beauty to match. Too bad he'd blown his chance with her long ago.

Not even hearing what she'd said, he carried on with his line of thought. "In the meantime, who knows where my parents are?" he said. "Or with whom? Most of the landline numbers for their friends have gone to new phone company customers because Mom and Dad's gang have all moved to Florida or Arizona. The couple I remember best," he went on, "is living in Mexico. If my folks went to visit one of their old friends, I wouldn't know where to even start a search. As for any new people…"

He looked hopefully at Molly, who only shook her head.

"I really don't know who might be in their circle now. Your parents are more social than Pop. Since he retired, he sticks close to home. He golfs occasionally with your dad, but that's all."

"Well, my folks are for sure not in town. No activity I can think of would keep them away this long."

"You didn't call them from...wherever on the way home?" Molly asked.

Brig shook his head. "When I finally got a military flight out, it was either jump on the plane with Laila while we had the chance or miss out and have to wait until whenever the next hop came." He paused. "I called home from Frankfurt, from my home base on the East Coast and then from JFK, even from here in Cincy. But I had to leave messages...." He trailed off. "The folks must have already gone. And then Laila was being a handful with the time change."

"I'm sure you did the best you could," Molly said.

Not exactly, Brig thought. He was always hard on himself—partly because he was the son and only child of a military family with strict discipline and even stricter expectations.

He knew his best wasn't always good enough. To prove it, he said, "Doesn't take most people I've seen twenty minutes to change a diaper. That was false bravado you saw last night."

"Practice," Molly murmured. "That's all you need."

He raised an eyebrow. "And about fifty books on child care."

She was rinsing potatoes at the sink, chopping them, then dropping the pieces into a pot of water. For whipped potatoes? Another of his favorites. He hadn't had them in months.

She pointed a paring knife at the backyard. "There's a library out in the center—my day care business behind the house. You're welcome to borrow any of those books, or all of them."

Which was another of his problems. Time to read—time to do anything. Brig's gut tightened. His emergency leave couldn't last forever. He needed to find his parents and get Laila into their temporary care before he had to take off again for parts unknown. Once he got that call, time would be off the table. He sure couldn't take Laila back with him into the danger that had ended her parents' lives.

He studied the play of light on Molly's hair as she set the pan of potatoes on the stove, then turned on the burner. Her vulnerable nape tempted him.

Brig shifted in his seat. "I, uh, appreciate the offer. About the books," he added. "But as I said, Laila and I had better clear out. We've taken up enough space here, and I don't want to rile your father."

"Nonsense. Stay for dinner," she said. "Just...stay. I'll handle Pop."

The words had slipped from her mouth as naturally as they might have years ago before Brig had left her. How many times had Molly or her mother invited him to dinner? Made him feel like part of their family? Thomas was right again. She had been so welcoming, when he didn't deserve it. She looked so good, he wondered how he had left in the first place.

Yet what else, really, could she say?

Molly had the biggest heart of anyone he'd ever known.

Which only made him feel worse, as if he *was* taking advantage.

Her father's warning echoed in his mind. Brig had brought Laila home with only one thought: find a safe place for her with his parents. He realized he needed a long-term solution, but that would require some hard thinking about what was best for the baby and for him. What he hadn't planned on was seeing a widowed Molly again, being attracted to her after all these years.

With a warrior's sense of danger, Brig

knew he was in trouble. Staying in Molly's house did seem more practical than staying in a hotel, but his proximity to her would only exacerbate the memory of their broken engagement, and renew the tension between them. She was now the girl next door all grown up, and she offered the brief haven a war-weary Brig badly needed. But…

He would *not* hurt her again, even as he wondered how to keep his hands off her. Before he left, as he would have to again, he needed to win Molly's forgiveness.

Maybe staying for another night could help accomplish that goal.

"WE HAVE A guest room," Molly reminded her father after dinner that night. "Brig might as well use it."

Molly had second thoughts of her own, but she'd already blurted out the invitation. She could hardly turn Brig and that sweet baby out into the night. The temperature had started to drop at noon. By the time her kids had gone home, the sky was black with clouds. It was already sleeting outside, and soon the roads would turn icy. The thought of Brig in a taxi, sliding along slick streets, then trying to cope with Laila in some cramped hotel room kept playing through her mind.

Yet how could she convince Pop it was all right for Brig and Laila to stay when she wasn't that sure herself?

As if to prove her point, Thomas cast a sour glance at the ceiling. Upstairs, Brig was struggling to get the baby to sleep, and Molly suppressed a fresh wave of frustration. She was still worried about Ann, but Pop wasn't helping her mood.

"What kind of son doesn't have a key to his family home? I can answer that," he said, not waiting for Molly to reply. "A man who doesn't care about anyone but himself."

"That's not true," Molly shot back, quick to defend him. Too quick, perhaps, but she could see he did care about Laila. "It's not Brig's fault his parents have apparently left town."

"Humph."

His mouth a grim line, Pop followed her into the living room. Molly sat opposite his faded blue wing chair and attempted to coax a smile from her dad. She knew he wasn't happy that Brig had breached his nightly routine with Molly: dinner, an extra helping of dessert that she wasn't supposed to notice on Pop's plate, his help with the dishes afterward, then their usual talk before he went up to bed. Sometimes they watched TV or a movie together, or he watched a sporting event while Molly pretended to enjoy it, too. She didn't mind keeping him company. But now...

She couldn't blame Pop for resenting Brig. It wasn't easy for her, either, to have him in the house. She'd really offered for Laila's sake, and as long as Molly kept her distance she'd be okay.

"Another day or two," she said, "won't hurt us. The baby doesn't belong in some stark hotel room, Pop, not when we have a good crib right here. And if she requires anything, the nursery in Little Darlings likely has it. Brig needs access to a kitchen for her, too."

"Huh," Thomas said. "So he stays and that little mite wraps her finger around our hearts. Then what?"

Molly felt his concern, his hurt, because they echoed her own. He had once wanted grandchildren just as badly as she'd wanted children. They would have been good for him. Ever since her mother had died, he'd been like someone lost in a wilderness, and Molly often felt helpless at easing his sorrow when she was still struggling with her own.

"About Brig's key..." She felt the need to explain, just as Brig had. "His parents changed the locks after his last visit." No, that didn't sound right. "I mean, remember they had that break-in a while ago and upped their security? New door included. They wanted to give him a key, he said, but he was overseas, and they never know quite where he is really." They had known about Afghanistan, though. And all that red tape. "I imagine they expected to be here when he arrived with Laila."

Thomas's features tensed. "I never heard a word about that baby. Maybe Joe and Bess aren't as good-hearted as you are, Molly. Maybe they decided to take off—go on a cruise—or maybe they just don't want to raise someone else's child."

Shocked, Molly leaned forward. "That's a dreadful thing to say. You sound like Ann when she talks about Jeff Barlow. What's with the two of you?"

Thomas seized the opportunity to shift the conversation.

"Ann?" He snorted. "You ever notice how she looks at him?"

"Yes, but...I notice more how she avoids him."

"Well, look again." The piercing glance he sent Molly made her squirm.

Did her dad also see how she looked at Brig when she thought no one would notice? She should just ignore his dark hair, his blue eyes, his broad shoulders and strong body. A body honed for war, she reminded herself, not love. Not her.

Eye candy, she tried to tell herself. Why not look if she did only that?

"We were talking about Brig's family." She hesitated. "There was a time when the Colliers wanted grandchildren as much as you did."

Thomas drew a breath. "What business does a man like that have with a baby? He's never home. He certainly doesn't have a wife...."

Ah. So that was it. Still.

"Pop. Don't." She paused again. "By the way, Brig told me you issued him some warning about me."

"Of course I did. You're my girl."

"I understand how you feel, but you don't need to worry."

He gave her another skeptical look, and Molly held his gaze until he had to avert his eyes. Lately, his protectiveness, his dependence upon her, had started to wear thin.

"I will worry," he said.

"I'm not interested in Brig. That's over."

Even Brig's mother had once told Molly that being married to a military man meant one long separation broken by short reunions. It meant moving again, often without much notice, just when you'd put down roots somewhere. And it meant always taking second place to duty. Maybe it was a good thing Brig had left and Andrew had stayed.

Her husband's steady devotion had suited her.

"Andrew and I had our differences, especially toward the end, but I'm not about to tarnish his memory." She took a breath. "Especially with a man who ultimately couldn't commit to me. I had Andrew," she said softly. And for a few months at least, they'd almost had the baby they'd wanted, that first grandchild for Pop. "I don't need anyone else," she added.

"You have me."

Molly tried to let his remark pass. But Pop looked afraid of losing her—or did she imagine this? And that troubled Molly even more. All at once she regretted her offer to let Brig and Laila stay. Not that she had any other humane choice, but her father's words only made her feel more unsettled.

You have me.

What kind of daughter was she? She loved Pop. Yet, sometimes, more often of late, she felt unsatisfied. As if he and Little Darlings and all her friends and family were not enough after all.

Frankly, she felt a little bit…trapped. Molly sure hoped Brig Collier's sudden reappearance in her life had nothing to do with that.

CHAPTER FOUR

ANN WALKER STARTLED at the first ring of the phone, though she should be used to it by now, since the phone had been ringing off and on all night. She had no intention of answering. In her darkened living room, she curled into her favorite chair, the TV set glowing but the sound muted. After the fourth ring she prepared to listen instead to her machine.

Jeff Barlow was finally leaving a message:

"Ann, if you don't want to see a movie—then we can do something else. Take a walk along the river. Go bowling. Drive up to Columbus..."

Drive? He couldn't have said anything worse. Frustrated, Ann snatched up the phone and launched right in.

"No," she said. "To bowling or a walk or anything else. Maybe—just a thought here—you should give up."

"Nope." She actually heard a smile in his voice. He went on in that same unhurried manner, as if he meant to stay on the line until she surrendered. "You know, we have a new K-9 recruit in the department, and he reminds me of you."

She tightened her grip on the phone.

"How flattering to be compared to a dog."

The smile-by-wire broadened. "No, see, he's this great-looking dog with honey-brown fur and big eyes that are kind of beige but gray, too, and a nice doggie smile, and he loves M&M's, his favorite treat."

Clearly Jeff was talking about her. "I don't eat candy," she reminded him pointedly.

"But sad to say," he continued, as if she hadn't spoken, "he may wash out of the program, which would be a shame—" here Jeff moved in for the kill "—because he has PTSD."

Ann said nothing.

"You know what that means?"

"Yes. He suffered some sort of mishap— and now he has nightmares."

"He's a dog," Jeff said. "Who would know?"

Her pulse was racing now. "He probably twitches in his sleep. His legs move as if he's running away from something."

"What are you running from, Miss Walker?"

"You," she said without even thinking.

"I understand that." She could almost see him lying on his sofa, the phone to his ear, that lazy "gotcha" smile on his face. Somewhere in his house or apartment or wherever he lived, his little boy would be fast asleep, the place quiet. Like Jeff. "What I want to know is, why?"

"How about because I don't like cops." Not true, except that they served as a reminder. She had her finger on the off button.

"Strange, because nothing showed up in your file. No arrest for resisting, or threatening an officer of the law—"

Her pulse lurched. "You looked at my file?"

"No," he said. "I was flushing you out. So there *is* a file?"

"That's none of your business! And if you call again—"

"Annie, don't hang up. I was kidding. I wouldn't hunt up someone's file just to get a date—even with you," he added.

She almost smiled. He was charming. And Ann couldn't resist.

"Then you don't know about the police brutality."

Obviously surprised, Jeff Barlow laughed. He had a nice laugh, rich and full and hiding nothing about him, which was more than Ann could say for herself. She envisioned his sandy hair and blue eyes and, yes, that uniform. And that was only his outer appeal. If the situation were different, she would want to go out with him again, test the waters at least. But Ann didn't dream anymore about love and marriage, or having a family of her own—the dreams she and Molly had once shared.

That night nine years ago, the worst night of her life, had changed everything for her. Jeff wouldn't learn about that, though, because they would never get that far. So it would do no good to let herself like Jeff Barlow too much. Which was why she'd decided to end this relationship now.

"Thanks for calling," she said drily, finger poised again on the off button, pulse still thumping as if she were a felon about to get nabbed, "but you're wasting your time. Goodb—"

"Is it because I'm a cop? Really?"

She froze. "Not you, personally, no. It's a general thing."

"Ah. I see. And it's not because of Ernie?"

"Ernie?" She had an instant image of the

little boy, small and chubby and full of life. He scared her more than Jeff did: Ernie was even easier to like.

"My kid," he explained, as if she didn't know. "You have something against kids? That a 'general thing,' too? Or is it mine in particular?"

She heard the edge in his tone, his instinctive protection of Ernie. Jeff never came into the center without swinging Ernie into his arms and smacking a kiss on his cheek. It was clear the boy worshipped him, too.

"I work with children every day," she said. "Why would I have something against them?"

"I don't know," he drawled. "Why would you?"

"Look. If I needed a counselor, I'd get one," she said. Over the years she had seen a number of shrinks. None of them had helped.

"I like psychology," Jeff said. "I like to learn what makes people tick. You intrigue me." That smile in his voice was back again. "And I don't see how we can come to some agreement here unless we get everything out in the open. So what is it, Annie?"

"Stop calling me Annie."

"Uh-uh. I like it. Takes some of the starch

out of you. Makes you seem more approach-
able. Like Molly."

"Then ask my sister for a date."

He whistled softly in her ear. "You are a
tough nut. Molly's a great person, but it's not
her I'm interested in." Then he homed in on
her again, his voice soft and soothing. "Who
hurt you, Annie?"

Her breath hitched, and to her horror the
words popped out.

"It was quite the reverse."

Had she shocked him? But the long silence
ended with "We'll have to get to the bottom
of that. Another time," he added. "I'll talk to
you tomorrow."

"No you won't—" she began, but Jeff had
already ended the call.

If only... But Ann didn't finish the thought.
She wasn't talking, because once he knew the
truth, he would certainly change his opinion
of her. Nobody wanted a guilt-ridden emo-
tional cripple for a girlfriend.

Blinking, not sure whether she was sad or
angry or afraid, Ann shut off the TV, doused
the living room lights and at ten o'clock
crawled into bed, where she struggled not to
pull the covers over her head.

In her dark dreams she must have been twitching like a dog.

"HELP."

Molly was in her room that night, intent on keeping to herself and brainstorming ideas for the presentation she would have to make to the town zoning commission about the center's proposed expansion, when she heard Brig's voice. Her mind still on an earlier meeting with her architect, she realized belatedly how frantic Brig sounded. Now he loomed in her doorway.

"What is it? Is something wrong with Laila?"

His face was paper white, and his mouth was drawn at the corners. There was no sign of the baby. He shifted from one foot to the other. "She, uh, had an…accident."

Adrenaline surged through Molly. She had already started toward the phone to call 911 when his voice stopped her again.

"Not an accident-type accident," he said, catching Molly's arm. "She, uh, well, she's a mess. So is her crib, the sheets—" Brig held his nose.

"Oh. I see." It didn't take much imagination to get the picture.

But Brig obviously felt the need to explain. "I guess I didn't put her diaper on right before she went to bed. She woke up screaming, and when I looked…" He made a face filled with distaste for the situation.

"No problem," she said. "I must deal with this at least three times a day. Where is she?"

"Still in the bed." He appeared guilty. "I should have picked her up, but…"

"I understand." So much for her plan to stay clear of Brig and the baby. Now that wasn't possible. "She needs a bath. I'll get my work clothes on. You wrap Laila in something warm—we'll wash that, too—and we can meet at the center. I have several baby baths there just for this purpose. She'll be good again in no time." Molly smiled. "And so will you."

The problem for Molly was that meant being alone with Brig in the nighttime Little Darlings with no hovering moms or staff to act as chaperones.

Moonlight washed the changing room with silvery light. The small space seemed that much tighter with Brig in it, too, but Molly appreciated that he didn't back out when she uncovered the baby and, indeed, discovered a mess. Molly fought the urge to cover her own nose.

"She probably hasn't adjusted to that new brand of formula," she said, a fistful of baby wipes in hand. "My fault for buying it. Poor little girl," Molly crooned. "Her system is in an uproar. I can imagine the digestive changes she must be going through after leaving a foreign country and doing all that travel."

"Now she's one of your Little Darlings," he murmured, standing close to Molly's shoulder.

Neither his comment nor his nearness helped her equilibrium. All at once she felt as unsettled, as much in alien territory, as Laila was. His next question only made her discomfort worse.

"I'm curious. Did you and Andrew ever want kids?"

Molly tossed a soiled baby wipe into the nearby trash bin kept solely for that purpose, then went back for another. She focused on cleaning Laila's small body with a light touch.

"I—we—wanted a big family," she said, trying to force a smile into her voice, though it wouldn't come. "But a few months before Andrew…before I lost him…we also lost our first—and, as it turned out, only—child." She took a breath. "I had a miscarriage."

He touched her shoulder. "I didn't mean to upset you."

"I'm not upset," she lied. "Of course, at the time it was dreadful—as you might imagine." But then, he couldn't. Brig had chosen adventure over her, and the six babies they'd planned on had been relegated to her dreams. If Andrew hadn't come along, if she hadn't loved him, too… Molly struggled to lighten her tone. "One day we were picking out baby furniture, planning what color to paint the nursery, which until then had been Andrew's home office, and the next we were putting back his desk and chair…" She trailed off. She hadn't been able to keep the tears, or the memories, from her voice after all.

"Did you own Little Darlings, then?" Brig asked.

"I didn't open this center until after Andrew… And before that Mom had died, too, and I decided to sell the house in Hyde Park and move back in with Pop. It was the right decision," she said, and aimed the last baby wipe at the trash. "I used my husband's insurance money to renovate this carriage barn. It's Andrew's legacy, really."

"You seem to manage pretty well." He paused. "I'm not managing with Laila at all. Her dad was not only one of my men but one of my best friends, and at times I just can't believe Sean is really gone—that he and Zada—"

Saying the words seemed hard for Brig, too, but clearly he understood loss. Since he'd left her years ago, they had both suffered, and certainly she couldn't help but admire him for accepting responsibility now as Laila's guardian. Maybe he wasn't as selfish as she had wanted to believe. Molly patted Laila's just-cleaned bottom, all the while whispering calming words to the baby to stop herself from giving in to tears. In front of Brig? No way.

Her voice was husky. "I know what you mean. I still expect Andrew to walk in the door. But he was too eager that night after work to get home—that's what I tell myself—and jumped a light in what passes for downtown Liberty. A truck hurrying through the intersection on the yellow hit his car broadside." The freak accident had robbed Molly of her dreams, all of them, for a second time. She no longer had the husband she had loved even during the worst of their bad weeks after her miscarriage.

But she didn't want to dwell on that now.

Not with Brig, no matter what his losses had been.

The little room was beginning to seem even smaller, tighter. Brig stood so close she could hear him breathing.

"That's sad, Molly," he said.

"Yes," she said, "but—as quickly as with Sean and Zada—that's what happened."

What if Andrew had convinced her to try for another child when Molly hadn't felt ready? What if she had a boy now like Ernie or a girl like Laila?

Straightening her shoulders, she reached down for the now-bare Laila. The little girl lay quietly in Molly's arms, her dark gaze searching the room and the overhead lights. "Let's get her into the bath. Babies usually love water."

"She didn't like it when I tried last time. Maybe I did too quick a job. I was afraid she might drown even in a few inches of water in your bathroom sink."

Molly didn't point out that such a tragedy was all too possible. But he hadn't asked her how to bathe Laila. She supposed he had his pride, too. It must be strange for him to admit he was inept at caring for a ten- to twelve-pound infant. Another thing they needed to do tonight: weigh Laila so Brig could chart her growth.

She moved to fill the plastic bath at the sink. Juggling Laila, she dribbled her favorite baby wash into the warm water, and finally lowered Laila gently into the bath. Her motions came as second nature, and Brig's gaze widened as he watched.

"Amazing." Laila was already cooing her delight.

"She likes feeling as if she were still inside her mother, where it was always warm and safe." Molly's baby hadn't been that lucky. But then, neither had Laila, who'd lost her mother almost at birth. "And again, it's only practice. Think of half a dozen like Laila, all squalling and ready for a bath at the same time. Good thing I have staff, especially Ann, to help."

"Maybe one of you would like to volunteer for nanny duty."

He was only half kidding, but Molly shook her head with a teasing smile. "You're on your own, soldier." Against her better instincts, she gestured for him to come closer. "Trial by fire," she murmured. "Just be sure to support Laila's head and shoulders."

"She's so slippery," he said, eyes filled with fresh panic the instant he touched her.

To Molly's relief, however, the baby was now looking up at Brig, her gaze roving from his hair to his eyes to his mouth as if she liked what she saw. The only daddy she knew. When she kicked her legs and water flew everywhere, Brig's shirt got soaked but he laughed and didn't let go. A good sign.

"She's strong. I'm always surprised by how strong she is."

"It's a survival thing, I'd say. She holds her head up really well for her age."

He shook his head. "Yeah, but I could deal with a raw recruit much easier—and I'm talking about some 'kid' who weighs two hundred pounds."

"Then Laila should be a piece of cake." She couldn't resist teasing him some more. "Don't tell me you'd let this little girl get the best of you?"

Brig glanced over his shoulder, keeping a steady grip on Laila.

"She already has."

But Molly knew he didn't mean her bath. The baby had definitely captured him. By the time he finished washing, then rinsing her, Laila was half-asleep.

Molly handed him a clean diaper and fresh clothing.

"No, please. You do it," he said. "I'm at my limit for tonight."

He stood over the changing table again, his sleeve now and then brushing Molly's bare arm and making the hairs on her skin rise, while she diapered Laila and slipped her into a clean sleeper. Then Molly stood back, forgetting how near Brig was, and bumped into him, their bodies touching. Instantly, she turned away so Brig couldn't see her flushed face.

She had to get out of there. The small room had become suffocating, and if she stayed any longer, there was a very real danger that she'd be tempted to slip into his arms. So much for her promise just to look.

Briskly, she bustled around the room, rinsing the plastic tub and shutting down lights until, to her dismay, they were standing in the now-dark space, and Brig was whispering, as if he felt the same temptation, "Molly."

Her name went through her like a welcome breeze and cooled her pink cheeks. No way would she let herself be lulled once more by

Brig's good looks and the newer, more tender side of him that she'd never encountered before. Soon enough she'd be seeing the back of him. Laila, too. So instead…

"I offered you some books on child care," she said, walking toward the door, "but you'll need more than that. Hands-on experience. If you'd like to avoid another mess in the crib, or at least lower the possibility, I could…give you a few lessons—for Laila—in diapering and so forth."

"And so forth," he echoed, following her out the door.

Molly hurried back to the house, to the light she saw still shining in her bedroom. She had to do at least some brainstorming before she went to sleep. She had to remind herself that too many years had gone by, with too many losses.

And she wasn't about to risk another.

"THERE SHE IS AGAIN."

At her father's voice Molly turned the next afternoon from plumping the sofa cushions in the living room. He had just awoken from his nap—a new habit of his that worried her, when he'd always been full of energy—and for some reason was staring out the side window at the Colliers' house next door.

The still-empty house, as far as Molly could tell.

Which was worse luck for her. Because after last night in the changing room at the center, she was trying to ignore her memory of Brig's closeness and her foolish urge to glide into his arms.

She'd decided then that any baby-care lessons from her would be given during daytime hours with her entire staff present.

"That woman," Thomas said. He was now looking out at the yard, taking care to stay out of sight, one hand pulling the curtains back just enough so he could see without being seen. "She's a friend of Bess Collier's." He peered harder at their neighbors' house. "Look, she's ringing their bell again like some town crier. Maybe they stood her up like they did Brig."

"Maybe," Molly said, "but she might not know they're away. Why don't you go out and say something?"

His hand dropped from the curtain as if he'd been burned. "I'm not stepping foot out of this house. Every time she spots me, she comes over to talk."

"Really," Molly said, wishing he might welcome some company.

But Pop was on a roll. "Last month she tried to get me to some potluck dinner at the community center. The Colliers were going, she said, so I wouldn't be a stranger—a ding dang double date, as if I couldn't see that coming a mile away." Molly noticed an odd expression on his face that looked to her a lot like...yearning? "Then only a week ago she had some notion I might like to join her senior bowling league."

Molly grinned. "You're a good bowler. I think she's sweet on you, Pop."

His face turned red. "That's all I need."

Molly wanted to say, *Maybe that's exactly what you need.* But that hadn't gone over well with Ann about Jeff Barlow. Molly was out of the matchmaking business.

Thomas eyed her as if she'd spoken anyway and didn't get his point. "Your mother was the closest thing to a saint I ever knew. She had a gentle way about her. Never said a bad word about anyone."

"I know, Pop." Molly's eyes stung. "I assume you said no to the potluck."

His frown deepened. "You were making your special meat loaf that night. I bet that woman's a terrible cook. She talks too much to pay attention to anything else."

Molly bit back a smile. "What if she has hidden depths?"

"You think this is funny? What if she's nothing but a man-hunting busybody?" he said, then stomped off into the kitchen for his afternoon snack.

Molly followed him. Unable to push just a little, she waited until he looked at her. "Pop, I know how much you loved Mom, but I don't want to see you bury yourself in this house."

"Hardly any chance of that," he said, rooting in the fridge and coming up with a block of his favorite cheese. "Not with Brigham here, too, and that baby that's not his."

"Now you're being unkind."

"Well, I don't see the good of it, Molly. If his parents aren't coming home anytime soon—"

"We don't know that."

"Then why doesn't he find an apartment or something?"

"For just a short stay?"

"And why isn't there someone else who can take care of that child? Makes no sense for a man who's little more than a drifter, a man who will likely head off tomorrow or next week for who knows where to play shoot 'em up."

Molly's stomach sank. She didn't like to imagine Brig in a firefight somewhere, in danger far from home. Not that home was high on his priority list. But to imagine Brig wounded, or even gone like his teammate, Sean…?

"That's Brig's business," she said, "not ours. All I can do is help him learn how to care for Laila properly—which I've promised to do while he's here—and keep my ears open for any news of his folks."

"Huh," Thomas muttered. "Well, I've been keeping my eyes open with him, and I doubt baby care is the only thing on his mind."

"Don't you dare say it," Molly cautioned him.

She was trying hard not to think about Brig, just as her father was trying hard not to acknowledge any interest in the woman still ringing the bell next door.

But, no. A glance out the window told Molly the woman was now steaming across the yard to Pop's front door.

"Uh-oh. There's no escape," she told him.

And went to answer the bell.

Unlike Pop, Molly welcomed the chance to distract herself.

She could only hope she wasn't occupying Brig's mind.

CHAPTER FIVE

MOLLY OPENED THE door—and any thought of Brig went flying out of her head.

Except for her red hair, the woman who'd been standing on the Colliers' front porch hadn't looked so…dazzling from a distance. Molly took in the purple sequined tracksuit and hot pink running shoes with their glittering silver reflectors. She wouldn't have been surprised if the visitor's shoes had sported those red lights that flashed when the wearer walked, as did some of the shoes the children at Little Darlings wore.

"Please. Come in," she said, gesturing with one hand. "I'm Molly."

"Natalie Brewster."

They hadn't officially met before, but Molly recognized the newest resident of the neighborhood. She had moved in last spring from across town, yet other than a wave or hello called from a distance, Molly had had no dealings with her.

Natalie Brewster's sharp gaze went roaming—with obvious suspicion. The living room was empty, except for her and Molly, and so was the adjacent dining room. She glanced out the side window where Molly's father had been hiding behind the curtains moments ago, then homed in on the archway to the kitchen.

"I thought I saw Thomas," she said.

Molly hated to lie. There was only silence from the other room, but she could imagine Pop sitting motionless at the table, behind the wall where he couldn't be seen, praying the woman would leave him in peace. Still, it wasn't Molly's place to turn him in. And if she got the chance, she had something in mind for their visitor that might help Brig.

"Pop isn't available right now. Can I do anything for you?"

Natalie Brewster's face fell. "I had something to ask him. I'll come back later."

Another swift look at the nearby kitchen told Molly their new neighbor didn't believe her for a second, and a twinge of guilt ran through her.

"Hmm," Natalie said, bright blue eye shadow shimmering in the light. "I hope he doesn't think he can avoid me forever. I need his help. I'm chairman of the rummage sale we're having soon at the community center." She refocused her gaze on Molly. "If you have anything to donate…"

"Let me check my day care. See what I can find." Molly tilted her head toward the backyard. "I might have some unclaimed lost items there that could be donated now, and a used baby crib or high chair that we've recently replaced, some toys…"

"We'd appreciate that. You can have Thomas drop them off. I bet he's a crack painter and in no time could turn that crib into something that appears brand-new." She turned to go, then whirled back, purple sequins sparkling. One manicured hand with Day-Glo green-painted nails waved in the air inches from Molly's face. "You at least must have seen me ringing the bell next door."

Pop, Molly thought, had fooled no one with his disappearing act. Still, she almost felt sorry for him. Natalie couldn't have been more different from Molly's mother if she tried. Her dad just didn't know how to cope.

Molly glanced toward the Colliers' house and seized the opportunity she'd been handed. "Mrs. Brewster," she began.

"It's miss, honey. I never took the plunge.

And call me Natalie. By the way, do you know where Joe and Bess have gone?"

"No, I was hoping you did. Or rather, their son is. He's been in Liberty for a few days now and expected them to be here, but they haven't come home. Brig is becoming more and more concerned."

"It's not like them," Natalie agreed. She cast another knowing look at the kitchen archway, her brow furrowed. "Now that you bring it up, I'm worried, too. Days, you said?"

Molly nodded. "I wonder who else might be in on their plans."

Natalie thought for a moment, then ticked off half a dozen names that Molly didn't recognize. Her usual contacts—the day care parents and her friends—were a lot younger than Pop or Miss Brewster or the Colliers.

"Let me see what I can find out," Natalie offered.

"Maybe you could give me their numbers, and I'll call. That would save you the trouble." But Natalie was having none of that.

"I left my phone on the charger at home, so I don't have any numbers handy, but I'd be happy to let my fingers do the walking later," she said with a gleaming, white-toothed smile. "Then I can come by to tell you what I've found."

And have another excuse to see Molly's father?

"Why not just call instead? It would save you a trip."

"Nonsense. I only live across the street." With a last, jaundiced glance toward the rear of the house, Natalie put a hand on the door-knob. "I'll be back," she said, as if it was a threat. "Once I set myself a task, I don't waver."

Molly did, though. Well, Pop would simply have to deal with his admirer when the time came. As she shut the door behind Natalie Brewster, she decided he was on his own— just as she'd teased Brig the other night.

And her thoughts returned to him.

Their time inside the darkened center, even with the baby between them and a bathing ritual for distraction, had been hard enough. Molly groaned. And unfortunately she'd already promised to start those lessons in infant care for Brig tonight.

"OH, BABY, IT'S all right." Late that afternoon in the nursery Molly cradled little Ashley Jones to her chest, whispering words of comfort. They were for herself, too. She was trying not to think about a classroom accident earlier involving Debbie Crandall's child and Ernie Barlow, and Molly's spirit always ached whenever one of her charges felt unhappy or unwell. "It's no fun cutting that tooth, is it?" she told Ashley. "But it will be over soon, you'll see. And you'll have a grand new way of dealing with the world." She was about to comment on Ashley having her first solid food when Ann walked into the room.

The baby kept crying. She tried desperately to shove a fist into her tender mouth but kept missing the mark, which only made her wail louder. Molly's attempts to help her out with a gel pacifier, chilled in the freezer to numb her gums, hadn't worked.

"Debbie Crandall is here," Ann announced with a frown.

"Ah, yes. Benjamin's mother." Molly held out Ashley. "Here, spend some time with this little one. She's miserable and needs a friend."

Except for the baby's cries, the rest of the center was quiet, the lights dimmed for nap time, the twos and threes in one room, the fours across the hall. Some of the older children were out in the play area with one of the other teachers. It seemed to reassure both parents and kids when Molly and her staff referred to themselves as educators in classrooms.

One more reminder that she was only a surrogate to other people's children.

Still, Molly took pride in her work. She loved her kids, and she was adamant about providing stimulation and opportunities to learn. Many of the older children were already reading simple books and counting to ten, and most could print their names and recite the alphabet as well as sing the alphabet song.

Ready for the battle she anticipated with Debbie Crandall, Molly glided into her office with a professional smile. The woman was on her feet, eyes flashing, before Molly stuck out a hand.

"Mrs. Crandall, it's a pleasure."

"Never mind the niceties, Molly. Benjy came home with my husband today weeping his eyes out. He's suspended? Whatever happened was Ernie's fault—"

There was a mischief maker in every classroom and at every age level, in Molly's experience. They all started young, but in this case Ernie wasn't the instigator. She easily remembered Benjamin pushing Ernie in the hallway yesterday when Jeff was here.

She sat at her desk. "It's true the boys are inclined to fight with each other, and I agree we have a problem here. But it isn't Benjamin's first time. Has something changed at home?"

"No." Debbie paced the small office. "I'm not here to discuss my situation. What are you going to do about Ernie?"

"Debbie, please." Molly clenched her hands. "I've been around children here for the past few years. Before that, I worked in several other day cares in Cincinnati. I think I know more about children—"

"Than a *mother* does?" She spun around. "Let me tell you. Until you have one of your own, Mrs. Darling, a child you carry in your body and give birth to and love more than your own life—"

Molly rose from her chair, shaking. "How dare you say this about me?"

Debbie Crandall didn't apologize. She didn't appear ready to back down, either, or want to listen to reason. "Oh, it's about you, all right. I can see that now. You would defend Ernie Barlow against my Benjy, show favoritism—"

"I try to treat all my children alike. But your son—"

"Has a behavior problem? Is that what you're saying?"

"Ernie Barlow has a two-inch gash on his forehead. When your son hit him with that metal truck—which he did more than once— he also laid Ernie's nose open almost its entire length. His father had to take him to the E.R. for stitches. He certainly didn't give himself those injuries."

"Ernie hit Benjamin first."

"So your son told you."

"My son is not a liar! He's a sweet little boy. He's only four years old."

"And I'm sorry, but he is showing aggressive tendencies."

Debbie Crandall ignored that comment. "As for Ernie Barlow, I wonder. He and his father are living alone without a woman's influence in the home—"

Oh, brother. This was getting completely out of hand. What could she say to salvage the situation?

Molly took her seat. "Please, sit down, Debbie."

Instead, the woman planted herself in front of Molly's desk, hands braced on top of it in an intimidating posture. "I don't need a seat." Her voice trembled. "Ernie is growing up with a cop for a father who probably has an arsenal of guns in that house. I saw Ernie only a few days ago with a *pistol*."

"A water pistol. And we don't allow them here. I asked Ernie to put it in his backpack to take home—and he did. Without, I might add, giving me an argument. Now, let's talk about Benjamin." Molly paused, searching for the right words. "Perhaps you could speak to him, urge him to come to me or one of my staff if he has a problem with another child. You and I can talk again, too. And try to channel Benjamin's energy in a more positive direction."

Silence. A heavy, condemning silence.

"There is nothing wrong with my son," Debbie said at last. Her face was still red as she started toward the door.

Molly tried again. "If you'd just listen—"

But Debbie was already striding into the hall, her back stiff with anger. Then, after only a few steps, she stopped and turned. Her gaze met Molly's, and her voice echoed in the empty space, loud enough to wake the sleeping kids nearby and even reach, Molly was sure, Ann's ears, her other helpers and the two mothers working as aides that afternoon.

"You don't begin to treat everyone the same way," she said. "And how could you understand?" She paused, then delivered the coup de grace. "My Benjamin, Ernie Barlow...they are not *your* children."

MOLLY SAT IN her office for long moments after Debbie Crandall left.

I try to treat all my children alike.

Benjamin Crandall wasn't a bad kid, but his parents, especially his mother, weren't doing him any favors by indulging his outbursts, then rewarding him with treats after he finally got his way.

But what did she know?

They are not your *children.*

She couldn't deny that Debbie was right. She should stop referring to the children as hers.

"Hey." Ann stood in the open doorway, holding Ashley Jones. The baby had quieted—Ann was always good with the youngest children at the center—and Molly hadn't seen them come in. "You all right?"

She sighed. "Getting there. I just needed a few minutes to myself."

"No wonder." Ann dropped onto the chair

in front of Molly's desk. "Everyone heard her in here."

"Benjamin needs his mother to admit there's a problem, then try to deal with it. Like that will happen. I could tell something else was bothering her, but she wouldn't say."

As if reluctant to ask, Ann looked away. "How's Ernie?"

"Jeff kept him home, but he called. Ernie's okay—probably better than Jeff, from the sound of his voice. The little fellow is a bit bruised and swollen, but nothing time won't heal. The doctor said he shouldn't even have scars."

"Those were some blows he took. None of us could arrive fast enough to prevent them. I'm amazed Jeff Barlow hasn't threatened to sue the Crandalls—or the center."

"He understands what's going on. I promised to keep a careful eye on Ernie, but I won't be surprised if Debbie Crandall quits the center."

"Her loss," Ann said. She gazed down at Ashley, who was almost asleep, her rosebud mouth working furiously at a new pacifier. "She likes this one better. Sometimes it's a matter of trial and error—maybe with Benjamin, too."

"Thanks, Ann," Molly murmured, feeling only a little better. "I hope no one else on our staff is upset."

"All I saw was a lot of eye rolling." She carefully rose to her feet, Ashley cradled close. "Here," she said. "You have her. You could use a bit of sweet, sleeping baby for a while. I'll help get the kids up from their naps and out to play while you take another few minutes."

Molly held out her arms. "You know me so well."

Ann tiptoed from the room, leaving Molly alone in the office with just the sound of Ashley sucking on the pacifier. The baby curled her fingers around Molly's hand, and warmth spread through Molly like a soothing balm.

Oh, yes, she had needed this.

But as she gazed down at the sleeping baby, tears filled Molly's eyes. *Don't cry. Don't.* There was nothing she could do. Andrew was gone, and these little ones were all she had. Yet despite the comfort they gave her, she could still hear Debbie's words.

They are not your *children.*

Neither was Laila. Molly needed to remember that, too.

She didn't relish seeing her, or rather Brig again, tonight.

Still, she had promised. For Laila. Because caring for children was what Molly did.

Hey, Collier. Too bad about your missing parents. What are you going to do? You promised us some pix of the little lady. What gives? H.

"CHECK THIS OUT," Brig said, turning his cell phone so Molly could see the latest message from his team. Henderson was the one keeping in touch. "For a bunch of hardened troops, they sure have a soft spot for Laila."

Molly's mouth tightened. "Very cute."

Brig watched her pull a fresh diaper from the stack on the dresser and prepare to show him how to put it on the baby, but their first lesson obviously wasn't going well.

Had he done something wrong? Earlier Molly had insisted they meet here in the house with Thomas nearby as a chaperone. Or was she still reacting to the bathing incident with Laila that had stuck in his mind, too: the intimate little room and the way he'd kept inhaling Molly's scent along with the smells of baby wash and powder?

Better to focus on finding his parents. But

no amount of running next door or gathering their mail had brought them home. Brig didn't know where else to look or what to tell Henderson.

And how long would he be able to stay here at Molly's, or even next door once his folks showed up? No lessons in baby care could change the fact that, sooner rather than later, he would have to return to duty. Maybe the email from the team had reminded Molly of that, too.

She held out the disposable diaper imprinted with colorful images of what she had told him were Hello Kitty figures in pink. He noticed that she avoided actually touching him and was holding the diaper by two fingers. Brig started to take it, then stopped. He couldn't handle any more of the tension.

"Molly. What's wrong?"

For a moment she didn't answer.

"Sorry, I had a bad day," she finally murmured. "One of my—one of the parents whose child is in the four-year-old group objected to something I suggested."

Brig waited for her to go on.

Laila was lying in her crib with the side down so it could double as a changing table, and was gazing up at him with unblinking dark eyes. He smoothed a hand over her little chest and smiled, although Laila didn't quite smile back. Instead, she kicked her legs and gurgled.

Beside him, Molly shifted. Her gaze stayed on the baby, too.

"I'm worried that her son isn't socialized properly even for his age—he's acting out with the other children, grabbing toys, hitting…" Then she told him about Ernie Barlow's injuries.

Brig winced at her description but was at a loss to respond. So he said nothing. He didn't know much about four-year-olds. He had enough trouble trying to figure out Laila's daily schedule—which so far didn't seem to be a schedule at all. With a frown of concentration, he took the diaper from Molly, opened it, lifted Laila's bottom and slid Hello Kitty underneath.

"That image goes in the front," Molly said.

Every movement he made with the baby still felt awkward. Brig wondered if he would ever become comfortable, at least before he had to leave her.

Molly reached over to fan the sides of the diaper to better cover Laila.

In a low monotone she told Brig about

Ernie Barlow's stitches. But that wasn't the whole problem tonight.

"What else?" he asked, because Molly was still avoiding his eyes.

She lifted a shoulder as if to downplay what she was about to next.

"I have this habit of referring to the day care kids as 'my' children. Debbie Crandall reminded me that it's only a fiction. That I can't possibly understand how she feels when I'm not a mother myself. Quote, unquote."

"Molly." He knew her well enough, even after an eight-year absence from her life, to guess just how badly that had wounded her.

Again she shrugged, then she forced her mouth into a stiff smile. "Reality hurts." She leaned closer, daring to cover Brig's hand where it rested on the diaper tape. "No, pull this tighter on both sides. You won't hurt her—the tape stretches—and trust me, you don't want to leave any gaps."

"Like the other night," he said, not meaning only Laila's mishap before her bath. He and Molly were still tiptoeing around each other. But every small meeting, every conversation had seemed to ease the tension between them. Until now. He wished he could give that woman a piece of his mind for hurting Molly and interfering with his efforts to win Molly's forgiveness.

"Like the other night," she repeated. Together, they strapped Laila into the diaper. "You take over now," she said. "I recommend putting an undershirt or a onesie on her tonight. We're supposed to get more icy rain, and the room you're in has some drafty windows. Then she needs her sleeper, that footed one." She paused. "If you think she still might be cold, you can zip her into her yellow fleece blanket sleeper, too."

He did as instructed. Having accomplished all this with only a minimum of thrashing from Laila, he stepped back, proud of himself.

"You're learning fast," Molly said. The faster, the better for her? "But then, having to think quickly and react in a heartbeat must be a part of you by now."

"You have no idea." Dealing with a ten-pound infant was different, though. Way different. "In Afghanistan I was lucky to find that local woman who took care of Laila in those first weeks. Didn't help to put my mind at ease much, though. Every time I collected the baby, I was afraid a bomb had been lobbed into her house, or that I would run over some

IED in the road. I was awful glad to get Laila out of there." He paused. "Caring for a baby with an M-16 slung over my shoulder also isn't my idea of being a good...guardian."

"You're on your way," Molly murmured with a half smile.

"You mean, on my own?"

His teasing tone and the reminder of what she'd said earlier widened her smile. Brig gazed at her mouth and wished there was a way to erase the past eight years, to have Molly see him at least as a friend again.

"You're doing fine," she said.

"You may be right. I had a pretty good day. After your dad agreed to lend me his car this morning, I managed to wrestle Laila's seat into the back and took her to a pediatrician."

"Which one? I could have recommended someone."

He told Molly her name. "A very nice lady who cooed and aahed over Laila, gave her a thorough checkup and told me she's at the light end of the weight scale. Understandable, when you consider her beginning, but I'm not to worry, the doctor said."

"Yes, I know her. She's very good."

"She adjusted Laila's diet. The formula

we've been giving her is okay, but she'll be better off with a different brand that'll be a bit easier on her system, as you suggested." He and Molly exchanged a glance rife with memories of the other night and of cleaning Laila up. "This new one has some kind of growth stuff in it."

"Good job, Brig."

He couldn't help grinning. "A first," he said, then sobered. "But, Molly, *where* can my parents be? It's like they stepped off the planet. I've been here three days. I should have heard from them by now."

"You did tell them not to call. And they didn't know you were on your way home." She hesitated. "What about the police? Have you phoned them?"

"Not yet. I couldn't file a missing persons report for the first twenty-four hours— whenever that was, maybe before I got here. But there's no reason to suspect foul play. Two adults have every right to go wherever they please."

Molly snapped her fingers. "Oh, wait. How could I forget? I talked to a neighbor today, Brig. She was ringing your parents' doorbell, then came over here." She paused. "I think she likes my dad, but he thinks she's just a busybody."

"Yeah, he mentioned her to me. And?" He picked up Laila, who was starting to fuss. Either it was time for a bottle or she was exhausted by all his prodding and poking and was ready for sleep. "Does she have any idea where my folks went?"

"No, but she's promised to call everyone she knows—all their mutual friends—and get back to me. To you, I mean."

"That's great."

Molly paused. "What about your grandmother? Have you called her?"

Brig felt a twinge of guilt. "A number of times, but there was no answer. I don't really expect to hear from her. She and I haven't been on good terms for a while."

Molly didn't have to ask why. Eight years ago his grandmother had blamed him for leaving Molly. Ever since, she'd avoided Brig except to send him happy-birthday emails and a care package overseas at Christmastime. He imagined Laila might soften her up, but the rift between them still ran deep.

"Because of me," Molly said at last.

"Because of you."

"Well, nothing has turned up yet from anyone. Let's hope Natalie Brewster has some luck."

"Let's hope," Brig said, referring to his tentative relationship with Molly, too.

CHAPTER SIX

ANN WASN'T GLAD that Ernie Barlow had been hurt the other day—how could she be? But his staying home for two days to heal was a more or less welcome thing, terrible person that she was. Seeing Ernie always meant seeing his father.

She was hanging up miniature coats and stuffing tiny mittens into pockets in the cloakroom just off the main entrance to Little Darlings when she heard a sudden commotion in the hall.

A familiar child's voice rang out. "Bella! William! I'm back!"

Ann had to smile. Ernie's irrepressible nature always had that effect.

Still, her breath caught in her throat. She wished there was a Mrs. Barlow around to bring her son to day care sometimes. But there wasn't, and in the coatroom Ann had nowhere to run.

Predictably, from the hallway she heard Jeff

Barlow's worried voice next, urging Ernie to slow down. That wasn't likely to happen. Four-year-old boys could barely contain their energy, and after two days at home, Ernie was obviously raring to see his friends again.

After another word from his dad, he barreled into the coatroom before Ann could prepare herself.

"Hi, Miss Ann! I'm here."

"Yes, I can see you are." Shocked by the sight of him, Ann clutched her throat. *Oh, would you look at that?* Her morning coffee roiled in her stomach. Ernie's forehead was red and purple and blue, lined with angry-looking stitches that also ran the length of his swollen nose. Yet he was beaming.

"Welcome back, Ernie," she said, her tone overly bright so he wouldn't know his wounds had shaken her. When he tumbled into her arms, Ann couldn't help herself. She let him stay there for a moment too long, just holding him, hurting for him. She was easing back, trying to compose herself, one hand lifted to smooth down Ernie's stubborn cowlick, when Jeff stepped in.

"Hi," he said, and Ann's stomach tightened. She hadn't answered any of his calls since he'd said, "I'll talk to you tomorrow," and now she was caught in a snare.

She nodded at him, then busied herself helping Ernie out of his puffy down jacket. She guided the boy to the empty hook in the cubby marked with his name. "I've got this," she said to Jeff Barlow. "You can go or you'll be late for work."

"It's my off day." He came closer. "In fact, I took several days after Ernie got whacked. Might as well use the rest of it today. There's never enough time to do chores around the house."

She ignored Jeff's words and busied herself tidying the cubby across from Ernie's. She heard, rather than saw, Ernie slam into Jeff's knees. When she turned, Jeff was holding his son by his narrow shoulders, his face a study in anguished love, eyes closed. Then he opened them and blinked.

"Have a good day, chief," he murmured. He was wearing jeans and a T-shirt today in place of his uniform—she should have realized he wasn't working. He planted a kiss on Ernie's rumpled hair, then gently aimed him toward the hall. "Remember what I told you."

Ernie didn't answer, just gave his dad a backward wave as he raced down the hall and skidded around the corner into his classroom with total disregard for his injuries. Jeff watched until he disappeared. His hands were knotted into fists.

Now that she and Jeff were alone, Ann felt another clutch of panic.

She couldn't help asking, "What did you tell him?"

"That if that kid comes at him again, he should knock him flat."

She rolled her eyes. "Combating violence with more violence. Now there's a strategy, Sheriff."

"The only one that works with bullies."

"Well, I guess we'll agree to disagree." *On that, too,* she added silently.

She took a step, intent on hurrying away to the nursery, but Jeff caught her arm. "Oh, no, you don't. There's no phone line between us now. Question—what do you think I want from you, Annie? And why does that scare you?"

"You've asked two questions, and you're missing the point. I thought I made myself perfectly clear."

"Yeah, well," he said, but there was still none of the usual smile on his face or in his voice. "In my work I'm pretty good at reading people. For instance, I can usually tell if a suspect is lying, and break him down fast." He paused. "Or if she's trying to cover up, I can sweet-talk her into telling me the truth."

"Good cop, bad cop," she murmured.

"So why won't you even talk to me?"

"I'm talking to you now."

He remained silent for a moment, seemingly mulling over his thoughts. At last he said, "I won't deny that speaking to your answering machine has already gotten old, and it ticks me off. But I'm also as stubborn as that cowlick on Ernie's head."

That was not what she wanted to hear. "My," she murmured, "being married to you must have been a walk in the park."

His eyes darkened. "It wasn't. I'll tell you about that sometime. After we get to know each other better."

"Jeff—"

"And maybe you'll spill the beans to me about yourself. Until then—"

She eased her arm from his grasp. "I need to go. I have babies to take care of." Then she paused. "I'll keep an eye on Ernie today. We all will."

And she saw Jeff's broad shoulders sag. He leaned against the door frame, blocking her exit. In that instant their nonrelationship and his unwanted questions ceased to be an issue. Jeff's thoughts had clearly shifted back to his son. "You can't imagine how I felt when Molly called to tell me Ernie had been hurt. It's the first time, really, except for his falling off his tricycle and bashing his chin last summer or skinning his knees when he tried to climb the tree in our yard. And those he did to himself."

"He's a typical boy."

"Yeah—all boy—and so was I. I get a kick out of that with him. But that other kid needs exactly what I told Ernie to give him." Jeff's eyes flashed with anger. "However. To avoid bloodshed I'd settle for talking to the kid myself. I'll set him straight in a hurry."

Ann took a breath. "I'm not a fan of the 'if you don't behave I'll call the cops' theory of parenting, but I can't recommend your dealing directly with Benjamin Crandall, either."

Jeff ran a hand over the back of his neck. "Yeah, I guess." When he spoke again, his voice shook. "Ernie's a tough little guy. I'd like to say that when I saw my son's face the other day, it hurt me more than it did him. But that's not true." Jeff studied the floor. "He didn't sleep all that night. The stitches and his bruises kept him awake. The pills they gave him at the E.R. didn't help much. His tears broke me in half. I shared his bed—and held him—and I swear, I wanted to hurt someone for hurting him. You're right, I shouldn't, and I won't, Annie. Except—"

She couldn't help but understand. Her first view of Ernie this morning had shaken her, too, even when she knew his bruises would fade, and his stitches were already starting to knit. Ernie was such a cute kid…a good person like his much bigger father.

Without thinking, Ann reached out and touched Jeff's cheek. She knew just how much he loved his child.

For Ann, it was a dangerous realization. Because she knew that he could come to love her a lot, too.

"Don't call me Annie," she said, but this time she pretty much whispered the words, and they held no heat.

Jeff smiled a little, which looked a lot to her like sympathy.

"You keep on covering up that soft side of yours for a while longer," he said, "but in the meantime, after school, Ernie and I are going to celebrate his return to day care with some ice cream at Graeter's. Why don't you join us?"

It was a siren call. An alarm.

"I'll think about it" was all she said.

MOLLY WAS IN the kitchen fixing dinner when the doorbell rang. She wasn't expecting company. She rapped a spoon against a pot on the stove. "Pop!" she called, then went back to stirring the spaghetti sauce that kept wanting to burn. "Will you get that?"

"On my way," he said, and she heard him shut the TV off.

It didn't occur to her who their caller might be. Her day at Little Darlings had been busier than usual. One of her teachers had called in sick, so Molly had monitored the three-year-olds along with seeing to her normal duties. She'd also been distracted all day by her churning thoughts about Brig and their first lesson for Laila. The last thing she wanted right now was to make small talk with a neighbor—unless it was one of the Colliers stopping by to say they were home.

Which they weren't, she knew, because she had a good view of their house from the kitchen window. So she stayed where she was, waiting for Pop to open the door.

"There you are, Thomas!" a woman declared.

Molly recognized the voice and sensed trouble brewing. She picked up on her father's silence as clearly as if he'd spoken. After a long moment he finally said, "Miss Brewster. What a surprise."

"I knew you couldn't hide from me much longer, you wicked man. I'm coming in, thank you very much—since you haven't asked me."

Molly heard the rustle of fabric, then the sound of the woman's bulk settling into a chair or the sofa. Natalie launched right into the reason for her visit.

"Your daughter offered to donate some things for our rummage sale. I volunteered you to deliver them. I'm thinking tomorrow would be good." Thomas didn't respond, and she rushed on. "I'll be there to help organize the displays. We've already gotten quite a few pieces of cast-off furniture, some of them not easy to move. You could help there, too."

Still no response from Pop. Molly knew she shouldn't keep listening, but the kitchen was right there, and she couldn't very well breeze through the dining and living rooms to the stairs. Besides, she'd risk blackening her spaghetti sauce if she left.

"I like a man with a solid look to him," Natalie said. "Not like some of my friends' husbands who are all skin and bones." She stopped, but only for a second. "They'll be there as well, so you'll have other men to talk to. Say, around noon?"

"I'm busy that day."

"Oh. Then how about the next? We still have time," she said. "And you, Thomas, need to get out of this house now and then."

"Now and then," he agreed. "But not tomorrow and not the next day—or any other in this case. I can't work myself up about a rummage sale."

She didn't comment, but Molly felt a twinge of empathy for Natalie Brewster.

"That's my story," he said with a faint smile in his tone. "And I'm sticking to it."

She sighed. "Do you think I didn't know you were lurking behind those curtains over there while I tried to rouse Bess Collier the other day? Hiding in the kitchen here while I talked to Molly?"

At the stove Molly gave the pot another stir, then lowered the heat.

Her father said, "I'm not a liar! I'll 'hide' behind the drapes if I want to."

Goodness, but he'd lost his social graces since her mother died. Or was his crotchetiness a sign of dementia?

Time to make an appearance. Molly felt as if she was about to break up some scuffle at Little Darlings. But what if Natalie had other reasons for dropping by now?

Molly strolled into the living room and again, caught a look on her father's face that reminded her of someone wanting something he didn't have.

"Hello, Natalie. I'd apologize for my dad, but that's his job." She eyed Pop pointedly.

"Sorry," he muttered.

Before Molly could say another word, he left the living room and went upstairs. Moments later a door closed on the second floor. Molly could only hope the sound didn't waken Laila or Brig, who were still adjusting to the more than seven hour time difference between Ohio and Afghanistan. Well, that and another sleepless night due to Laila's refusal to accept her new schedule.

She turned to Natalie, whose face looked as black as a thundercloud. In contrast, she wore a cheerful flowing coral-pink shirt and pants as if dressed for a social occasion. Man hunting, Pop might have called it. Or would he?

Now Natalie was all but shaking her head.

"He needs a woman in his life—besides his daughter. I hate having to say that, dear, because I know you love him and you're alone, too, but it's true."

Again, Molly wasn't that certain. A few hobbies might suit Pop better. Her mother was a hard act to follow, and Natalie wasn't his type—in the same way Brig could never be right for Molly. Yet she'd seen that look. Twice.

"Anyway." Natalie dismissed the issue, at least temporarily. "I've been making those calls," she said.

Molly held her breath, hoping for good news.

The bath incident and diaper lesson had brought Molly into much too close contact with Brig, and she couldn't help but hope Brig and Laila might soon move next door—for her own safety.

"I've learned nothing," Natalie said at last. "I've called everyone in town—our mutual friends, plus those I remember are either Bess or Joe's—and even tried contacting their doctor. He's the same one I use. He couldn't tell me anything. Their dentist, too. I hoped maybe Bess had an upcoming appointment that had been canceled with some explanation that would help. If you ask me, this is very strange. They would have told someone they were leaving town, don't you think?"

"Yes," Molly agreed, her spirits sinking. This wouldn't be good news for Brig, either.

She heard footsteps on the stairs. Molly crossed her fingers that Pop was still in his room. And it was Brig who appeared.

"Brig, this is Natalie Brewster." Molly looked up at him. "She's made a ton of calls—"

"All to no effect, I'm afraid," Natalie interrupted with a sympathetic look.

Molly watched Brig's face fall. "Thanks for trying."

At which point Molly sniffed the air and realized the spaghetti sauce was now burning on the stove. Her parents' electric range was never easy to regulate. With a last few words of appreciation to Natalie for her efforts, she left her in the living room to talk with Brig and went to save the dinner. And herself.

BURNED SPAGHETTI SAUCE WAS the least of his problems. Brig had spent the past few hours walking the baby around the bedroom he shared with her and wishing Natalie Brewster had found out something he could use to locate his parents before he did something dumb with Molly.

Standing next to her while he learned how to diaper Laila like a pro had been slow torture. The scent of Molly's freshly washed hair, the way the light played over her nape, her confident movements with Laila all made him long to escape. And at the same time to stay.

Fat chance there.

He knew that for sure when he wandered into the living room and saw Thomas flipping channels. Thomas glanced up. "You see the news?"

"Not tonight," Brig said, his empty stomach starting to burn. "May I?"

Thomas handed him the remote control. To Brig's surprise, he and Thomas had reached a tentative truce since Brig had borrowed Thomas's car to take Laila to the doctor. Brig guessed the truce was all because of the baby, not him, but he was grateful nevertheless. He'd topped off Thomas's gas tank today, put air in his tires and run the car through the automatic wash at the service station. His way of saying thanks.

As soon as Brig snapped on the cable news channel he preferred, dread soured his insides like an ulcer boring through his gut.

"It's always something," Thomas muttered.

Silently, Brig swore. If only the news had been about the Cincinnati Reds, but the season hadn't started. Instead, the Middle East was heating up again. He studied the map onscreen, calculating the odds of U.S. boots on the ground and his own chances of avoiding more conflict this soon. They didn't look good. The first guys in anywhere were teams like his.

He sighed. "Maybe things will settle in a few days."

Frustrated all over again, he said goodnight to Molly's father, who didn't answer, and wandered into the kitchen. Might as well try to soothe his fiery stomach with some leftover pasta or a sandwich. And hope Laila stayed down for the count. Brig made a mental note to lay some cash on Molly tomorrow for his share of the food. He certainly didn't deserve a free ride here. She and her father had done enough.

To his surprise, she was seated at the table

with a piece of apple pie and a half-full glass of milk. Brig didn't feel like talking, and he certainly didn't want to be this near her right now, but when he turned to go, Molly stopped him.

"Don't worry about Natalie," she said. "Something will turn up."

"It already has." He slumped into the chair across from her, then mentioned the news.

"Would you like something to eat?"

"I'll get it." He'd only picked at his dinner. In the middle of moving salad greens around on his plate, Laila had let out a wail from upstairs and Brig's meal had been over. Not that it mattered. He'd lost his appetite and didn't have one now, either.

The images from the TV were still playing through his mind, reminding him of things he wished he could forget. But he knew better. The nightmare would be with him for the rest of his life. The guilt, too. "Everything's blowing up," he said at last. "I'm not good with Laila. My folks have vanished. Now the part of the world that I know too well is about to erupt again."

"Laila's fine," Molly murmured. "Your parents will surely turn up soon." She paused. "Does the news mean you'll have to leave?"

Again, she thought but didn't say, *like eight years ago.*

"Probably," he said with resignation. "Once I get orders, I could have only a few days before I'm due back on base."

"Which is where?"

"D.C. area. A launching point for my unit." He gave her a weak smile. "And that's all I can tell you about that."

He had stepped out of one mess in Afghanistan into another right here in the U.S.A., and if experience was any teacher, he was about to fly into yet a third in the Middle East. From the living room he could hear a round of gunfire on the TV, the sounds of people running, shouting, and all at once he was back there, too, even farther from home... and Sean was—

Brig swiped a hand over his face. After a few minutes, with only the tick of the kitchen clock to break the silence, Molly said, "Are you okay?"

No, he wasn't okay. He would never be okay about Sean.

"Sometimes I get caught up in stuff that happened," he told her.

She wouldn't let his remark go at just that. "What are you caught up in now?"

In the midst of his blue funk, it occurred to him that since he'd returned home, he and Molly had never really talked details. About Sean, or about years ago.

"I was remembering Laila's dad. Her mom. And how they looked after that explosion. I was Sean's commanding officer. I had to identify them." He took a breath. "You should have known him, Molly. He was this big, goofy kid with a killer smile. Everybody liked him. It was impossible not to. He came from a family of miners in Kentucky, and the military, he always told me, was his way out." Brig shivered. "But he always planned to come home and buy a little farm. He and Zada talked about that all the time, about being outdoors in the sun in a place that was safe…."

Molly laid a hand on his arm. "You've honored your promise to take Laila out of that horrible war zone and give her a better life. That's more important, Brig, than knowing how to warm her bottle, bathe her or change her diaper. I'm sure even Laila knows how much you care about her. That's what matters."

"You think? But what happens when I have to—" He couldn't say the rest. Instead, he said, "You know why I went into the service in the first place? Not only because my dad, my grandfather, his father before him, were military." He half smiled. "Not because my dad—"

"Ran a tight ship? I always heard that, but I never saw it myself."

"He had his expectations, but that's the easy answer," Brig said with another smile he didn't quite feel. "No, maybe the best reason I had for joining up was Sean. I didn't know him then, but he's a perfect example of all the guys on my team. We're a small, tight-knit group. Elite. We share the same ideals—to serve this country, to make a difference in the world. I know that seems corny—"

Molly's voice sounded tight. "You're a patriot. So are they."

He met her open gaze and the brightness in her eyes. "But that didn't help you eight years ago, did it? There you were with your white dress and all the plans for our wedding—and I ground them into the dirt with my boot heel."

"You did what you had to do—what you're doing now."

"And the way I left didn't make you angry?"

"Of course it did. But I told you—no grudges. They're unhealthy."

Brig couldn't quite believe her, and he wouldn't let himself off the hook.

"Molly, the day I broke our engagement, I had just talked to a recruiter. In my own mind I was already gone. Nice guy, huh?" He didn't wait for her answer. "I suppose I had some notion that I'd charge off to war—wherever that was—then come back when I was done, and we'd pick up where we left off. We had time, I thought. Arrogant, huh?"

"We're different people now," she said with a finality, as if she didn't want to pursue the subject any longer. "I'm sure you're very good at what you do. I know you love it."

Another rush of memory overcame him. That ruined hospital wing, the dust and shards of concrete and twisted metal everywhere, the blood. There hadn't been much left of Sean or Zada. He couldn't help them now, or ever make amends for what he'd done to get Sean killed.

And the fact remained: he'd let down Molly just as much.

Now there was Laila, and she needed him, too. This time he'd do better.

"But enough about me," he said, trying to sound light. "What about you?"

"You already know about me."

"I know about Andrew and your unborn child…but that's not you, Molly. That's not *your* life now."

"I have Pop," she said, "and Ann. I have Little Darlings. *That's* my life."

None of it was enough, but he didn't say so. Brig scraped back his chair, went to the window over the sink and stared out at the dark night, stared at his own reflection in the glass. And thought, *Yes, I love what I do.*

And in that moment he hated himself.

He didn't hear Molly leave her chair. He didn't really see her set her plate and unfinished glass of milk on the counter. He felt the touch of her hand, though, on his back, warming him through the fabric of his shirt.

"I'm sorry," he whispered. "I'm so sorry, Molly. For everything." Her hand moved up and down his back, soothing, accepting. At that moment it was all he needed.

Filled with remorse, Brig turned blindly into her waiting embrace. He buried his face in her hair, pressed a light kiss to her there and they held each other close, the TV blaring from the other room. Duty loomed again. He would answer its call, but this time he'd be leaving with regret.

CHAPTER SEVEN

BRIG TUCKED LAILA in for what he hoped would be a morning nap and then went downstairs. At the kitchen table where he and Molly had shared last night's heartfelt discussion of the past, he nursed a second cup of coffee and read his emails.

The last one brought a smile, as usual.

Hey, Collier. Thanx for the photos. About time. The little lady looks great—and big! You probably don't see that but we do. Cutest kid on the planet. Good for you, buddy. See you soon. Give L some xxxxs. From all of us. H.

See you soon. Brig fired back a quick message to ask what intel the team had about the latest crisis in the Middle East, then dialed his grandmother's number, another item now in his daily routine. One that grounded him in the here and now.

Still no answer. After staring at the display for another few seconds, he snapped his phone shut and slid it across the table in frustration.

Why wasn't Grandma Collier picking up? Even if she was still angry with Brig over his broken engagement to Molly, and she was one to hold a grudge, surely his increasingly frantic calls would force her to answer—if only because of his parents.

Brig knew phone communication wasn't that simple. He couldn't leave messages. His grandmother didn't have an answering machine or even a cell phone. "Newfangled gadgets," she called them. If her landline had happened to include some kind of message service, which it didn't, she probably wouldn't know how to access it or care to learn. And unless his parents showed up there…

The TV news for public consumption this morning was no better than the night before. Brig had begun to startle last night every time another update flashed onscreen.

That startle reflex had hit him again in the middle of the night, and Brig had been trying to suppress it ever since. Now he sat up straighter in his chair. Coffee sloshed over the rim of his mug. Wait a minute.

What if his mom and dad were still home

after all? What if something had happened to them? On his last visit here Brig had urged his father to get their sooty fireplace cleaned so as not to risk carbon monoxide poisoning. If his dad hadn't—he tended to forget things—and his folks had built even more blazes during this cold winter to take the nighttime chill off the house, they could be in real trouble.

He had an instant vision of his parents lying unresponsive in bed. Or what if they'd both fallen ill? Molly had told him before she left for work this morning that a flu bug was going around. What if they'd become too sick even to call for help? *Feverish, weak, unable to lift a hand...* the horrific images wouldn't quit. Like his memories of Sean. What if all this time they'd been right next door and helpless behind those new locks?

He shoved back from the table. At the doorway to the dining room he called out to Molly's father, who was obsessively watching the news.

"Thomas? Would you listen for Laila, please? I'm going next door."

"Again?"

"I just had a thought." He was out the back door as Thomas muttered his agreement. He sounded cross, but if Brig knew him at all, the older man would be up the stairs at the first peep from Laila—if he even needed that excuse to hold her again.

Under different circumstances Brig might have smiled. Thomas Walker might seem crusty, but inside he was as soft as bread dough. Brig didn't smile, though. With one purpose in mind, he picked his way across the icy yard. Today was just as chilly and damp as every other day since he'd been back, and Brig shivered, wishing he'd pulled on a coat. Not that winter in Afghanistan wasn't even harsher. He should be used to freezing his tail off.

At the rear door that opened onto his mother's kitchen, he rapped a fist against the glass, but as usual got no answer. He peered inside at the old range that should have been replaced years ago, another possible source of poisonous gas. Then he checked the table, where he'd eaten so many meals during his late teens and early twenties after his father retired from service and they'd moved to Liberty. The town where his dad had found work was located midway between Grandma Collier's home in Indiana and his other granddad's place in western Pennsylvania. He could almost smell his mother's baking, but clearly she wasn't here now. The house looked cold and empty.

And what was that? Brig groaned. His dad's cell phone was lying on the kitchen counter. That looked ominous. His dad wouldn't go anywhere without his cell.

He went around to the front of the house. It was a good thing his folks had vanished during winter. If it were summer now, their grass would be knee-high. He climbed the porch steps to peer into the living room. The house was laid out pretty much like Molly's next door, and he could also see through into the dining room. But there was no evidence of anyone there, either.

The big table was bare, with no abandoned coffee cups. So was the living room, where the sofa showed no signs of having been recently used. Normally Brig would have seen the cushions indented from his father's heavier frame.

He'd observed all this before, of course. Nothing had changed. Which didn't give Brig any comfort. If they were, as he'd imagined, upstairs…if they'd gone to bed one night, then gotten ill or…

He sped back across the ice-encrusted

lawn, slipping and sliding, to the Walkers' front door and knocked. When Thomas lumbered up from his chair to answer, Brig said, "Can I borrow a ladder? The longest you've got. I want to take a look at my parents' second floor. They often watch TV in my old bedroom, which they converted to a den after I left home."

"At the front of the house," Thomas said, nodding. "Joe and I watch the Reds there sometimes in the summer. But why would they be there now?"

"That's what I want to know."

Thomas must have heard the worry in his tone.

"Let me get my coat. I'll go with you."

"No. Please. Stay here. Laila could wake up any minute. I'll be right back."

He hoped. If he saw nothing, he'd be back to square one, but his parents would be okay, just off on a vacation somewhere, maybe. Brig retrieved the ladder from Thomas's garage, then lugged it next door. In the front of the house he didn't need its full extension to reach the porch roof. From there he looked inside.

The TV room was empty, the television set showing a blank screen. He scanned the area, finding nothing out of place. No still bodies lying on the floor.

Not as relieved as he wanted to be, he climbed back down to haul the ladder around to the side. There was no way to see into the bathroom, but he would have a good view of his parents' bedroom.

With his pulse ticking like a bomb, he scaled the ladder once more.

Please, he silently prayed. *Let me be wrong.*

Brig was leaning to his left, hanging off the ladder by one hand and looking in at his parents' bed, when he heard sirens.

AT THE FIRST sound of the siren, Molly dropped a sheaf of new student applications back onto her desk, then hurried from Little Darlings, grabbing her coat on the way. One glance toward the street told her the commotion was at the Colliers' house. Molly's breath froze in the frigid morning air. Her steps began to drag with dread.

Frankly, she'd been dragging all morning, weighed down by her talk with Brig last night, the feel of his body against hers. She wondered if he was all right.

The first thing she saw was Jeff Barlow's cruiser angled at the curb. He flung open his door and got out. "What's happened?" she called.

"Don't know yet." Jeff glanced around, then with his hand on his gun holster, he walked to the side of the house. He looked up. "Stay there, Molly."

But of course she couldn't. What if someone had discerned that the house was empty, that the mail was piling up in the box, and had decided to burgle the place while Brig's parents were away? But that couldn't be, because Brig had collected the mail.

She followed Jeff. By then other people had begun to gather on the normally quiet street, her father among them. He came out of their house with Laila. Obviously he'd wrapped the baby hastily, in a blanket, because one tiny arm was sticking out. Molly noticed some of the neighbors.

Oh, and wouldn't you know? Here came Natalie, questions flying as she hustled up the front walk.

"Who's hurt? How can I help?" she asked, bustling around to the side of the house before Molly could get there. "Is it Thomas?"

Now, why would Molly's father be involved?

Natalie obviously hadn't noticed him there

with Laila, maybe because Pop was edging around the perimeter of the yard, hoping not to be seen. Where Natalie was concerned, he'd developed his own radar. Still, he was in plain sight.

Molly kept walking. If this was a crime scene, it had already been trampled by at least a dozen people. All of them had gathered by now under what Molly knew to be the Colliers' bedroom.

Was the burglar still inside? Jeff was standing at the foot of what appeared to be her father's extension ladder. She looked up, too—and saw Brig, frozen on one step.

"Come on down," Jeff said. "Looks like there's something we need to talk about here." His hand lingered on his holster.

"Sheriff, I can explain—" Brig began.

"Now," Jeff said in a harder tone, tightening his grip on the butt of his gun.

Like Molly, Ann came skating across the slippery yard from the center, her breath frosting in the cold air. "What's going on?" she asked, slipping her arm through Molly's elbow.

"It must be a robbery," Natalie announced, drawing her pink chenille bathrobe tighter around her. "But the cops got him." *Thanks to me,* she might have said. The look of triumph on her face said she was the one who'd called the police.

"Wouldn't you know?" Ann murmured.

Brig clambered down the ladder and held out his hand. Jeff didn't shake it.

"Start talking," he said. Keeping one eye on Brig, he turned to the crowd. "Go home, everybody. It's all over. I'll take it from here."

Some of the others started to drift off, but Natalie stepped forward.

"Sheriff, you'll need my statement."

Jeff sighed. "I know where you live." He'd probably taken a dozen statements from her about various "crimes." Natalie was her own Neighborhood Watch. She sashayed toward the sidewalk. And stopped next to Molly.

"I've just heard from the neighbors that you want to enlarge your day care center, Molly. None of us are happy about that. I know Thomas owns that triple lot, but building on it would be in violation of the town's zoning laws. This is a residential area."

"Yes. I know. I'll be speaking to the commission about an exemption."

"As a member myself, I have other worries, too." She patted Molly's arm. "Noise, for instance. But we'll talk about those another time." She continued through the yard and crossed the street.

Thomas carried Laila over to Molly and Ann. "What was all that?"

"Nosy neighbors," Molly said. "But it seems as if Brig's in a bit of trouble."

He and Jeff were talking quietly by the corner of the house now, their expressions earnest. "I didn't break in," she heard Brig say. "It's my family's home," and then he elaborated in a softer tone, words she couldn't make out.

Thomas moved closer and cleared his throat to get Jeff's attention. "He's okay," he said, much to Molly's surprise. "I've known Brigham Collier since he was in high school." Laila's arm waved as if to second the statement.

Jeff didn't look impressed. "I've known a lot of guys who, during or after high school, decided to become career criminals. I appreciate your vouching for him, Mr. Walker, but—"

Molly also made a move. "And you know me, Jeff. I mean, Sheriff Barlow." She didn't want to undermine his authority. "Would I lie? Brig is a highly decorated soldier, the commander of a top-secret black-ops unit. He served in Iraq and Afghanistan—"

"Thanks, Molly. Thomas," Brig added, looking poleaxed that her father had stuck up for him.

Ann might have added her two cents' worth as well, but Brig wasn't her favorite person since he'd left Molly. Now she turned away from him, obviously unwilling to add her endorsement.

"The man is staying in my father's home" was all she said. "Do you really think he'd allow a felon in? And what about this baby?"

"She's a cutie," Jeff agreed, reaching out to let Laila grasp his finger, but the look he gave Ann could have melted steel.

After a few more words of support from the lingerers in the crowd and some more conversation with Brig, Jeff appeared satisfied. He rubbed the back of his neck and smiled at Brig ruefully.

"Well, I suppose I could take you in— family place or not, you don't have the right to prowl. But considering the circumstances, I'm letting you go. I'll be talking to your folks, though." As if Brig were still a teenager.

"Good luck with that," he said.

Jeff snapped his holster shut, then gave Brig a quick salute.

"Thanks for your service," he said, already walking toward Natalie's house across the street. He gave Ann another look, and Molly heard him sigh again as he passed her, his notebook in hand.

ANN RAPPED ONCE on the back door, then let herself into her dad's house. Why hadn't she said even two words to Jeff about Brigham Collier? It was time she confronted that issue head-on. Thank goodness Pop had met up in the Colliers' yard with an old friend from work. To her amazement, the two retirees had decided to have lunch at their favorite café in town. Ann knew Molly was back at Little Darlings, working through her own lunch break, and Brig had gone into the house with Laila.

This was her chance. She'd been waiting for the right opportunity ever since Brig had all but moved into the house. Waiting for his parents, Molly had said. Ann didn't buy that for an instant.

"Hello?" she called out.

Brig came from the living room with the baby in his arms.

"Hey, Ann." She couldn't miss his wary regard. "What can I do for you?"

Get out of Molly's life, she wanted to say.

Instead, she told him, "Congratulations. You won't have a rap sheet after all. Or should you?"

Brig merely gazed at her.

"But the real question is—" she took a breath "—what are your intentions with my sister?"

Brig almost laughed. "You sound like the outraged parent in some Victorian novel," he said, but his eyes shifted to the baby in his arms. He wasn't as confident as he appeared. He knew what she thought of him.

"That doesn't answer my question."

"My *intentions?* That's between Molly and me," he said.

"Assuming you have any—honorable ones, that is."

"For heaven's sake, Ann. I realize I'm not your idea of the ideal man, for Molly or anyone else. I know how you felt years ago when we canceled our wedding—"

"*You* canceled," she said.

"Right. I did. And that was between Molly and me, too."

"So now, eight years later, you barge back

into her life and we're all supposed to say, 'Fine, Brig, never mind what happened then. It's all good now. Everything's forgiven.'"

"Not with you, apparently."

The baby fretted, and Brig spoke softly to quiet her. After a moment she fell asleep again. When he lifted his gaze to Ann once more, she saw anger there and something else. Regret? Guilt?

"No one is sorrier than I am for what I did to Molly. But I don't owe you any explanations," he said.

"You don't understand what you did to her. How she felt. Well, I do. I was with her when she put her wedding dress, which she looked so *beautiful* in, back in its box and paid for an ad in the paper to sell the dress. I was here when she cried herself to sleep night after night for six months, when she could hardly drag herself to work in Cincinnati every morning. I mailed that diamond ring to you myself because she couldn't bear to even look at it again. Did you know that?"

He flinched. "Ann, stop. This won't do any good. What's done is done."

"Is it? Really? Or is that simply your neat little way of evading responsibility?"

"I accept the responsibility. Molly knows

that. And I realize that you and your father have had a very low opinion of me—for good reason. I'm trying to earn Molly's forgiveness, at least—and to maybe change Thomas's mind." He gazed at her for another long moment. "I see it won't be possible to change yours."

Ann couldn't fail to notice the earnestness in his eyes, and maybe she *had* come on too strong, yet she wanted Brig to be clear on where she still stood.

"Well," she said, "just so you know, I'm with my father on this. I'm aware of what he told you. If you hurt Molly again, you'll answer to both of us."

No one understood better than Ann that whether eight years had passed, or a century, guilt lasted forever.

ANN WORKED LATE that night. She'd lost time that morning during the "burglary" next door, and the assistant she'd left in charge of her room then was never as thorough or neat as Ann liked. Besides, she felt uneasy about her earlier confrontation with Brig.

There were always things to be done at the center after the babies went home. When she had finished in the nursery, Ann decided to tidy up the older boys' play area down the hall. Then there were the girls' dress-up costumes—tiaras and gauzy ballet skirts, a nurse's outfit with a Red Cross cap, even something that looked to Ann like Snow White's dress—strewn all over the threes' room.

Little Darlings indeed.

An image of Ernie flashed through her mind. Not that he was inclined to take part in the girls' playacting. Ernie preferred the yellow trucks she had already organized by size and function.

The image of him, unfortunately, brought another image with it: of Ernie's father. Jeff, who had looked, as always, much too good in his sheriff's uniform that morning, had given her more than one withering glance at the Collier house.

When there was no more left to do, she locked up, cast an eye toward the lights glowing in her father's house, but rather than stop in as she sometimes did, she trudged the few blocks to her own apartment. With Brig and the baby sharing Molly and Thomas's quarters, tonight she would just go home.

Her stomach growled. She should go grocery shopping. That morning before work her

refrigerator had contained two slices of bo-
logna, a half pint of milk past its sell-by date
and some dried-up cheddar cheese she had
neglected to wrap.

A bowl of cereal for dinner seemed her
only option, because she couldn't summon
the energy to walk five more blocks to the
convenience store. Ever since she'd talked to
Brig and before that seen Jeff at the Colliers'
house, she'd felt guilty. And depressed.

Her mood lingering, she ignored her car in
the parking lot near the front entrance to her
building. Pop had changed the oil a few days
ago, as if hoping Ann would start to drive
again. And maybe she would...someday.

Walking with her head down, she didn't
notice the car that pulled in next to hers. Jeff
Barlow got out, strolled toward her and gave
her another of those looks.

"You stood us up," he said mildly in that
always too-patient way that made her feel
even worse about herself. "You missed our
ice cream social yesterday."

"Jeff, I'm sorry. I just...couldn't."

"When I came to get Ernie at the center
then, Molly told me you had left to run an
errand. She didn't know if you'd gone for the

day." He paused. "We waited for you until six o'clock."

Ann's empty stomach tightened. She couldn't tell him she had stewed and fretted all afternoon, "thinking about it," when she'd known all along she wouldn't join them. She had leaped at the chance to wheel a batch of books to the library using one of the center's strollers.

He leaned against the hood of his car and peered at her in the dark.

"You don't like ice cream?"

"I love ice cream."

"Favorite flavor," he said.

She didn't hesitate. "Butter pecan."

"Mine's black cherry. Ernie never gets anything but *dulce de leche*."

Ann blinked. "What?"

"Means *sweet milk* in Spanish. Basically, a lot of caramel. I figure he likes it because it's all sugar. The only time he gets the stuff."

She started up the path to her building. "Tell him I said hi. I'll see him tomorrow."

She took a single step before Jeff said, "He's here now." He tilted his head toward his car. Ann could just make out Ernie's small form buckled into his car seat in the back.

When he saw her, he waved. She could make out his mouth moving. *Hi, Miss Ann!*

Ann waved, too. "How's his face?"

"Better. See for yourself." He unwound his long frame from his slouch against the hood. "So here goes. Ernie and I have a bag of fast food." He reeled off the menu, every one of Ann's favorites when she allowed herself to indulge.

Her stomach growled a third time.

"It's cold out here," Jeff said, "and getting colder. Why don't I shut off the car, grab that bag and Ernie and we all go inside before the food freezes?"

For a too-long moment Ann hesitated, once more not knowing what to do. That Jeff was sticking way too close for her comfort should have alarmed her more than it did. Why hadn't he given up? And why—if she was honest with herself—didn't she want him to?

Confused, she worried her bottom lip. Jeff's gaze followed the motion. "You haven't eaten dinner? You must be hungry."

"All right. Fine," she said at last, starting up the walk again. "Come in." *See if I care.* The childish thought arrived all too easily, as had her surrender. "We'll eat—Ernie must be starving—and then you can go."

"Gee, Ann," he said, opening Ernie's door, "you really know how to make a guy feel welcome."

She didn't want him to feel welcome, even though her mother would have scolded her for that.

Jeff and Ernie followed her into her apartment before Ann could think of any excuse not to open the door.

Jeff moved around her kitchen as if he owned the place.

"Plates?" he asked, and Ann pointed at an upper cabinet. "Knives and forks?" She indicated the middle drawer. She didn't dare help. It would involve standing too close to Jeff.

By the time he served dinner and poured sodas for Ann and him and chocolate milk for Ernie, her mouth was watering.

"I'm only allowing this because I'm hungry, too," she said.

"Whatever you need to think."

"Isn't this great, Miss Ann?" Ernie asked around his cheeseburger. Ann was happy to note that his face indeed looked better. The bruises were now interesting shades of acid green and yellow, and the skin around his stitches didn't look as red. The injuries didn't seem to bother him at all.

"Don't talk with your mouth full, chief," Jeff said.

After they ate, and before Ann could object, he hustled Ernie off to her second bedroom, which she used as an office. He told his son he could watch *Finding Nemo* again on Jeff's iPad, but he had to use the earbuds. Then Jeff sank onto her living room sofa.

"He'll probably last ten minutes. He's always exhausted after day care. I'll end up carrying him to the car."

"Maybe you should leave now."

"Ann." Jeff studied her for a long moment in that way he had. "Admit it. You liked your burger and fries. Not to mention having company instead of eating another meal alone." He hesitated. "Don't you ever cook? Or shop for food? Your fridge is a disaster."

She blushed. "Thank you so much for looking inside."

"I was trying to find some ketchup for Ernie's fries." He sighed. "What is it with you anyway?"

"You don't want to know."

"Yes. I do," he said. "I'll tell you what I see. An attractive woman who loves kids. A woman whose face crumples when she looks at Ernie's stitches, who hurts for him just as I do. But I also see this other person."

"The one who shuts you out."

"Exactly. If you're not interested in me, okay. But I think you are. That's not male ego talking. I get the vibes, the same ones you get from me. Give me a break, Annie. I'm just divorced," he said, "not a serial killer."

Ann tried to shift the topic. "You said your marriage wasn't easy."

"Understatement of the decade. No, it wasn't." As if he sensed her interest, he went on, "You want to know how I got to this point—giving up a job I loved with CPD? Moved Ernie from Cincy to Liberty Courthouse and became a sheriff's deputy here? We live in a house half the size of the one we had with her. But all that's okay." He gazed into the middle distance as if seeing his old life, his marriage. "Kay and I were never a good match, though neither of us knew that at first. There was some heat in the beginning, as there usually is, and then…there wasn't. We argued a lot. She had a big spending problem, a need for some kind of anger management. Not that our issues were one-sided. I had my share."

"You don't have to say any more, Jeff."

The more she learned about him, the more she risked liking him. The more she risked having to reveal herself. Because then he wouldn't let the relationship be one-sided for them, either.

"No, you need to hear this." His face hardened. "The evening I arrived home from a lousy day at a double homicide scene and saw her about to smack Ernie, I packed his stuff and mine and called a lawyer."

"Do you two have joint custody?"

"Nope. The court finally agreed Ernie is better off with me."

His story touched her. "You're a wonderful father, Jeff. I see some who aren't at the center. I'm afraid Benjamin Crandall has one of those—his dad is either on the road for business or unavailable emotionally, and if the child doesn't get some guidance, I hate to think what will happen to him."

Jeff's features softened again. "I love Ernie with everything in me. I would have had a dozen kids if Kay and I had…but we didn't last. Leaving was the best thing for Ernie and for me."

"He's a lovely little boy," she said.

Jeff grinned. "Don't let him hear you say

that. *Lovely* isn't a word boys like Ernie care for."

"How about cool, then?"

"Way cool is even better."

From the other room Ann heard the soundtrack for *Finding Nemo*. Jeff said, "That's my cue. He probably fell asleep, and the earbuds popped out. We'd better head home so I can tuck him into bed. Morning comes early, and before I catch forty winks, he'll be bouncing on my chest ready to get to Little Darlings."

"He does have enthusiasm."

Jeff stood, then looked down at Ann. "I realize you herded me like a sheepdog right into talking about Kay tonight. But I'm still waiting to hear about you."

She paused, heart beating too fast. "It's really not that interesting."

"Oh," he said, "I'll bet it is. Once we get past that we can—"

"Jeff, thank you for dinner. Somehow you sensed my weakness for junk food. And thanks, too, for dinner that one night. I had a good time when we hiked with Ernie. But you're wasting your time if you think this— whatever it is—can go any further."

"Further than what?"

"Being…well, acquaintances. Tonight was for Ernie," she said. "He's one of my favorite kids at the center. And maybe there is some spark between you and me, but that's all it is. All it can be. So you should really—"

"Don't tell me what I should do." He kept looking at her in that way that both fascinated and scared her.

By now her pulse was hammering triple time. She drew herself up, her words brittle as she tried to protect herself. "Don't make anything of this just because you have a cute little boy. I was acting in my official capacity tonight. Call it a parent conference if you like."

To her surprise, Jeff only laughed.

"Tell yourself anything you want, Annie. But don't expect me to believe it."

CHAPTER EIGHT

MOLLY WAS IN her room that night editing her still-balky presentation for the zoning commission when she heard a cry from across the hall. Laila was up again.

She could hear Brig talking softly to the baby as he paced. But Laila only cried harder.

Molly wasn't in the mood to give another lesson on caring for an infant—as if there was a cure for sleeplessness at this age—but she was out of bed before she realized what she was doing. Her mind was still whirling from the ladder incident that morning, so it didn't take much to break her concentration tonight. Besides, Molly was a caregiver, not a writer.

She opened her bedroom door, stepped into the hall and ran smack into Brig. At the brief contact with his solid chest, she jerked away.

He gave her a drowsy smile, Laila nestled in the crook of his arm.

"Guess who doesn't want to sleep?"

"She's definitely clock shifted," Molly

agreed. She reached out to smooth the baby's damp hair but drew back when her fingers brushed Brig's hand. She didn't need to see Laila's red face to know she was working herself up into a real state. One tiny fist smacked Molly on the cheek. "She must think midnight is time to get up."

"Well, it *is* morning over there," he said. "The problem is how to get her turned around."

Molly peeled aside the blanket and took another look. Immediately the baby kicked out her legs, then wailed even harder.

"I don't think the clock is her only issue. Maybe we've been missing the obvious. With most babies who cry at the same time every day or night, it's colic." She didn't stop to ponder her use of the word *we*.

He groaned. "That doesn't sound good. You mean, like a horse?"

"Similar, I suppose. In either case, belly pain hurts."

The dark circles under Brig's eyes stood out like bruises.

"What's the treatment?"

"I hate to say this, but time. She'll outgrow it as her body develops. Usually by four months."

"I thought the new formula would do the trick."

"That helps. Her digestive system has been better, don't you think? But for now..." Molly gave a little shrug.

Brig sighed. He was jostling the baby in his arms, trying to comfort her with the motion. "Guess I'll head downstairs so as not to wake the—"

He didn't even finish before Pop emerged from his room, a worried frown on his face, his hair sticking up in spikes, his bathrobe tails flapping. "Is she sick?"

"Not exactly," Molly said. "Go back to bed, Pop. No sense in everyone losing sleep." She turned to Brig. "Let me take Laila. She can help me with my presentation," she joked, "and you need rest."

"Molly," he began, shaking his head, but she deftly slipped the baby from his arms to cradle her close.

Perhaps not the wisest decision she'd ever made, but it was either that or watch Brig become ever more sleep deprived. Then there was Laila. That first night in the spare room when she'd gazed down at this baby and loved her on sight had been a cautionary moment. She'd done her best ever since, even during

their lessons, to keep from any too close contact, using the excuse whenever she could that
Brig needed to be hands-on so he could care
for Laila on his own. But she'd been fighting
a losing battle.

"Put a pillow over your head—you, too,
Pop—and I'll see you both in the morning."

Which soon left Molly in her room again,
sitting in the rocking chair she liked to read
in, holding a bundle of blanket and baby and
giving up another piece of her soul. Well,
she'd volunteered—again—hadn't she?

Alone with Laila for the first time, Molly
sang to her, but the lullaby didn't help. Nothing did. Molly tried every trick she used at
Little Darlings, but Laila continued to kick
and squirm and scream. She screwed up her
little face until it looked like an angry prune.

So they just walked. The metronome tick of
the grandfather clock in the hallway seemed
to soothe the baby's wails, and Molly soon
dared to plant a soft kiss on Laila's hair, like
the soft kiss Brig had given Molly in the
kitchen. A kiss Molly had done her best to
forget.

"It's just you and me tonight, babe," she
murmured. "I know you don't feel well. It will
be all right, though. You and me," she added,

settling back into their nest in the rocking chair.

Molly's room was warm and cozy, a retreat, with her treasured things. The comforter from the bed in the house she'd shared with Andrew. His favorite shirt, still hanging in her closet here because it smelled of him, woodsy and masculine and…safe. Her favorite wedding picture of her and Andrew, and next to it the silver-framed sonogram of their unborn child.

What if their child had been born healthy and alive like Laila? And Molly had been given the chance to hold her baby and walk the floor on colicky nights like this. That wasn't meant to be. She had to accept this reality.

She wouldn't feel sorry for herself.

Laila had finally quieted and, exhausted, fallen asleep. But Molly wouldn't take her across the hall to her crib and Brig, and be reminded of so many years ago when she had loved him and thought he loved her, too.

Now they were both different, and after all he'd seen and done in war, he might not even be capable of love. She wondered if she was, either.

They both cared for Laila, though.

Molly smiled down at her, rocking, rocking. In the darkness, she held the baby close, this latest borrowed child, one body warming the other, warming her inside.

What if…

BRIG HAD JUST waved at Jeff Barlow's retreating cruiser the next morning when he spied Thomas rounding the corner of his house with Laila in a stroller. He grinned at the picture they made, the small baby wrapped in a lavender bunting, an extra blanket tucked around her, the older man with his neck swaddled in a bright red plaid scarf and wearing a navy blue parka.

Brig was feeling pretty good this morning, thanks to Molly's offer to sit up with the baby last night. He'd actually gotten a solid seven hours of sleep. His stubborn jet lag, which usually didn't bother him, was finally easing. The air didn't hold quite the chill it had for the past few days, and he didn't see a snow cloud in sight. The sun was even shining in a blue sky.

If he could ignore the news in the paper and on TV, he'd be fine.

Thomas, stroller in hand, joined him on the

sidewalk. "I saw the sheriff's car," he said as if urging Brig to explain.

Brig decided to hold off on that subject. He was still pondering his team's tight-lipped response to his query about intel. "Where'd you get the stroller?"

"From Molly's center."

"Good thinking." He fell into step beside Thomas. "I like Jeff," Brig said when they were rolling along the sidewalk. "He's a solid guy. I couldn't help thinking he'd make a good fit for my team."

"He's a good man. As I keep telling my daughter Ann." He paused. "One of these days she'll have to let go of the past. Until then, that accident has ruined her life."

Brig bit back the words that wanted to come out. He knew about her accident years ago, and he'd wondered more than once about Ann's lifestyle now—staying to herself, always walking everywhere, refusing a lift the time he'd offered on his way back from the pediatrician's office with Laila in the car he'd borrowed from Thomas. But Brig knew better than most people that sometimes keeping quiet was the right thing to do. Certainly he had his own demons. And Ann had made her opinion of him clear.

"Sorry to hear that," he said instead. Then, "Jeff came by this morning to ask about my parents—and offer some help. He said he could probably put out an APB, but I doubt my father would appreciate being pulled over somewhere by the cops."

In the stroller Laila was cooing to herself. She stared up at the bright sky, kicking and waving in obvious approval of the outing.

"My grandmother in Indiana also seems to have disappeared. I can't help feeling that the two things must be connected. I know Mom worries about her. She says every time the telephone rings, she jumps, concerned that something has happened to her mother-in-law or something has happened to me."

"That's what parents do," Thomas murmured. Brig could almost see him thinking about Ann, then Molly. "I have to say I was mighty relieved when Ann started to work at Little Darlings and Molly left Hyde Park to live here with me. It's easier to keep tabs on them," he said with a smile.

Brig could relate to that. He watched Laila like a hawk, like his parents watched his grandmother. "My folks want Grandma Collier to come live with them, but she's still active and in good health as far as I know. She's not ready to give up her independence and sell her house. Four bedrooms, three baths plus a walk-up attic full of things from the past fifty years. Weeding out stuff and packing up would seem daunting."

"Joe told me they've met with some major resistance."

Brig bent to straighten Laila's blanket, which had come loose and now threatened to trail on the sidewalk or get caught in the wheel. She gave him one of her new, perfectly sunny smiles.

It occurred to him that her night with Molly might have done her some good, too. Molly had a way of calming her that was all her own.

It also occurred to him that he and Thomas had never held such a lengthy conversation, especially without Thomas snarling or Brig feeling guilty for every transgression committed years ago.

"Thomas, I appreciate you standing up for me yesterday."

Thomas grunted. "No sense you getting run in to jail, leaving Molly to care for this child and her center at the same time."

And you, Brig thought, but didn't say that, either. He'd watched Molly pick up after her father, cook his meals and do his laundry. It

irritated him that Thomas let her, without of-
fering to help.

"Nice touch," Thomas said, surprising Brig
again. "Bringing my car back with a full tank
and shiny to boot."

"You're welcome." By now they had made
a full circuit of the block. Considering their
temporary truce, Brig ventured the rest of
his latest theory. "So what if my folks are in
Indiana right now? With Grandma Collier?
Which doesn't explain why they wouldn't answer the phone."

"Maybe they took her with them somewhere else."

"Maybe." But Brig had a bad feeling. His
grandmother wasn't the most enthusiastic traveler. Although she had a dozen activities in her hometown, she tended to not
stray far. "Barlow's going to make some calls
to local law enforcement there. See what he
can learn."

Thomas turned in at the front walk. By
now Laila was beginning to fuss. Either she
was wet or she needed a bottle. Certainly she
couldn't be cold. The temperature was ris-
ing, the sun warming the air, and Laila was
bundled into so many wrappings that she
had a too-rosy pair of cheeks. And would

you look at him? Postulating what the baby's trouble might be. He'd even managed to diaper and dress her earlier without a hitch after Molly left for work without more than a good-morning to him and a quick acknowledgment of Brig's "thanks for last night."

"I'll take the stroller back to Molly," Thomas announced.

"Let me have Laila," Brig said. "Come on, cupcake."

"Why don't *you* heat her bottle? I'll carry the baby home after I return this rig."

Brig hid a smile. The old guy was crusty, all right, but he sure liked Laila. His intention was as clear as the morning sky. Brig had noticed how he liked to hold her whenever he got the chance and talk nonsense until she punched the air with a fist or flung out her legs in delight. His growing love for Laila showed in his eyes.

"Okay, I'll go heat her bottle," Brig said.

He had started toward the back door of the house when Thomas stopped him. And their pleasant walk ended with the words that brought Brig back to reality.

"You think they're in trouble? Bess and Joe?"

"I hope not."

HOPING SHE HAD half a chance of securing the town zoning commission's approval for the expansion at Little Darlings, Molly frowned at the papers on her desk. At half past eight she was still at the center, profiting from the weekend quiet there to do more work on her presentation. But Molly wasn't getting far with her editing.

Her thoughts kept returning to the house. To Brig and Laila, and last night when she'd rocked and sung to the baby she was coming to care about far too much. The man, too, she had to admit.

And where could that possibly lead?

The TV news kept getting worse and worse. The president was scheduled to speak right now about probable military intervention because of human rights violations, but Molly didn't want to hear what he had to say. Sooner rather than later, Brig would leave for wherever in the world he was needed.

Squaring her shoulders, she shuffled papers until she found the page that most needed work. She was still pleased with how the original renovation had turned out. The character of the carriage house remained, but now the place had new and larger windows, more safety features.

The play yard, though, could use new equipment; for example, a base of recycled tires to cushion falls from the slides or swings. Molly had also added a small climbing wall to the new design. If the commission approved her plans, she'd be able to open more new classrooms, plus enlarge the nursery. Her architect had carved out space, too, for another much-needed bathroom, with kid-size sinks and toilets.

One more if, she thought with a sigh. The commission—specifically Natalie, who Molly hadn't even known was a member until she'd objected to the expansion—might be a big stumbling block.

She covered her face. All she could do was hope for the best.

"Molly?" Brig's voice brought her head up. "Am I interrupting?"

"Please, do." She sat back in her chair. "Trying to make this presentation for the zoning commission into something peppy they can't resist is driving me crazy."

Brig was holding his cell phone. "News," he said. "Good and bad."

For a second she feared it was his next foreign assignment.

"Jeff Barlow tracked my parents down.

Good thing we met when he almost arrested me yesterday. I needed his help on this after all."

For an instant she held her breath. "Where are they?"

"Indiana. Staying at my grandmother's. That's the good part."

"Then why didn't they answer her phone?"

"I don't know. My grandmother doesn't have a machine, so they weren't getting messages, either."

Molly leaned forward. "What about your parents' cell phones?"

"You won't believe this—but yesterday when I checked their house, I saw my dad's cell sitting on the kitchen counter. I guess they left in a hurry—and if I know him, he was cracking the whip over Mom's head to get on the road. She doesn't have a phone of her own. One of Dad's economy measures after he retired. He still likes to be the guy in charge."

Molly could think of only one reason for the lack of communication.

"I assume your grandmother's not well."

"No, she's not, and that's the bad news."

His worried expression made Molly ache for him. "Poor Mrs. Collier."

"Apparently she was cleaning out her garage, tried to pull a carton from a stack against the wall—and fell, hard." He flinched as if he could feel the landing. "She shattered her hip. The prognosis is actually pretty good, considering, but after surgery to repair it, she might have suffered a ministroke. My folks probably aren't coming home anytime soon."

Molly knew what that meant. Brig had found his parents, but there was still Laila to worry about. "What are you going to do?"

"Leave for Indiana first thing in the morning."

Molly took a breath before she plunged in and said, "I'd be happy to look after Laila while you're gone."

"Well, uh…" He trailed off, obviously unwilling to impose on her.

"Really, it's no trouble. Even with colic she's a 'little darling,' as you said."

But Molly wondered if she was losing her mind, tormenting herself all over again by getting close to Laila when she knew the arrangement was only temporary. Yet how could she not offer to help Brig? The last thing he needed now was a baby to consider. A colicky baby who could be demanding.

"During the day I can keep Laila at the

center with me or in the nursery with Ann. No charge," she said with a smile she hoped was encouraging. "When we're not able to help, Pop is always here."

"I know, but…"

"He's not the easiest person, but he does like Laila."

Brig frowned. "He and I had a nice talk this morning, but to be honest, Molly, I wouldn't like leaving him with the responsibility. The other night he was watching Laila in the living room, but when I walked in she was all caught up in the covers, her face scrunched into a pillow he'd put on the floor for her. If I hadn't come in, she could have smothered."

Molly frowned, too. Had her fears about Pop been right? Was he losing his edge? "I didn't know that. Sometimes he does get distracted."

"He's become addicted to the news on TV."

So had Brig, but Molly didn't point that out. Actually, so had she. Brig wasn't the only one who jumped now whenever the phone rang.

"I'll make sure Pop isn't alone with her," she said.

But still, he didn't seem to like any of her solutions.

"You told me a flu bug is going around at

the center. I'd rather not leave Laila there. She's so young and underweight, and likely still hasn't built up many immunities—" He broke off, then tried again. "I was kind of hoping you might come with us instead."

Molly blinked. "To Indiana?"

"Why not? It isn't far. A few hours' drive is all. We could be there and back in one day. I just need to check on my parents, see how Grandma Collier is doing."

Hours in the car with both Brig and Laila? In such close quarters? After the night in the kitchen with him and then the night alone with the baby, she would be risking too much. Yet he wanted her help. Someone in need was always a lure for Molly. Still, it was also a chance to leave Liberty for a day, to escape her ever-increasing restlessness and the sense that no matter how she loved Little Darlings and Pop and Ann, she had begun to envision something else, something more....

"I suppose I could go with you."

Brig's face relaxed. "Thanks, Molly. Can we use your car? I'll drive, and that way you can deal with Laila whenever necessary. I think she'll be okay, though. She likes the motion of a car, and it might help her catch up on some sleep. If we're lucky, she'll get clock shifted to the right time zone."

She gave him a weak smile. "If we're lucky."

And if *she* was, Molly added silently, she wouldn't sink deeper into the abyss of her growing feelings for Brig and Laila.

CHAPTER NINE

MOLLY STEPPED OUT of the car and stretched her cramped legs. The drive from Liberty had taken less time than she'd expected, and Brig had been right. For the most part, Laila had slept soundly in her car seat. Molly, riding in the back with her, felt grateful for the distance from Brig. Conversation wasn't necessary, and she had asked to stop only once so she could diaper the baby.

"I'm glad my mom finally called," Brig said as he unstrapped Laila from her seat. Halfway along the interstate, his phone had rung.

His mother had been ecstatic to hear Brig's voice. "You're back in the States? At our house?" He quickly disabused her of that notion, filling Bess in on his search for them and about the missing door key. "I'm so sorry we didn't leave a note," she'd said. "But your father wanted to get going fast, and we had no idea you were on your way home."

That didn't matter now. Brig had assured her that he was already near his grandmother's hometown outside of Indianapolis. Molly noticed he hadn't mentioned either her or the baby.

"Can you believe the communications gap in all this?" Brig led the way now across the parking lot to the hospital entrance. "It took the police calling all the hospitals to find them."

"At least your mother phoned right away this morning."

Walking with Brig into the hospital, Molly decided she was definitely out of her comfort zone. Instantly the typical smells assailed her nostrils. Antibacterial cleaning products, mingling with the heavier scents of various medications, she supposed. Molly had wanted to wait outside with Laila, but Brig wouldn't hear of that. The late winter weather was still frigid, and, after yesterday's reprieve, fresh storm clouds threatened.

Instead, she and Brig and Laila were in the elevator, riding up to the third floor as if they were an ordinary family coming to visit a beloved relative. Which they were…except for the family part.

Molly was just a neighbor.

As soon as they walked out of the elevator, Brig's mother spied him. With a happy
shout, Bess Collier flew into his arms. Just
in time he handed off the baby to Molly, who
blended into the background. "My boy," Bess
said with tears in her eyes. She held him tight
for a long moment before drawing back to
study him from head to foot, a mother checking for damage. "You're safe," she said at last,
the tears rolling down her cheeks. Then she
stepped away for a better, even longer look—
and saw Molly.

Shock, then more joy showed in her face.
"Molly, how are you? I know, we should have
told you and Thomas we were leaving town."
Brig's mom was a very pretty woman, slim
and straight, with the same dark hair as Brig,
but clearly the family crisis had taken its toll.
Molly noted her pale face and the dark circles that were a perfect match for Brig's. "In
fact, I thought we had," she said in an exas-
perated tone. "Joe promised to call your father after we got here—then forgot. He's been
so stressed." She moved as if to draw Molly
close, then stopped.

Bess's gaze snapped to the baby in Molly's
arms. She glanced at Brig.

"You've brought Laila, too!" A second later

she was holding the baby, talking to her. The look when she gazed down at the little girl was instantly one of pure love. "Isn't she beautiful? Yes, this is your...grandma. Hi, darling. Welcome to..." She shook her head. "I keep forgetting. We're not in Liberty." She looked again at Brig. "You can't imagine how hard this past week has been."

Assuring her that he could, Brig asked about his grandmother.

"She's doing better. She still has a long way to go," Bess said, "but she could be released to rehab by next week."

Molly heard a distant chime, and Brig's gaze shifted to beyond the nurses' station to the bank of elevators. His father stepped out. When he spotted Brig standing there, he loped straight for his son. Laughing, relieved, it seemed to Molly, he clapped Brig on the back, as if not to let emotion overcome him.

Joe Collier was a rough-and-tumble sort, she had always thought, with an almost rigid bearing that bespoke his long military career. He still had a head of thick brown hair, though it was lighter than Brig's, but the same blue eyes.

"You're a welcome sight," he said in the gruff tone Molly had heard ever since the

Colliers had moved in next door. Like Bess, he pulled back, eyes glassy bright to assess his only child. "When did you get here?"

"About fifteen minutes ago, sir."

"No, I meant Liberty."

Brig told him, then added, "Sorry I couldn't give you a heads-up. You know how those military hops can be."

"Quick and dirty," Joe agreed with another laugh. He stopped smiling when Brig explained about the new key for their house. Molly noticed he still called his father *sir*.

"So where have you been staying?"

"At Molly's." Brig gestured toward her. "Next door."

"I'm sorry I forgot to call Thomas." Joe's gaze homed in on her. "Seems we're having a real reunion here." He leaned to kiss her cheek. "Great to see you, Molly." He took another step to grin at his wife, then peeled back Laila's blanket. "Hello there, too, angel. Aren't you something? Look at those dark eyes, Bess, and have you ever seen such little hands? She's like a miniature."

"Sheer perfection," Bess murmured.

Brig said, "She's certainly got a good set of lungs."

"Cries a lot, does she?" Joe didn't appear worried. "I can't wait to hear that."

Brig grinned, too. "Be careful what you wish for."

Oh, yes, Molly thought. *Be very careful.*

BRIG DIDN'T CARE for hospitals. Sean's tragic death was still too fresh and stark in his mind, and he and Zada weren't the first losses Brig had experienced in his unit. He'd begun to sweat as soon as he entered the hospital, and was halfway to a full-blown panic attack before he and Molly had even walked into his grandmother Collier's room.

Blood. Tissue. Body parts...the screams of survivors.

He couldn't stop the replay. And always there was his own sense of guilt.

Brig hesitated in the doorway. All at once he was glad one of the nurses had told them infants weren't permitted to visit, so Brig's parents had taken Laila down to the lobby to wait, obviously eager to become better acquainted with her.

Now he heard the familiar rhythmic beeping of monitors, smelled the stomach-turning scents of rubbing alcohol and about a dozen other things he couldn't identify but didn't like. Molly must have felt the same. She held back, and for courage himself, he grasped her hand. His parents loved her. So did his grandmother, even if Molly didn't appear to feel she belonged here.

"Oh, no, I don't think I should," she said, tugging at his hold. "I'll sit with Joe and Bess—"

"My grandmother will want to see you."

He took a breath, then strolled toward his grandmother's bed. She'd been dozing, her mouth half-open, and looked way too much like a corpse in Brig's view; for an instant he couldn't breathe. The faded hospital gown she wore wasn't even close to the brightly colored clothes she favored, always with a bit of bling, and her hair was stringy and damp. Then, as if sensing him there, she opened her eyes, and he saw that familiar flash of blue.

"Brigham Collier." Her scolding tone—weaker than normal—didn't fool him, but if she'd suffered a minor stroke, it hadn't affected her speech. "Where have you been? I have no protection here. That son of mine and his wife are a couple of bullies."

Brig grinned. Surprised that she was glad to see him, considering their rift, he let go of Molly's hand and bent to kiss Grandma Collier soundly on the forehead. "What's this I hear about you trying to hurt yourself? Now, look," he admonished. "You're locked up in this place as though you were in a solitary cell in the brig. I say we spring you and head for somewhere warm and sunny."

"The Caribbean," she murmured, but when she lifted her hand to touch him, it fell back onto the sheets. Brig picked it up and held it, feeling the brittle bones beneath her skin. "Sounds lovely, but there'll be no world travel for me. I've turned into a useless old woman."

"Don't say that." He softened his tone. "You'll be on your feet in no time."

"I was up the first day after my surgery. If you think you know pain, you don't."

Brig patted her hand. "Well, don't give up. We can talk later when you feel better about getting you some help in cleaning out that house."

"I was only clearing some junk," she said. "I have no intention of moving. I've been in my home for over half a century, and when I leave, they'll carry me out—just like those paramedics did when I broke my silly hip."

"Let's not argue. You concentrate on getting well first."

She made a disgruntled sound. "You're just like Joe after all."

Brig didn't press the issue. He turned to find Molly perched on a chair by the empty second bed in the room. She was studying her hands and biting her lower lip.

"You have another visitor," he told his grandmother. "Will the senior Mrs. Collier please stop worrying about tomorrow— It's Molly, Grandma."

The woman's sharp gaze sought Molly's softer one. "Come right over here. I haven't seen you in years." She cast Brig a chiding glance as Molly all but fell into her arms with a half laugh, half sob. They clutched each other. Molly and his grandmother had once been friends, and neither had forgotten.

"Shame on you, Brig. Letting this woman go," she said in her most stern manner.

Brig had heard the lecture more than once—when she was still talking to him. His grandma was so candid and forceful that at times she could make Brig's dad appear like a wimp and not a onetime military man.

"Molly is prettier now than she was even then." She squeezed her with her good hand. "You listen to me, Brigham. Why I expect you will when you never have before is another matter, but sometimes we mortals do get a second chance."

"Grandma."

"That is, if Molly would even be willing to try again. Getting dumped practically at the altar is any woman's worst nightmare. Shame on you," she went on, then paused. "On second thought, you don't deserve her."

True enough, Brig mused.

"Mrs. Collier, please." Molly was blushing. She knew his grandmother could be plainspoken, so that was no surprise, but she couldn't meet Brig's gaze. "Eight years is a very long time," she added in a shaky voice.

But his grandmother didn't agree.

"Eight years is no time at all. When you get to be my age, it's a blink and nothing more. The important thing is not to waste what time you have left." She gestured at herself, then planted a kiss on Molly's cheek. "Of course, that's up to you. I wouldn't trust this one myself." She pointed to Brig.

"And you'd be right," Brig murmured, remembering his vow to win Molly's forgiveness and then her friendship. If he didn't deserve either, he surely didn't deserve her love a second time.

"You can't play soldier forever," his grandmother told him. Brig could hear a growing faintness in her tone. She was getting over-tired. "Someday you'll have to come home, Brigham." The words were all but whispered. "Don't wait until it's too late."

"IT'S MY FAULT," Brig said to Molly. His grandmother had unexpectedly taken a turn for the worse later that afternoon, which had upset Molly, too. "I shouldn't have pushed her about moving."

"I'm sure that's not why she started to run a fever."

He and Molly walked out of the lobby and headed toward the parking lot with Laila. Molly pulled in a deep breath of cold night air, and not just to clear her sinuses of those hospital smells. She needed to purge her emotions, too. Like Brig, she was worried again for his grandmother. And she couldn't stop hearing Mrs. Collier's words, all the while knowing they had come too late for her and Brig.

As she followed him to her car, Molly tried to think instead of the few years she and Andrew had shared after Brig left, and of their wedding that had actually happened.

She didn't dare entertain the fantasy of

finding that kind of contentment again, this time with Brig.

Trusting him not to hurt her or to leave her behind wasn't possible.

"I hope your grandmother's fever wasn't *my* fault," she said. "The flu is really sweeping through Little Darlings now. One case the other day has become six. Even the teacher for my three-year-olds has called in sick for tomorrow, Ann told me. Maybe I'm a carrier."

"I doubt the incubation period is only a few hours. That's all we spent at the hospital before Grandma's temperature spiked."

Brig unlocked the doors, then slipped Laila into her car seat. He glanced up at the sky. The night air felt heavy and threatening. The clouds were already thick in the sky. "We shouldn't drive back tonight. The weather forecast doesn't look good and is getting worse by the hour. We don't want to get caught in this coming storm on the road to Cincy, especially with the baby—plus I can't leave my parents when Grandma Collier is worse."

Bess had already given them the key to his grandmother's home. She and Joe would be along later, or not at all if they stayed the night at the hospital again. Laila was already at her limit, fussing and most likely crampy. She needed a warm place, a bedtime bottle and perhaps more of someone walking the floor with her. Did Molly want a night with Brig, too? Maybe alone? Yet she couldn't risk Laila's safety.

"Another day won't matter," Molly finally said without the confidence she wished for. "I'll call Ann about my replacement for tomorrow. Two, in fact, counting that sick teacher."

When they were all buckled in, Brig started the car and swung out of the lot. "Let's stop at the grocery store for some dinner fixings and anything Laila will require for the night."

"More formula, for sure. We only brought enough for today, with a few extras. We don't want to run out in the middle of the night."

There it was again, that *we*.

"Truer words were never spoken."

AT THE HOUSE Molly put their purchases away while Brig, as if eager to demonstrate his new parenting skills, changed the baby into her sleeper for the night.

Molly was putting their frozen dinners in the microwave when he came into the kitchen carrying Laila. The baby looked as cute as could be in her clean night wear, with its pattern of little lambs. "Any idea where she can bunk down?" he asked.

"Oh. Of course." Molly thought for a minute. "How about a dresser drawer? My mother used to press one into service whenever a guest arrived with a baby. That's why I eventually bought the crib Laila's been using. But a drawer will work for one night."

Brig liked the suggestion. He grabbed a fresh bottle for Laila, then went back upstairs to tuck the baby into her new "bed" while Molly heated their meals. His parents were using his grandmother's master bedroom, or had been until their latest vigil at the hospital. Brig and Laila would take the first of two guest rooms, and Molly would have the second to herself.

Laila fell asleep after dinner, at least temporarily. Which meant Molly and Brig were alone, as she'd feared.

She could hardly avoid him now. With Laila quiet upstairs and the dinner dishes cleared away, Molly went into the living room, wondering whether going to bed early would be the wiser course for her. If the weather held off, or the system shifted and Brig's grandmother stabilized, they could leave for Liberty after breakfast.

Outside the windows, the first flakes began to drift down. To Molly, who dealt with snow every winter, they didn't even appear close to becoming a blizzard. Her four-wheel-drive SUV with snow tires would provide the necessary traction for driving in such weather, and if Indiana cleared roads around the city as promptly as the crews did in rural Ohio, she didn't foresee any problem.

In the living room Brig sat glued to the television set. He had muted the sound, probably not to disturb her or Laila, but when he saw her, he snapped off the TV with the remote, shutting down the endless cable news show.

"More bad news?"

"No surprise," he said, "but there's nothing to do about it now." He patted the sofa cushion beside him. "Sit. I want to ask you something."

Obviously whatever it was troubled Brig, because he was frowning. But when he spoke, the subject surprised her.

"Ever since we visited my grandmother, I've been thinking. About hospitals, in part. I know about your miscarriage…but what happened after that?"

What on earth had made him wonder? Molly didn't welcome another trip down memory lane, but Brig had been forthcoming about his teammate, Sean. She owed Brig the same honesty.

"I was a mess," she admitted. "I couldn't sleep, I didn't want to eat, I had no interest in the world around me. All I kept asking was *why?* Why did that have to happen to me? To Andrew? I suppose I had prepartum depression instead of postpartum."

"Did you try to have another baby?"

Molly shook her head. "Andrew wanted to as soon as I felt physically well again. He thought we'd feel better if we had something joyful to look forward to. But I was still grieving for the little girl I would never have."

"You know it was a girl?"

"From the sonogram, yes."

Brig reached for her hand. "Not that a new baby would have been any kind of replacement."

"No, and he understood that, too. As I look back on all the 'discussions' we had, he was simply trying to help me out of my depression. But the real cure was time. As for Laila's colic." She paused, feeling Brig's finger brush over her palm. She told herself she should pull away. But she didn't. Couldn't. It had been a long while since a man had comforted her, as she had tried to comfort Brig that night in the kitchen.

"You blame yourself that your marriage didn't heal."

Molly had never thought of Brig as the sensitive type. But the intervening years had changed him.

Her throat tightened, and for a few moments she sat there, letting Brig hold her hand, feeling the warmth of his skin on hers. Loving his understanding.

"If only I had relented about becoming pregnant again just after my miscarriage, but I felt too sad. I couldn't see why we needed to rush. I wasted the time we had left on senseless arguments," Molly admitted. "Allowed our growing tensions to overwhelm our love for each other."

Brig said with a sigh, "Sean didn't have much time, either. He and Zada were together for slightly less than a year. There we were in the midst of that disaster of a war, cold and miserable and often undersupplied, and all of a sudden Sean was in love." Brig smiled.

"Together, they just lit up the place. I stood up for them when they got married. How they managed that, I'll never know, considering the military's regulations. Probably the JAG office had to help—and then Laila was coming and Sean's future wasn't a hardscrabble mining town any longer. He was a husband, a father-to-be...."

Brig shook his head and gazed down at their joined hands. He and Molly had both been talking about the same thing, really. About love and loss, about regret.

"But that's not something for tonight," he said.

Molly disagreed. "I'm a pretty good listener. And I owe you one. You listened to me."

He glanced up. "You wouldn't want to be around when my head gets that messed up. Still, you have a point." Shaken, he took a deep breath. "I guess you heard my grandmother today."

But he didn't go on. That conversation threatened to become far too personal. She guessed what he almost said: that they, too, had squandered time.

"She's a wise woman," Molly murmured.

"I hope *she* hasn't run out of time."

Molly started to withdraw her hand from Brig's, but he held on. His next words surprised her all over again.

"What an idiot I was back then," he said. "Thinking I could do my thing for a few years, then come back to Liberty—and find you waiting."

"I did wait," she admitted, "for a while."

He cleared his throat. "I'm glad you didn't wait for too long. I'm glad you met Andrew, got married, bought a house, planned that family." He paused. His voice was husky when he spoke again. "I'm glad your marriage was mostly happy."

She had no idea what to say after that.

"You're way ahead of me there," he added.

His gaze fixed on hers, and something dangerous passed between them.

"Molly," he whispered in his thick tone.

At the same time, Brig tugged at her hand to pull her forward. And despite her instinct to retreat, she felt herself leaning toward him, looking into his eyes with a message of her own, one that she shouldn't even think of delivering.

Gathering the remnants of her courage, Molly moved back just in time.

Without initiating the kiss she expected, as

if he'd come to his senses also, he released her hand. The tense moment drifted away like stale smoke, leaving behind the too-well-remembered ashes of their long-ago engagement. Molly never wanted to hurt like that again.

CHAPTER TEN

THE SNOW HAD sifted down all night, but by morning it was falling in thick, heavy flakes and piling up fast on his grandmother's back lawn. Brig stood at the window with a mug of hot coffee in his hand and stared out at the endless blanket of white. He could barely make out the neighbor's house, no more than fifty feet to the rear. The sky was murky gray. The snowfall would not abate soon. He yawned again.

"Baby all right?" his father asked, sitting at the table with his morning bowl of corn-flakes.

"She's had colic for the past few nights. Hope we didn't keep you awake."

"We slept like babies ourselves. We got home from the hospital around 2:00 a.m. and just fell into bed. Did you get any sleep?"

"Here and there."

"I hope you aren't thinking of driving back to Liberty today, Brig. The roads are a mess and the plows can't keep up. Why not wait until the snow stops?"

He smiled a little. "In Afghanistan the snow never stops until almost summer—such as it is there. I'm used to snow, plus I'd like to get Molly home. She's short staffed at the center."

Before he could ask about his grandmother, Molly walked into the kitchen. Avoiding Brig's gaze, she helped herself to coffee, then sat across from his father. "Ann has taken care of all that," she said. "She stayed overnight with Pop, too. But what about your mother, Joe?"

He grunted, reminding Brig of Thomas. Neither man was a morning person. "Bess and I will head for the hospital soon. I've phoned, and the nurse said my mother had a 'restful' night. Her fever's down a little, but she's weak and achy."

Molly looked guilty. "Flu?"

He shook his head. "No, they're calling this a 'fever of unknown origin,' possibly a reaction to her medication or to the new hip. Hope it's not infected. She's not contagious," he finished, "as far as they know."

Still at the window, Brig watched a house sparrow on the lawn, leaving bird tracks in the fresh snow. Molly still wouldn't look at him, and for the hundredth time he wished he hadn't moved toward her like that last night, spooked her with a near kiss—as if that could ease things between them. What could he say now to make amends?

Molly spoke. "We can't possibly leave today, Brig. As badly as I want to help Ann and the rest of my staff, I don't think we should leave your parents here alone. Even if your grandmother seems better this morning, is she really out of the woods yet?" She paused, daring a glance at him. "I heard you up with Laila for most of the night. There's no way you should drive, especially with the roads getting slicker. I could, but what if the highway shuts down when we have Laila in the car?"

She had voiced Brig's concern. "You don't mind staying another day?"

"It's what we *should* do," she said, though she didn't sound wild about the prospect.

"I agree," Joe added. "Your mother would have a fit if you tried to leave. The Weather Channel says we could get a foot of snow before dark, and the storm's heading for Ohio. You'd be taking it with you." He looked at Molly. "My wife has her son back for a little while. I'd hate to see her waving you off so soon."

And that ended that. Brig turned from the window. The little bird had disappeared between the two houses, possibly without the food it had been searching for in the snow-covered grass. Brig made a mental note to fill his grandmother's empty bird feeder.

"All right," he said, "but we need a plan. Can you stay here a little longer this morning, Dad, and watch Laila? Molly and I could run to the store again and stock up more before the shelves are stripped. It won't take us long. Then maybe you'd like to borrow Molly's SUV to drive to the hospital—if she's okay with that."

"Of course."

Brig noticed she still wasn't looking at him. The thought of spending time alone with him obviously didn't appeal, even when keeping Laila safe did.

They left his parents to dote on the baby, and ventured into the storm. His father and Molly had been right. The roads were already treacherous. Brig had agreed to let Molly drive—he really was too tired, as she'd pointed out—but even though she handled the

SUV with skill, it took them twice as long to make the short trip to the store.

Molly had prepared a list, the better to shop quickly, she claimed. She tore it in two and handed Brig one half. Split up, she and Brig could get the shopping done even faster. The place was crowded with folks eager to buy batteries and bottled water and all the other things people judged essential to have on hand in a storm. There was an air of camaraderie, a coming-together mood, but the aisles were tight and the shelves were rapidly becoming bare.

Brig threw a two-pack of cinnamon rolls into his cart. Molly, cruising past him toward the cereal aisle, spotted them. "Not on the list," she said, gaze fixed on the packages, not him.

"Feel-good food. You can't be snowbound and not have these."

Brig turned his cart into the baby section. The store was family owned, not big box, but with a wide selection of goods for its size. He tossed in several packs of diapers for Laila, then startled when Molly moved in beside him. She must have had the same idea, list or not.

She noticed a wall display of packaged onesies and other baby clothing. "Laila is already growing out of the things you brought with you. Do you want to get a few new items?" Her face lit up. "Oh, look. Isn't this sweet?"

"Sweet," Brig agreed, though it wasn't a word he'd use. He watched Molly slip the beige-and-cream outfit printed with giraffes into her cart. Then in a corner he spotted a collection of plastic baby baths, booster seats, mesh security gates, and...

Molly saw it the instant he did. Their eyes met—the first time this morning she'd allowed it—and two lightbulbs went off in their brains. "A baby swing!"

Brig inspected it. Sturdy enough, and it even played music.

"This could do the trick. Maybe cut down on some of those nighttime marches with Laila."

"A genius idea." With room left in her cart, Molly let Brig stow it. She stepped back as he did so, clearly to avoid the possibility of touching him. "Get this baby bath, too. She needs a wash, and a warm bath might help relax her. Make her sleepy."

"Aren't we smart?" he said.

"Let's hope Laila thinks so."

Brig chose more food items to leave with

his parents when he and Molly went back to Ohio, and by the time they shoved both piled-high carts through the freezing slush in the parking lot to her car, he felt much better than he had earlier that morning.

Even considering Molly's reluctance to engage with him today, he grinned to himself as he loaded the SUV. He felt like a pioneer, a hunter. And hadn't his parents loved the idea of spending time with Laila while they were gone?

More alert now, he took the wheel, not wanting to let Molly navigate the increasingly icy roads. He looked forward to being indoors, warm and dry, and there was nothing better, in his view, than getting snowbound in a house with a pretty woman. Later, Brig decided, he would chop some wood for a fire to add to the coziness—and his own macho sense of being a provider.

LIKE BRIG IN his more masculine way, Molly spent the whole snowy day being domestic. It wasn't often that she got time off. Normally, she took care of food and laundry and cleaning for herself and Pop while he carried out the garbage, mowed the lawn in summer and ran the snowblower in winter. Theirs, she had to admit, was a conventional division of labor along traditional gender lines. But with her duties at Little Darlings and the myriad problems that cropped up there every day, she rarely had time to herself or time to bake.

That afternoon, after Brig's parents had plowed their way through the storm to see his grandmother, she whipped up a double batch of brownies, then slid a fruit pie into the oven and finished off with mountains of chocolate chip and oatmeal cookies. The former was Joe's favorite; the latter was Brig's. Along with his cinnamon rolls, she guessed they were set for the duration, however long that would be. At least they had plenty of carbs on hand.

Done with her baking, she made all the beds and ran several loads through the washer and dryer. Joe and Bess hadn't found time to launder what clothes they'd brought with them. Not expecting to stay last night, Brig and Molly had packed only some changes for Laila, so at the store earlier Molly had bought a few basic outfits plus a big T-shirt to sleep in. Brig had added jeans and flannel shirts to his cart, plus some for his dad. He'd thought to buy his father underwear, while Molly chose tops and jeans for his mother, guessing at her sizes. Both of them, plus Brig and Molly, were the owners of new boots, scarves and hats. None of them had come prepared for a blizzard.

Finished at last with her chores, she sat down in the living room with Laila and smiled at her. The baby had been a dear all day.

"She loves this swing."

Brig glanced over from reloading the fireplace with more wood. Molly was thrilled— nothing like a crackling fire to lift her spirits. But she looked away quickly from the sight of his strong back and shoulders as he piled logs on the hearth, added extra kindling and poked at the leaping blaze.

"I have a good feeling about tonight," he said. "I'll position the swing right by the bed, and every time she gets up, I'll just crank the mechanism, and she'll be off to dreamland again."

He and Molly exchanged quick smiles before he took Laila and the swing upstairs. The wind was howling now, and as darkness descended, the snow picked up even more, big, moisture-laden flakes falling from a leaden sky. A late-winter storm always dropped this kind of heavy, wet stuff that would be hard to shovel. Brig had already cleared the walks and porches twice.

The silence when he came downstairs made her search for something to fill it with.

"Have you heard from Joe and Bess?"

"Not in the past few hours. Dad said earlier that my grandmother's doing well enough, but her hip hurts and so do the rest of her joints. He and Mom will likely head home soon. Dad didn't want to get stuck all night at the hospital." Brig jabbed at the fire, looked out the window at the snow and pulled his cell from his pocket. "He won't be able to see the street from her hospital room. I'd better give him another call. Tell them to start out before this gets any worse than it already is."

To Molly's relief, the Colliers soon came stomping in the back door, shedding jackets and gloves, their faces red from the cold. Even the short trip from the garage into the house had chilled them. Molly was glad to see them. Now she and Brig were no longer alone.

"What do I smell?" Joe asked with a look of rapture.

"Beef stew. Biscuits," Molly said. "Blueberry pie."

"And what are the rest of you having for dinner?"

Brig laughed. "I'd fight you for it if I had to. Sit down. Let's eat."

In the cheery dining room they gathered... like a family, once again reminding Molly that years ago she had expected the Colliers to become her in-laws.

"How's your mother doing tonight, Joe?"

"I think she's turned the corner. Her doctor reminded us that at her age people get fragile—not only that hip—and they can sink, then rally on a dime." He paused. "When she gets released from rehab, she's coming with us to Liberty. I've had enough of her 'I can manage on my own' nonsense, let me tell you. If I have to, I'll clean out this house myself—"

"And toss out everything she loves?" Bess put in. "No, you will not, *Admiral* Collier." The fictional nickname suited him. "Don't be stubborn. We'll all sort her belongings together. Then you can put the house on the market," she said.

"If Grandma agrees," Brig added.

"Oh, she'll agree," Joe said. "Believe me."

Molly focused on her plate. If she did say so, the stew was delicious, and they finished it all. The biscuits, as well. The pie vanished, too, along with a half gallon of vanilla ice cream. The blizzard seemed to increase appetites.

"A magnificent dinner, Molly," Bess said with a smile. "And doing the laundry plus putting fresh sheets on our bed? If I'm ever snowbound again, I know just who to call."

She and Joe did the dishes while Brig checked on the baby upstairs and Molly folded the last load of wash.

All in all, the day had been a breather of sorts from Molly's usual routine, and in the evening she collapsed contentedly on the living room sofa to stare at the fire. She could get used to this, even when she knew having it was impossible.

To pass the time tonight she might find a good book on Mrs. Collier's bedroom shelves to read and curl up right here on the sofa with a cozy blanket, nowhere she needed to go and nothing else she needed to do.

How long had it been since her last break? The week she'd had a strep throat and Andrew had done all the cooking and cleaning and caring for her?

Tonight she was content to look into the fire or out at the falling snow, hear the silence on the street, feel cocooned in white as long as she had the warmth inside.

She rose to get a book, but Brig clattered down the stairs right into her path. He gave Molly a grin and a thumbs-up. "Mission accomplished," he said. "Laila's out like a light. So far, so good." He grabbed Molly's hand. "Let's go."

"Where?"

"Out," he said. "I was going to shovel the walks again—and I will—but first—" He opened the front door, letting in a blast of cold air. Brig handed Molly her boots and her coat, then shrugged into his own. "Come on, Mom. Dad!" he yelled toward the kitchen. "Snowball fight!"

THE SIGHT OF four adults building opposing forts in the front yard, then piling up their weapons made Molly grin. It had been years since she'd participated in a good snowball fight. At Little Darlings, it wasn't allowed. Someone might get hurt, the current thinking went. But, oh, what fun everyone was missing.

"Hey!" Brig called when the first snowball hit him in the chest. His father had fired one before the agreed-upon signal to begin. "You wanna fight dirty?"

The next landed on his father's head. Bess laughed, her breath frosting in the night air as the snow continued to drift down around them.

"Incoming!" Joe shouted, lobbing another ball at Molly this time. She retaliated with the biggest one in her arsenal.

Bess joined in, slamming Brig in the back before he could pick up more ammunition. In no time he and Molly had exhausted their stash. There was a brief time-out while he went inside to check on Laila, who was still sleeping. Then, with a fresh supply of snowballs, the fight resumed, even fiercer than before.

In the heat of battle, Brig's eyes—his father's, too—were alight with something Molly couldn't even name. Excitement, of course. Determination, maybe. Focus? She wasn't entirely sure. But adrenaline and testosterone were obviously flowing. For Molly, peace was more her thing.

Brig's gaze held another, different spark when the truce was finally called.

"We'd better get the walks cleared now,"

Joe said, "or by morning we won't be able to open the doors."

"In a minute, Dad." He stalked toward Molly with that light in his eyes. She took a step back, lifting her arms as a shield.

"Oh, no, you don't."

"Oh, yes, I do." He closed in, one hand behind his back. Brig caught an arm and, with his parents watching nearby, moved to push the last snowball into Molly's face.

"You!" she cried in mock outrage.

But at the last minute, Brig lobbed the snowball away from her like a live grenade. Molly was laughing, too. After evading Brig, she scooped up more snow, packed it into the tightest ball she could and chased after him, but he was already running across the lawn, having guessed her intention. "Stand still," she called, gasping as she ran.

When she caught up—because he let her, most likely—Brig wasn't even breathing hard. Through his coat his forearm felt steely in her grasp, but she didn't get the chance to deliver her missile—not that she really meant to. Brig tumbled her back into the snow. He straddled her, his lower body weight on her, leaning on his elbows, his broad shoulders blocking everything from view. Then he framed her face and looked into her eyes. Not smiling at all.

"Brigham, let the poor girl up," she heard his mother say.

"We're just playing," he murmured. "Molly needs to play. So do I."

Their closeness lasted only a minute, even less, but for Molly it was a time-travel moment into the past when she and Brig had laughed like this so freely.

No wonder she had avoided Brig all day, avoided anything that stirred the daydream of being part of his family again, part of his life.

"You've been in black ops way too long," she whispered.

Then, needing to end the moment, as if to fire, she raised the snowball she held close to Brig's neck. He howled.

"That does it." He bounded to his feet. With a strength that always astonished Molly, he pulled her upright.

As if they were on a parade ground, Brig marched her across the yard, away from their forts, to a big patch of virgin snow. She could sense his parents behind them, wondering and perplexed as they gazed at Brig and her.

"Get down, recruit," he ordered in a mock growl, as if also pulling himself from that other moment. But he didn't bark out an order to do push-ups, as Molly had expected. "Give me…a snow angel."

Brig flopped beside her on his back. Limbs moving in a wide arc, they made twin angels, something Molly hadn't done since she was ten years old.

His head now turned toward her, Brig grinned like one of her boys at Little Darlings. Like Jeff Barlow's Ernie. In that one instant, Brig's war was gone. Their time to play had freed him for now from his memories of Sean.

Smiling, yet strangely moved, Molly gazed into his eyes. She saw the more carefree Brig she'd once known. And yearned for what they both had lost of each other.

THE SNOW STOPPED by dawn. At noon the angels he and Molly had fashioned were melting. Brig again left Laila with his parents to take Molly to the hospital. Miraculously the little girl had slept half the night and swung the rest until six in the morning. He and Molly would visit with his grandmother one last time before they had to leave for Liberty. Joe and Bess seemed more than happy to play with the baby and get a brief respite from all the stress.

Molly carried a bright bouquet of yellow prespring tulips into his grandmother's room. She was sitting up in bed. To Brig's relief her face showed some color again, and her eyes had their normal sparkle.

"Thank you, dears. April can't be far away, but isn't this snow something?" She glanced toward the window that looked out onto the parking lot. "Makes a person want to go skiing. What are you two doing here when you could be having fun?"

"We did," Molly said. She told Grandma Collier about their snowball fight and the angels. "I wish you could have joined us. Now we're bringing some fun to you."

Brig stood back as Molly pulled an old Parcheesi game from her bag. She'd found it, she'd told him, on his grandmother's bookshelf.

For the next hour they played the game his grandmother had always loved, and the color in her cheeks grew even brighter. Then Brig showed her the pictures of Laila he'd snapped on his phone that morning. In his favorite one, Molly was holding her with a Madonna-like smile on her face. And not Madonna the singer, either.

His grandmother studied the photos, her gaze occasionally swinging from Molly to Brig and back again. He could almost see her thinking, *What a good match these two make.* Which, as she hadn't hesitated to let everyone know, she'd always thought so.

Molly, he was sure, had another opinion. And why wouldn't she after he'd walked out on her years ago? So what had he done last night? Stepped way over the line. Trapped her beneath him in the snow, all but kissing her right there with his parents looking on. No wonder she once again wasn't talking to him except when she had to.

"She's lovely, Brig." His grandmother's voice called him back, but she wasn't referring to Molly. "Laila you said her name is?"

He smiled. Meeting Laila even secondhand had raised his grandmother's spirits more than his and Molly's visit. "Right. You're a great-grandmother now."

She straightened, setting the lid back on the Parcheesi box. She'd won, of course. She always did. "As soon as I get out of here, I'm coming to visit. I know a thing or two about babies."

Brig didn't dare mention her possible move to Liberty this time. Leave that to his father. Instead, he leaned down to kiss her. "You behave yourself now. I'll be getting regular updates from Mom and Dad. See you soon, Grandma."

A promise he wasn't sure he could keep.

She reached up to take his face in her hands. Her eyes held his. "I love you, Brigham. The only thing I want in this world before I depart it is to see you happy." Her gaze shifted to Molly, who was packing away the game box. "You know what would make *me* happy," Grandma Collier said. "I wonder if it isn't the same thing we both want."

Dream on, Brig thought. He couldn't mistake her meaning.

Too bad he didn't have a chance at being more than friends—if that—with Molly. "We need to go," he said. "The snow has finally stopped and the roads weren't bad on the way over here. I want to be in Liberty before dark."

"I only have one grandson, you know," his grandmother murmured, and looked toward the television perched on a wall mount. "I see the news. And I'll worry about you. Please, stay safe, Brigham."

"Yes, ma'am. I plan to." *For now, I am safe and so is Laila,* he thought. He'd had an overwhelming sense of peace last night and all day yesterday. Chopping wood, shoveling the driveway, going to the store with Molly. Simple tasks with no threat involved. Like today's visit at the hospital. Not like that day with Sean.

And yet he all but champed at the bit to get back in the action.

No need to tell Molly that. She already knew.

So did his grandmother. Reminded of an issue he hadn't settled with his parents, he gave Grandma Collier one more kiss, then hustled Molly from the room.

In the car on the way home, Brig worried himself into a headache. On duty he missed his family. And, always, he missed Molly.

She seemed to occupy some part of his mind no matter where he went. The day his mom had told him about her wedding to Andrew, Brig had punched a hole in the mess hall wall. Not that he'd had any right to object. Brig had given her up. She belonged to another man.

He jerked his thoughts back to the present. "I need to get Laila's care figured out fast. I have to talk to my folks as soon as we get home."

As if waiting for Brig to return, his mother sat in the living room when they got back. Laila swayed in her swing to the tune of "Twinkle, Twinkle, Little Star" and Bess watched the baby's every motion.

"There you are," she said to Brig. She was wringing her hands, a habit when she felt tense, and that worsened his headache. "We've had a wonderful time with the baby."

"Will you think so at four in the morning when she's screaming?"

Bess cast another longing glance at Laila. "You don't think you used to yell loud enough to wake the dead yourself?"

His father wandered into the room carrying another load of firewood. He deposited it on the hearth, then brushed off his hands, as if ridding himself of some problem. "Roads pretty good by now?"

"Yeah. Molly and I need to leave." Brig took a breath. "But I wanted to see first about Lai—"

"Joe." His mother glanced at his father, who, when Brig spoke, had squared his shoulders as if he was about to address a unit of his men facing some terrible firefight.

"Your mother and I have been talking. About your grandmother. We wanted her at a rehab facility near us in Liberty, but she won't hear of it."

"She wants to stay close to home," Bess said, "at least for now. She'll have a faster recovery if her friends can visit here and keep her spirits up."

"It's not likely," Joe said, "that they'd make the trip to Ohio."

His mother looked at the baby. "We've had a great visit with Laila…she's everything we could want in a grandchild…." She didn't finish.

Brig's pulse began to thud. The grandchild he had never given them. Because of all the emotion underlying the arrival of a baby in his parents' lives, he had hated to ask them to care for Laila even for a short time, but they had agreed.

"I know the situation has changed since Grandma's fall," Brig said, but couldn't go on, either. By then, he already knew.

Molly was still standing by the front door. In the silence she cleared her throat and said, "I'll go upstairs to pack. For you, too, Brig."

She left them alone to talk. Brig didn't want to hear the rest.

"This whole thing has made us think. We're not getting any younger." His mother picked up the speech she and his father had obviously rehearsed while he and Molly were gone. He'd been half expecting it since he arrived in Liberty and found them missing. "If there was any way, believe me, we'd be happy to…but with your grandmother's condition still uncertain, and considering her age, the extra care she may need…moving her eventually…."

She was on the verge of tears. Yet Brig couldn't stop her. He was as frozen as Molly had looked by the front door.

"Mom, it's okay."

"No, it's not. But, please, honey. I hope you can understand. We're part of the sandwich generation, and having an elderly woman who will struggle to adjust to that new hip for months, plus a small baby in the house…" She shook her head. "I'm so sorry, Brig."

"I know this puts you in a real bind. But even for a few weeks—" his dad delivered the final blow "—we just can't take Laila."

CHAPTER ELEVEN

IT HAD BECOME ever harder for Molly to resist Laila, and after their trip to Indiana and Brig's parents' decision, she'd all but stopped trying. Her fresh memory of making snow angels with Brig told Molly, too, that she and Brig were in a different place emotionally. What to do about that?

Dressed for success—she hoped, because tonight was the dreaded zoning commission meeting—she walked into the kitchen. To her surprise, Brig and her father sat cross-legged on the floor with metal objects scattered between them that seemed to have something to do with the sink. Both men had greasy hands, and Pop sported a matching streak across his forehead.

"What kind of plumber are you?" he asked.

"Not even an apprentice," Brig answered, frowning at the plumbing parts. He glanced at Molly in her go-to-a-meeting outfit, and his eyes widened. "Wow. On a scale of one to ten, you're over the top. That's a killer dress."

"I hope so." Molly ignored her father's sour glance at Brig and took a deep breath. She really wasn't looking forward to this. Still unsatisfied with her presentation, she wanted to stay home. Like Pop. "If Natalie Brewster isn't happy with what I have to say…" Reality in the form of their neighbor and her place on the zoning commission had intruded again. "And with the blizzard and those few days away, I haven't begun to get my donations to the rummage sale in order. I'm sure she's aware of my oversight."

Pop grunted. "I'll drag 'em over to the community center tomorrow. Tell her I said so."

Brig grinned at Molly. Aware of Natalie's interest in her father, he handed him a wrench. "I can help, Thomas. Provide cover," he said. "Together we'll have the stuff there in no time. Then you can help me move the baby gear next door."

Pop didn't reply. For the past few days he'd shied from any mention of the baby leaving this house.

"What's wrong with the sink?" Molly asked.

Brig shrugged. "We started with a clogged trap and went from there."

Molly's father scowled at all the parts on the floor. "Now we're thinking of rebuilding this whole kitchen."

"This sink is a relic. It's also an amazingly complex piece of…metal."

Molly rolled her eyes. Men. She assumed Brig had been about to say *junk,* but he didn't want to offend her father, who took pride in his home. Strangely enough, he and Pop continued to enjoy a détente. Certainly Pop had been happy to see him when she and Brig had driven in a few nights ago from Indiana.

Already Thomas had had a project waiting. Molly suspected her dad welcomed a bit of male companionship, something she never would have imagined he might find with Brig.

The baby had been sound asleep in her car seat when they'd arrived. Brig had produced the new key his parents had given him to the house, but silently they'd agreed there was no reason to wake Laila. Moving to the Colliers' could wait until the following day.

Three days later Brig and the baby were still at her place. She knew he was trying to locate someone in Sean's family who could help with Laila in the short-term, but so far he'd run into a wall. Maybe sharing this household task with her father took his mind off the problem.

"Laila's asleep," Molly informed the two men. "You'll hear her if she cries?"

"My hearing is excellent," Pop said, turning the wrench in his hands. "Why would you think we'd neglect the tyke?" This from the same man who had almost let Laila smother in her blankets while he watched the news on TV.

On the other hand, he took every opportunity to be with the baby, and their daily walks around the block—by sled this week—had become something of a neighborhood show.

"Trust us," he went on. "We'll have this sink back together in no time. There's an old movie on tonight—*Saving Private Ryan*—we might watch. You okay with that one, Brig?"

"Yep." He didn't appear that happy about it, and Molly could see why. The movie was way too much like his job, plus it would remind him of Sean's death. Nevertheless, to please Thomas, he would sit through the film.

"We'll be in the living room," Pop said. "Soon as we finish here."

Molly cast a jaundiced eye at the pile of

whatever those things were on the floor. Pop was fiddling with the wrench, tightening or loosening some, uh, bolt.

She felt another twinge of a responsibility that wasn't really hers, except her nurturing instincts didn't end at five o'clock when she left Little Darlings, at least where Laila was concerned. She wasn't sure about Pop, but Brig would be on high alert. She told herself she had nothing to worry about, save her presentation.

"I have to go or I'll be late. I left clean clothes and more diapers on the dresser in your room, Brig. You won't even need to turn on a light."

"I've developed an even more awesome dexterity in the dark," he said with a smile. "All that training for my team has paid off. Go knock 'em dead, Molly."

"Break a leg," Pop murmured, casting another suspicious eye at Brig.

He was obviously sending Brig a silent warning: *We're okay as long as you stay away from my daughter.*

As if he had anything to worry about. She and Brig hadn't been alone together since their return from Indiana.

Tonight, her drive across town through

still-snowy streets seemed to take forever. At last she was locking up her car, hoping the mechanism wouldn't freeze by the time she came out of the zoning commission meeting. When she opened the door to the community center, a different anxiety overtook her concern about a frozen door lock.

Molly's already shaky confidence took a sharper nosedive.

The first person she saw, already seated at the long table in the front of the room, was Natalie Brewster.

Hey, Collier. Would you believe? Jacoby dropped out today. Second guy to quit the team this year. The rest of us have decided to make the little lady our official mascot. You like? H.

BRIG LAY ON the bed in the spare room he shared with Laila and glanced at his email. But Henderson's post didn't bring a smile. And there would be no movie for Brig tonight. Predictably, Laila had wakened just after he and Thomas put the sink back together. Her face had screwed up like Thomas's expression earlier when he'd sent Brig that warning glance. And its unmistakable message.

Molly's message this past little while was equally clear. In the few days since they'd been back in Liberty, she'd worked extra hours at the center either on day care issues or on her presentation. When she finally came home, she hurried through dinner, then disappeared. Late at night he could hear the small television in her room, the murmur of voices and occasionally a laugh track. Which Brig hated. Like Molly's renewed distance.

Those two nights in Indiana had been an interlude, as had the snow angels before his stupid urge to kiss her.

He should make that move next door as he'd planned. What was keeping him? He had hoped to contact Sean's father in Kentucky by now, but he wasn't having much luck. He must have made a half dozen calls to the man, only to get a busy signal each time. The guy must be a real chatterbox.

Frustrated, Brig snapped his cell phone shut again and gave the baby swing by the bed another nudge. Nope, it didn't make sense to linger here, keeping out of Molly's way, remembering what she'd said that night in the snow.

You've been in black ops way too long.

She'd been laughing at the time, but she had a point. On some level Brig had known for quite a while—certainly since he'd accepted guardianship of Laila—that he would have to make another change sooner or later.

Right now Laila was showing off her fine pair of lungs again, yelling so loud he could hardly hear himself think.

From the hallway Thomas called, "Baby okay?"

"Just shattering eardrums, nothing new."

Brig plucked the red-faced baby from her swing. The gizmo wasn't doing as much good as it had in Indiana; if anything, her colic seemed worse. After a minute he heard Thomas go back into his room, then shut the door.

"Guess we'll have to ride this one out," he told Laila, draping her across his chest. "Tell you what. Let's try your grandpa once more."

Brig didn't mean his own father. Sean's dad, the miner in Kentucky, was the baby's closest blood relative. Brig didn't like what little he'd learned from Sean about his relationship with his dad, so Brig would size him up on the phone first. Make his judgment. For Laila's sake.

He waited until she fell asleep against him, her small body warming his. He ran a hand lightly down her back, inhaling her familiar scent, letting her calm him, too. You know, he wasn't half-bad at this baby care thing after all.

Not that the baby caring would last much longer.

He hit Redial on his phone.

"Yeah?" a grainy voice demanded at the other end. For a second Brig couldn't believe someone had actually answered.

"Mr. Denton?"

He heard a wheezy cough on the line. "That's me. Who's this?"

Brig braced himself for a difficult conversation. "I'm calling about…Sean." He hesitated, mindful that he might not be this man's favorite person. Some people welcomed contact with someone their son or daughter had served with. Others wanted no part of them. Or the reminder. "I'm—I was—his commanding officer."

"Collier, right? I got your package."

"It wasn't mine, sir. Our unit sent it." Sean's dog tags. All the letters he had written home but never sent because he and his dad didn't get on. The medals Sean had won, and the old laptop he swore at all the time. The cell phone he'd called Zada on ten times a day, dented and useless after the blast. Brig had included a letter to Denton telling him what an honor it had been to serve with his son. "I'm glad you got his things. I'm sure they must mean a lot."

Denton's voice hardened. "How well did you know him?"

"In combat there aren't any strangers. He was…more than a friend. He was like a younger brother."

"Huh." The man paused for a long moment. His voice had turned hoarse. "What was it? Almost three months ago," he said, "since some uptight officer knocked on my door. Before that, I hadn't seen or heard from Sean in over two years."

Brig was shocked. He'd assumed Sean at least had notified his father of his marriage. Was their uneasy relationship that bad?

"Then you didn't know he was married? You never heard about Zada, his wife, or—?"

"All I know is he's dead." Denton paused. "I'm sorry for that. I am," he repeated, and Brig could hear the sadness in his voice. "But there's the end of it."

Brig swallowed. And why hadn't that officer told Denton about the marriage? About Laila? Now Brig was flying blind. He didn't know how to soften the blow. He waited, then said, "This will probably come as another shock, but Sean and Zada have a child. Her name is Laila."

Another long moment followed before Denton spoke. "Say what?"

Brig looked down at the baby. "Sean named me as her legal guardian, but I'm still on duty, Mr. Denton—except for an emergency leave to bring her to the States. I'm in Ohio now but not for long. As much as I'd like to keep her with me, I won't be in a safe place. Even if I could take Laila with me, it wouldn't be fair to her." He hurried to get this over with, "I was wondering if you…"

The man started coughing again.

He sure didn't have healthy lungs like Laila. She continued to doze against Brig's chest, his free hand still moving on her back. Denton wheezed again, then cleared his throat.

"I guess that's supposed to change things. Since you were like *brothers,* I suppose he told you my wife died years ago. I've been on my own ever since. He was still a kid then. Turned into a wild one. Got into trouble with the local law. I told him—they told him, too—it was either join up if the service would take him or plan on spending time behind bars." He hacked some more, the sound echoing over the line.

Brig's throat tightened. "I wasn't aware of that, but rest assured, the military made a man of him."

"That so? And now you want me to raise that woman's child?"

"Sean's child," he said.

The silence stretched again. Brig thought he heard a soft curse over the line and then a sigh. "Let me tell you where I stand. I used to be a strapping guy, big and all muscle. Now I'm a cripple, on full disability—thanks to too many years down the mine. I have enough trouble scraping by. On top of that I just got out of the hospital—again—and the doctors say I prob'ly won't see sixty." His voice tightened. "So you tell me. What would I do with a months-old *baby?*"

Give her a home, Brig thought, even when that wasn't going to happen. He laid his cheek against Laila's silky dark hair, feeling hopeless. And what kind of a home would it be? Unstable in the end and filled with resentment from the start. It would probably be the same childhood Sean suffered. No, Brig thought. Never. No matter what he had to do.

"Sorry to bother you, Mr. Denton. Hope you feel better. I'll make other arrangements for your granddaughter," Brig said resignedly.

He hung up to the rasps of another coughing spell that wouldn't quit.

"NATALIE'S GOING TO vote no at the next meeting. I can feel it." Molly paced the floor of her small office the next day, venting her frustration on Ann. "I liked her, but maybe Pop was right." The memory of Natalie Brewster's set face the previous evening wouldn't leave her mind. "I was so disappointed, so mad on the way home, that on an icy patch I almost spun my car into a tree. I haven't been able to tell Pop about the meeting yet for fear I'll end up in tears."

Molly stopped. She wanted to bite her tongue. The mention of any accident, or potential for one, would upset Ann. Her sister's face had paled.

"Your presentation didn't go over well with the others?"

"It went over fine. I guess. There were a few nods and smiles from the rest of the commission, but if you ask me, they'll give us a thumbs-down."

"You won't know until the next meeting." Ann gazed out at the parking lot, where parents were beginning to roll in to collect their kids. "Maybe you're overestimating Natalie's influence."

"Maybe. I doubt it, though. I guess I'll know when they vote."

Ann didn't quite agree. "I've always thought Natalie was okay. She certainly keeps an eye on Pop."

"And the rest of this neighborhood." Molly sank onto her chair, still fuming. She'd stalked into the house last night, looking neither right nor left, then marched up the stairs. She hadn't even checked on Laila, as she usually did if Brig wasn't in bed in that room. She hadn't noticed that the kitchen sink had been repaired.

"Remember how 'someone' reported me for watering the Colliers' garden during last summer's dry spell when they were on vacation? Of course I knew about that town ordinance to preserve water. I gave all the plants just enough to keep them alive until Joe and Bess got home."

"You are a model citizen."

Suppressing a laugh, Molly threw a pencil at Ann, missing her by a mile as she'd intended. But at least Ann's color had come back.

"Where is my sister?" Molly said in a teasing tone. "I must have mistaken you for her when I laid my frustrations on you."

"Molly, I'm only trying to make you see. You could be wrong. Maybe it wasn't Natalie who reported you then. Last month I fell on the sidewalk near her house, and she was out the door in a flash asking if she could help."

True, and when Brig had presumably burgled his parents' house, Natalie was almost the first to arrive. Of course, she'd called the cops, too, which reminded Molly now of Jeff Barlow. For the entire time Ann had been in Molly's office, she'd also been watching the parking lot through the window. He'd be picking up Ernie any minute now, since the center's half day Saturday session had just ended.

"Who are you looking for?" Molly asked in a singsong voice.

"No one." The answer came too quickly.

Molly grinned. She welcomed any distraction that might help her stop thinking about the center's threatened expansion. Teasing her sister or her sister teasing her was a lifetime habit of theirs. "How is our hunky sheriff lately?"

"Oh, you think you're so smart. You want to know how he is?" Another swift glance toward the window. "I walked home one night and he met me at my apartment. He had Ernie in the car." She paused for dramatic effect. "And a bag from McDonald's with every single thing I love."

"Wow. That should be a felony." Molly grinned again.

Ann's eyes shot daggers of suspicion. "Did you tell him what I like?"

"Fries and a Quarter Pounder? Who, me?" *"Did you?"*

"No," Molly said. "I didn't." She paused, taking a moment to weigh her words. If she said the wrong thing, Ann wouldn't speak to her for days. "Did you eat the burger?"

Ann sighed. "Yes, and that's how weak I am."

"You let him into your apartment," Molly guessed. Oh, this was good.

Ann sighed. "Ernie, too. He watched a movie on Jeff's iPad while the 'hunky sheriff' tried to pump me about my accident." Tears glittered on her lashes. "If he knew me better, he'd probably take Ernie out of Little

Darlings, quit his job, and move away from Liberty."

"You're underestimating Jeff."

Ann's voice broke. "I'm a monster, Molly. Because of me, an innocent man's whole life changed in an instant."

"That part is true. And so did yours. You can't change that, but, Ann, you can't keep on like this, either."

"You're a fine one to talk."

Molly looked away, remembering that night in the snow with Brig and a past and future she couldn't seem to reconcile. "That may be," she said, "but I'm not the one who won't even get behind the wheel of a car, who won't drive herself to work even when it's pouring rain or snowing. How does that approach make your life better?"

"I can't hurt anyone," she said.

"Well, you can't move forward, either. And that makes me sad."

Ann looked out the window again.

"Don't you *see?*" Molly asked in frustration.

"I see that one bag of French fries isn't enough to make me spill my shameful secret to a man I barely know." She started toward the door. Then stopped. "Speaking of men, I notice Brig is still at the house."

Ann had obviously been saving that ammunition.

"He's trying to make some arrangement now for Laila."

"Nothing more? Come on, talk. You've gotten Natalie Brewster off your chest, but you haven't told me what happened in Indiana." Ann's gaze narrowed. "Pretty suspicious, if you ask me, you taking off with him and the baby, staying there for days...."

"We had to stay. There was a blizzard. It was snowing here, too."

"Hmm."

Molly didn't pretend to misunderstand her tone. "Brig and I have a mutual concern for Laila, that's all."

"Even more interesting. And dangerous. I spoke to him, you know—"

"Ann, I wish you hadn't. As soon as he finds care for Laila, he'll be gone."

Ann's gaze returned to the window like some obsessive-compulsive person. "That's a little too cut-and-dried even for you." She paused. "You know, years ago I wanted to kick that man for hurting you. Now I have to wonder if you aren't guilty of the same thing I am."

"Ann, that is—"

"Ridiculous? I don't think so."

Molly sighed. "Let's just say I don't hate him anymore and leave it at that."

"We'll see." She faced away from the window. Jeff's car had just pulled into the lot. "I need to tidy up the nursery—" which stood at the opposite end of the hall from Ernie's group "—then start some wash. You wouldn't believe how many crib sheets we used this week. I'm wearing out the center's dryer, too."

She was out of the office, hurrying along the hall, Brig likely forgotten for the moment, before Molly could respond.

At least Molly had finally stopped thinking about Natalie Brewster.

About Indiana in the snow. And angels.

CHAPTER TWELVE

Hey, Collier. Denton? No surprise there. Find anyone else for our princess? All the guys wish we could adopt her. Wouldn't that be a blast? First girl ever to have a dozen "fathers." Good luck, boss man. H.

AFTER HIS CALL to Sean's father, Brig had written to the team. And he couldn't stop thinking all the next day about the night he and Molly had made angels in his grandmother's snowy yard. What if he hadn't broken their engagement years ago to follow his own star? What if they had married, and Brig, not Andrew, had waited at the altar to watch Molly come down the aisle in that long white dress? By now they might have two or three kids and plenty of room in their lives for Laila.

But they didn't. As the newest email reminded him, he was searching for someone to keep the little girl for a while. He was still doing things he couldn't tell Molly about in places she'd never been. Indiana was probably the farthest she had traveled from Liberty in years, if not ever.

In the spare room, he diapered Laila, then set her in the swing. He didn't hear Molly coming up the stairs. He still had his back to her when suddenly she spoke. So much for his keen sense of imminent danger.

Her words only made Brig feel worse. "Every day when I get home," she said, "I expect you to be gone."

His shoulders tensed. "Is that what you want?"

"No, but you've been talking about a move next door...."

Now he was getting crazy. No doubt she hadn't meant that at all.

"I'm moving," he said, "at least in the right direction. I rented a car yesterday— declaration of independence—so you won't have to cart us around."

"Brig, even Pop says not to hurry." She walked over to the swing and wound up the music. "Itsy Bitsy Spider" began to play. "You and Laila are settled here. Why change that now?"

"Yeah, but she's pretty loud at night. I hate to bother you guys."

Molly touched Laila's hand. "I hear babies crying all day. And if I'm not mistaken, Pop loves her. It's been good for him to have you here."

Brig turned. For a moment he couldn't speak. After what he'd done to Molly long ago, after her father had made it plain he wasn't to hurt her again, they were asking him once more to stay.

"I don't know," he finally said. "If we can borrow the crib—"

"Of course you can. But think," she said.

And he saw what appeared to be distress in her eyes. After days of keeping away from him, she seemed upset to have him go. Maybe he hadn't messed up again too badly the night of their snowball fight after all. Or was it Laila?

"After work I'm home and on weekends, and Pop is always here," she went on with a rueful smile. "If necessary, Ann's usually available. And with Laila's colic lately, wouldn't you rather have our help than be alone over there—" she gestured toward his parents' house "—with no one else around to give you a breather?"

Brig smiled. "Sounds like some TV reality show where the parents have eight kids at once and the whole town steps in to help out."

He dared himself to put an arm around her shoulders, but he didn't move. "Which reminds me…the zoning commission meeting." Caught up in his own issues, he'd almost forgotten. But then he hadn't seen her much until now. "How did it go?"

"Don't ask."

"Your presentation was good, Molly." She had shown it to him the day before the meeting. "How can they refuse to grant the exemption?"

"I think Natalie Brewster's against it. And other neighbors are concerned. They'll have a chance to speak at the next meeting before the vote." She paused. "Did you connect with Sean's father?"

He told her about Denton.

"That's too bad," she murmured. "What will you do now?"

"Make more calls." Brig's spirits lifted. "Denton's not the worst guy in the world. Would you believe he called me back today and gave me a number for one of Sean's cousins? Seems Sean was close to several of them. But I'll give this woman a try first. If that doesn't work, maybe she can tell me where to find the others." He added, "I think Denton was more shaken up about Sean—and Laila—than he let on."

"What about Zada's family?" she asked.

He shook his head. "Not a chance. They disowned her—the whole bunch—when she married Sean. It's a cultural thing, I guess, but they apparently consider Laila tainted blood somehow. He said they weren't big on Americans." Brig paused. "Besides, that would mean taking her right back into the same dangerous environment I finally got her out of." He added, "She's also a U.S. citizen, thanks to Sean. With her very own passport." He touched Molly's shoulder, then quickly withdrew his hand. "Laila can stay in this country."

She frowned. "Pop says the situation overseas isn't getting better."

He sighed. "Yeah, and I need to find some solution here fast."

"Could you get an extension on your leave?"

"I've already had one. Requesting it was the first thing I did after I realized my folks were among the missing. My team's an elite unit, and we don't live by the normal rules in the mainstream military. We're more flexible—at least when there's not trouble to fly into somewhere. How much longer before that happens, I don't know."

"Maybe one of the team could help."

"They're in the same position I am. Prepared to ship out. But here." He showed her his phone with the latest post from the team and saw her smile.

"It's a good group."

"The best," he agreed.

Molly paused, as if uncertain about her next words. "Is there any chance you could… leave the service? If you did, that could be the solution for Laila. You'd be here, too."

"In D.C.," he said. He was one of those many people in the CIA and other low-profile organizations who, when asked about their jobs, answered only that it was in government.

But Molly had a point, as she often did.

"I know someday in the not-too-distant future I'll have to make that decision to opt out—as several members of my unit did this year. What we do requires lightning-fast reflexes, top-notch physical condition and a razor-sharp mind. Lives depend on that. And on my skills. It's a young man's job. Once the body starts to decline even a little, the end is in sight."

But Brig was still at his peak, and the adrenaline rush that went with his job was like an addictive drug. He'd always been a daredevil. And Molly wasn't.

"I'm not ready to leave all that behind me," he said. Not the way he had left Molly years ago. "I can't hang it up just yet."

Had his words hurt her again now? She gave him a look, one of those female things he couldn't interpret. Or was she simply thinking about Laila?

"I guess you'd better make that call," she said.

I'M NOT READY to leave all that behind me.

Molly carried another carton from her car into the community center. The place was hopping, and she shouldn't even be here. But Pop had missed delivering the donations after all.

"What do you mean, you forgot?" she'd asked. "You and Brig promised to take the stuff days ago—and there's a ton. With Ann and the rest of my staff helping, we really cleaned out Little Darlings." Making room,

Molly hoped, for new items in the wished-for expansion.

"Brig was on the phone or that computer of his all the time," Pop said. "I hardly saw him. We'll do it tomorrow."

Tomorrow was here. Molly had taken time off from work again to make sure Natalie couldn't fault her for not making the almost-too-late donations. She fought her way through a group of ladies from the church who were setting up a display of crocheted pot holders. She doubted they were castoffs. Over time the twice-a-year rummage sale had become a half discarded items, half crafts fair. Molly had happy memories of coming here with her mother, playing hide-and-seek under the tables with other kids, then, as she got older, "graduating" to actually helping out.

Still upset with Pop, who was outside with Brig unloading the car, she almost didn't see Natalie bustle over from a booth, selling raffle tickets for a huge, shrink-wrapped basket with a springtime theme. Wearing an emerald-green tracksuit, she stepped into Molly's path.

"I'd given up hope," she said, eyeing the box in Molly's arms. "Let me show you to your location." Before Molly could say a word, Natalie rushed toward the far corner of the large room. The rumble of people talking everywhere, the clatter of glassware and china, the harsh blare of a toy horn made her ears ache. And so did Natalie's words.

Molly's location?

She set her burden down with a thud on the table Natalie pointed at. "I thought you sorted all items into categories—toys, housewares, gifts, clothing, furniture—for your volunteers to sell."

"This year we decided to change things a bit."

Here we go, Molly thought. "Natalie, I hope I'm not expected to man this booth." She'd planned to simply drop her donations and go.

"Didn't you get our flyer in the mail?" Another oversight on Molly's part. "They went out a month ago. No one else has objected," she said.

"I'm not sure I can spare the time."

Natalie patted Molly's aching arm. "You'll find a way, dear. Thomas can pitch in," she added, then hurried off to badger someone else.

Molly wondered if the whole idea of this exercise was to get her father out of the house and close to Natalie. With a booth to manage, Molly would have to press Ann, who was watching Laila today, into service, which meant giving her a ride to the community center. Maybe other Little Darlings staff could donate a few hours, too. Frowning, Molly rummaged—*not to make a pun*—through the box of toddler toys, most of which looked the worse for wear. Maybe she should have crocheted a few new pot holders.

"Trouble?" Brig shoved the box aside to set his first carton on the table. Like the muscles in his arms, the box bulged, but with board games. A blue ball rolled around on top, threatening to fall out and bounce across the floor.

Remembering their discussion about his military service, Molly moved a few inches away from him.

"I've been sandbagged," she said, not meeting his eyes. "Natalie has 'donated' my time. Apparently I'm to stand behind this table for two days—and try to sell every piece we hauled over here."

"It's your civic duty," he said with a smile in his voice.

"I suppose. We all have our duties, don't we?"

With that, Molly marched off toward the

exit and her car to retrieve another load. To her utter irritation, their last eye-opening conversation shouldn't have surprised her, yet it had. That didn't give her the right to snap at Brig. He actually loved the heat of battle, pitting his strength and skills against an enemy, another reminder of how different they really were.

As she reached the door, Pop came through it carrying a well-used porta-crib, his face red and his breathing labored. Why hadn't he picked something lighter and less bulky?

Brig brushed against Molly's shoulder. "Let me get that, Thomas."

"Think you're the only one here with muscle?" Pop said.

He was about to argue further when he glanced over Molly's shoulder—and spotted Natalie. Molly didn't see her, but there was no mistaking the woman's voice.

"Thomas Walker, you sit down right now. Your face is as red as Santa Claus's coat. No one is having a heart attack on my watch."

"She's right," Brig said. "Here's a chair that's not being used. You rest while Molly and I get the other donations."

Natalie moved in to hover over Molly's dad, who was panting.

"Okay, okay," he said, giving in more easily than Molly had expected. "Fuss all you want."

"He'll be okay," Brig told Molly. "Miss Brewster is obviously a force to contend with, but she'll make certain he doesn't do anything foolish."

He pressed a hand to her lower back, then steered Molly from the community center. His touch sent another wave of yearning through her, like that night in the snow, followed by a surge of resentment for the other night, before she could move away. In the parking lot he grasped her shoulder to turn her around. His gaze swept the area as if to make sure they weren't about to be run over by any of the cars and pickup trucks streaming into the lot. "What's the problem here, Molly?"

"I'm a little peeved with Natalie, that's all."

"That's not all. Your face is an open book. Always has been." He hesitated until several people carrying boxes of books went by. "I don't blame you for being ticked because Thomas and I forgot to bring your donations."

"Well," she said drily, "you were busy."

"I should have remembered anyway."

The commanding officer, she thought. *The buck stops here.*

Molly's tone tightened. "I know you're worried about Laila," she began.

"Right now I'm more worried about you." After skirting a parked compact sedan, loaded to the roof inside, he walked her to her SUV. "Is this about the other night? Because if it is, I want you to know, I was only trying to make you see where I'm coming from."

Molly attempted to brush the remark away. "No, I understand. I myself am troubled about Laila. In a perfect world she'd have a home with you—" pause "—but the world is far from perfect."

"And so am I," he murmured. "Is that what you're really saying? Don't even try to back down, Molly, and tell me that my job is important. I already know that." Brig turned away. When he swung back to her, he said, "Look. Nobody would like more than I would to take care of that baby every day, every minute, until she leaves for college. But that isn't what I do, Molly." He rubbed the back of his neck. "And you saw me when I got back to Liberty. I couldn't even manage a diaper change. I almost scalded her with that first bottle in the microwave."

"You've learned since then," she said, "and I know you've been reading those books from the center every night—when Laila isn't up crying."

"Come on. Stop pulling your punches." *Fight like a man.*

"What I mean is—"

"I know what you mean. I know exactly what you think of me. I've known it for eight blasted years!" His eyes had darkened until the blue was all but gone. "I still feel guilty about you, and now Laila. That make you feel better, Molly? But there's nothing I can do now except find someone to care for—and love—Laila when I have to be gone."

"In a perfect world," she repeated, then, "that might be me. And Pop."

As soon as the words spilled out, Molly clamped her mouth shut. She hadn't meant to say that, but Brig studied her for a too-long moment, as if he'd never thought of the same solution. But he must have, even if Molly couldn't possibly offer to take Laila on any kind of longer-term basis, until Brig decided to "hang it up" at last. She wasn't that big a fool. That would be more difficult than their brief trip to Indiana when she had struggled not to imagine being Laila's mother and Brig's... No, she wouldn't even think that.

He glanced at the gravel under his feet. "Let's get your rig unloaded. I need to get back to the house—"

Before he finished, his cell phone rang.

Brig turned away to take the call, and Molly moved to the trunk of her car to give him privacy. Could it be one of his superiors, ordering him back to Washington and then elsewhere? She had just hefted another box filled with baby clothing and a few left-behind winter jackets when Brig joined her again.

"Great news," he said. "I hope," he added, their almost quarrel set aside for now. "That was Sean's cousin. She wants to come to Liberty. To meet Laila."

ANN FUSSED AGAIN with the smaller items on the Liberty Courthouse rummage sale table. She couldn't imagine why she'd let herself get talked into working when she needed time to clean her apartment, walk to the grocery store and do her laundry. But she had decided to make the best of it. Molly did a lot for her beyond giving her a lift whenever she needed one. This was Ann's chance to repay part of her debt.

She rearranged a collection of toy miniature cars. They were Ernie's favorite, and the thought of him reminded her of Jeff. *You can tell yourself anything you like....*

To her surprise, as if she'd conjured him up, a familiar little boy called out, managing to make himself heard above the din in the high-ceilinged room.

"Miss Ann! Hi!"

Ernie raced the length of the big room, bumping into people and threading his way at waist height through the crowd to her table. Excitement danced in his eyes. He stopped just short of plowing into the display Ann had been arranging.

"Good morning," she said with a smile that was always automatic when she saw him. "How are you, young Mister Barlow?"

"I'm fine!"

Ann fought the urge to skirt the table and scoop him up for a hug. She could never resist him, even when she tried to block out his father. And wouldn't you know? Here came Jeff, looking handsome in a rust-toned rugby shirt that brought out the color of his eyes. Today's Western-style boots made him seem even taller than usual. His journey from the front entrance to the far corner took a while, in contrast to Ernie's. People kept stopping Jeff to pump his hand or clap him on the shoulder. Clearly he was popular with the locals as the new sheriff's deputy. Natalie Brewster talked his ear off for a good two minutes before he smiled and moved on.

The whole time his gaze stayed on Ann. She hadn't seen him since the night they shared fast food, when he'd said, *Just don't ask me to believe it*. She had become an expert at avoidance.

Even Ernie had noticed at Little Darlings. *Why do you run away when my daddy comes to get me?* he'd wanted to know.

Ann had no answer for that.

Keeping her eyes now on Ernie, who was searching the tabletop for a car he liked, "the shiny silver one," she didn't look up as Jeff finally joined them. "You got a bunch of toys here from my school," Ernie said. "Did you carry it all?"

"No, sweetheart. Molly and my dad brought them." Ernie didn't know Brig, so she didn't mention him.

"That was a lot of work," the little boy noted with a solemn look.

Jeff was still staring at her. He laid one hand on Ernie's narrow shoulder, and Ann could feel her neck warm. As she sifted through the metal cars with Ernie, her hand shook.

Jeff hadn't said a word.

Finally, Ernie gave a shout, then held up the silver roadster he wanted.

"I played with this every day!" he told his father.

Jeff grinned at Ann, or in her direction. "Leave it to him to pick a Porsche."

Ernie glanced over his shoulder with a worried expression.

"Does it cost too much?"

"Well, let me see...." Jeff pretended to study the tag on the rear of the car. "Maybe we could swing it."

Hope sprang into Ernie's eyes. "Can I have it, then, Daddy?"

"May I," Jeff corrected him, but he was still looking at Ann, one hand on his son's shoulder. He dug in his jeans pocket and pulled out a twenty-dollar bill.

Ann couldn't resist. She said, "You can buy even more cars with that."

That set Ernie off again, scrabbling through the pile for a red fire truck, a blue convertible and a miniature yellow backhoe. He clutched them to his chest in his two small hands, and Ann couldn't help thinking how excited by the world he was at only four years of age.

Ernie should have whatever he wanted.

She might wish the same for Jeff. He'd already told her about his broken marriage. Here in Liberty, taking part today in the rummage sale amid the throng of smart shoppers, with the tantalizing scents of popcorn and cotton candy, he and Ernie were making a new life for themselves. Remembering her talk with Molly, Ann felt left out. Even more, she felt small and mean for pushing Jeff away to safeguard herself. He'd been nothing but nice to her. More than patient, too.

What was she really trying to prove?

"That's enough, Ernie." Jeff eased him from the table, his gaze shifting from Ann. "We'd better pay for these, then go. We have lots to do." He was still holding the cash.

"With your change, you can buy lunch at the hot dog booth," she teased.

"We don't need change." He glanced at her. "This is for a good cause."

As if he was talking about her, not the rummage sale profits for charity.

"Can I look over there at the bikes?" Ernie asked. "I see a big-boy one."

"Sure. But stay where I can watch you. It's crowded in here."

When Ernie charged off but Jeff stayed, Ann wasn't as upset as she expected to be. She put the cash in the money box. In the silence between them, without Ernie for a chaperone, she had to say something. "Looks like you may be going home with a new—or not quite new—bicycle, too."

"Ernie isn't ready for a two-wheeler. Maybe next year. He's had enough 'crashes' on his trike."

Jeff had told her about that, but Ann cringed at the word *crash*. Still, his choice of words aside, if she was honest, she'd have to acknowledge that he melted the ice around her heart. Which scared her even more.

Because baring her soul could invite his scorn, his disgust.

But had Molly been right? Ann couldn't go on like this.

Before he could turn away from the table, she cleared her throat. And, metaphorically, stepped off a cliff into thin air.

"Jeff, wait. I was, um, wondering…if you'd like to have dinner again some night.

It doesn't matter when. If it ever fits your schedule…"

His eyes widened, and for a few seconds he just stared at her.

"I know it's loud in here, but did I hear you right?" He smiled, a slow smile that went all the way to his eyes, lighting them with a hope that reminded her of Ernie and the toy car. "You're asking me for a date?"

She was in it now. And falling fast to the bottom of that cliff.

"My treat," she said. Maybe it would even be a good thing to let him know who she really was, to unload her burden. Like Molly venting over Natalie Brewster's possible vote against the center's expansion. Afterward Ann wouldn't have to dodge Jeff at all. He would know.

For a moment she expected him to include Ernie in her invitation, which would have seemed safer to Ann. But Jeff shook his head as if in wonder and told her, "I'll get a sitter."

They quickly settled on a day—tomorrow!—and a time, then Jeff was moving toward Ernie. Halfway across the room his son was about to jump on a black-and-gold bicycle that was too big for him but obviously held some mini-macho appeal. Jeff touched one finger to his temple in a small salute to Ann, then hurried off to rescue his son, having insisted he would pick Ann up at her apartment. "See you then."

She wasn't sure he heard her, but she said it anyway.

"I have something—bad—to tell you."

CHAPTER THIRTEEN

MOLLY WASN'T TALKING. For the past two days she'd tried to suppress any thought of her "discussion" with Brig in the parking lot. She worked her shifts at the rummage sale and stuck to business. If she was more than normally chatty with the residents of Liberty who cruised by the Little Darlings booth, no one seemed to notice. Except Brig. The two of them were working together today.

After Natalie Brewster had collared her father to make him rest, Pop had refused to join Molly again. Ann had begged off this morning, too, saying she had "things to do," but would try to come by later. That had left Brig to volunteer while Pop babysat Laila after vowing he wouldn't take his eyes off her. Molly had already called him twice.

She couldn't deny Brig was a big help. Carrying the day care center's donated porta-crib out to the new owner's car would have taxed Molly's strength, but Brig toted it effortlessly. What she did try to deny were the looks he kept giving her, part exasperation, part amusement.

"Okay," he finally said, "enough of this silent treatment."

Molly disagreed. For the moment no one seemed interested in the items remaining on their table. She decided it was time to inspect and do her usual trade-off with other people's leftover offerings, a tradition started by her mother, and that many others also observed on the last day of the sale. Without asking Brig to keep an eye on the booth, she stepped from behind the table.

But he caught her arm. "No way. Let's have this out, Molly."

"There's nothing to—"

"You're right. There's nothing to be angry about."

"I'm not angry." Her tone said the opposite.

Because Brig wouldn't let go, she all but dragged him to the table across the aisle—not that she could budge him if he didn't want to be budged. Brig couldn't very well continue their discussion when the vice chairman of the rummage sale was standing there in front of a display of hand-decorated linens.

Giving the woman a smile, he stuck his

hands in his pockets while Molly examined a baby-size pillowcase embroidered with flowers.

"Everything is half price now," the woman said. "So many people are leaving, already taking down their things early."

Molly murmured her agreement. It was always like that on the last day. Business had been slow for the past hour, making the time with Brig close at hand seem even more difficult. But he was wrong. She was more disappointed than angry. He'd stated his position about his military career. Why be surprised?

The truth was, she couldn't blame him. Molly held up the pillowcase.

"Isn't this pretty? It would be perfect for Laila when she's a little older."

As if he and the baby would be here then.

He drew out his wallet to pay for the item as though he and Molly were a couple. "Let me. She needs to start collecting girlie things."

"No, Brig." Molly tried to hold on to the linen, but he pulled it from her.

"Done," he said.

With the air of command that was so much a part of him, except of course in his earliest attempts at child care, he handed the paper bag with the pillowcase to Molly, then walked her farther along the aisle.

Playtime, her main competition for day care in town, boasted a huge play area and six more classrooms, and had manned a booth near the door during the sale. It had been all but cleaned out by now, but Brig had a mission in mind.

"What do you think? For Laila, too?" He bent to check out a used stroller. "With some cleaning and chrome polish, this would be great. Spring will be here soon, and you'll need your center's stroller." He glanced at Molly. "This even has a rain shield. And plenty of storage space."

"Sold," Molly said weakly. Didn't he hear what he was saying? This was another reminder that he and Laila wouldn't be here by spring. Pop wouldn't be taking the baby anywhere. Yet wherever Laila went, she would need a stroller. Or whoever cared for her would.

That was the last she and Brig said to each other before Molly closed out her cash box an hour later. By then the community center looked like the aftermath of a storm, with litter everywhere, empty tables with torn paper bunting hanging from them, fallen popcorn

crunching underfoot, its stale smell lingering in the air, and a general forlorn look that
echoed Molly's mood. The scene reminded
her of one of her parties. Brig carted the un-
sold items out to her car.

"I won't unload these," she said, still trying
to maintain her business-only attitude with
Brig. "Tomorrow they can go to Goodwill."

At that moment another car pulled up behind hers, and Molly saw Ann in the passenger seat. "Hi," she said. "I brought a few more
things from the center. Are we too late?"

Molly said they were. But she didn't miss
the look Ann gave her or her sister's pointed
glance at Brig. He nodded at her, said a few
words to Ann's friend, then stepped back, but
his gaze stayed on Molly, whose face soon
warmed. And he stood too close. There was
no telling when Ann had first seen them now
or what she might make of the obvious tension in the air between them.

Brig waited until Ann had left with her
friend. Then, by the tailgate of her SUV, he
turned her to face him. "I meant what I said
before inside. The other day, too. I don't like
you giving me the cold shoulder. You need
to understand that I don't have a choice right

now. When the order comes, I'll have to leave. That's how I earn my living."

"I understand. Perfectly," she said.

He shook his head. "No, obviously you don't. I'm not an insurance agent or an engineer, a car mechanic or a teacher. I never will be—because as right as those jobs are for other men, they aren't right for me."

"I know." She started around to the driver's-side door, but Brig was right with her.

"Molly, I need your help. With the baby."

They might have been the only words that would stop her. Molly had her mother to thank for her caring gene, but even sometimes-grumpy Pop had a soft spot for others. Especially Laila.

She gazed into Brig's eyes. "Forgive me. I'm being a…" She shrugged. "You know."

He took her face in his hands. "Why are we fighting?"

"We're not."

"Sure feels like it to me. The only thing that matters right now is Laila." He paused. "I've made arrangements with Sean's cousin. I'll see how that goes," he said, not looking happy about it. "What I need to ask is, will you be there with me when she arrives?"

Molly frowned. It was one thing to know he

and Laila were leaving. It was quite another to help make it happen. "I don't think—" *I can do that,* she thought.

"You have experience with kids," he said. "You'll know the right questions to ask. Laila's well-being depends on my choice of caregiver. I don't think Sean's cousin will be anything like his father. She sounded nice on the phone. I've talked to her twice now, but I need your input, your advice—"

"Yes," Molly said, unable to refuse. Unable to hear any more. "Yes, I'll be there. For Laila." That was always her rationale. "I'll help in any way I can."

WITH THAT PROMISE ringing in her ears, Molly hadn't been home more than a few minutes when she heard the doorbell. Thomas had the TV on so loud he didn't seem to hear—or was he hiding again? When Molly opened the door, she saw Natalie Brewster.

Today their newest neighbor was wearing a silvery jacket and pants. Purple feathers were woven into her hair, and her eyes danced with excitement that almost knocked Molly over in the doorway.

"The rummage sale earned more this time than ever! As soon as we finished counting the money from the cash boxes at each booth I had to come thank you for your contributions." She swept inside without waiting for an invitation. "Thomas, we couldn't have done it without you."

An exaggeration in Molly's view, but she smiled. Her dad was already twitching in his chair, trapped as he had been at the community center. He didn't meet Natalie's gaze. "Bunch of junk, if you ask me. Why would anyone pay for someone else's clutter, then drag it home instead of to the dump? I never understood why Molly's mother kept going year after year."

"I'm told she was one of our most dedicated volunteers." Natalie stood over him like a teacher scolding an unruly student. "I'm glad you decided to take her place this year."

His eyes lifted, and Molly thought she saw him assess Natalie.

"No one could take her place."

"Well, that's not exactly what I meant," Natalie backpedaled. "It must be very difficult to lose someone. I've been an independent single woman all my life, so I don't have a family of my own and I wouldn't know, but—"

Thomas looked past her.

Natalie followed his glance to the television set. The Cleveland Cavaliers were playing the New York Knicks. Her eyes lit up again. "A classic rivalry! And I'm blocking your view. But who could miss it?" She plunked herself on the sofa beside his chair. "What's the score?"

He waved toward the screen. "Read it and weep."

The Cavs were behind by twenty points. "Pop," Molly murmured, afraid he was going to say something rude to Natalie. Even after so obviously checking her out, he couldn't be relied on to keep the peace.

His gaze shot to Natalie. "I'd like to watch this game."

Natalie didn't move. "So would I."

"Please, stay. Would you like something to drink?" Molly asked her. There really was no polite reason to kick her out. And Molly had her own reason for the invitation to stay.

"I wouldn't mind a cup of tea." Natalie settled into the sofa and plumped a pillow behind her back as if to tell Thomas she meant to stay awhile.

"Pop, let's have a basketball party," Molly said. There hadn't been an occasion since Valentine's Day, and that had put all of her current problems in motion. "Give me a minute. I'll get some food together."

She went to the foot of the stairs to call Brig. Molly would give Ann a ring, too. Maybe Molly would be able to forget her earlier wrangle with Brig, not to mention her agreement to sit in on the interview with Sean's cousin.

To her satisfaction, the house felt lively again before long. Even without Ann, who, to Molly's amazement, had a date tonight with Jeff. In spite of Pop's first efforts to ignore Natalie, she kept the conversation going, and soon he was joining in. Molly served wings and chips with onion dip, cheese and crackers, even rice cereal for Laila, who'd gotten the go-ahead from her pediatrician to start solid food. She was cranky, but it wasn't colic.

"The baby had her vaccinations, too," Brig said, "and I think she's feverish. I just gave her a baby painkiller."

Molly could have smiled. Maybe child care wasn't Brig's forte like black ops, but he certainly looked and sounded now like a fully involved father. Fortunately, the pill and the cereal seemed to help Laila's mood.

Nothing could soothe Molly, though. With Brig and Laila in the room, she was reminded all over again that they would be gone too soon, probably in different directions and for good this time.

At halftime she refilled the spicy wings platter. When she came back her dad had Laila on his lap. To her surprise Natalie was shoveling more cereal into the baby's mouth. Without warning, Laila spewed a mouthful into the air, which hit them both. She actually giggled at her new trick, but to Molly's relief and delight, her dad and Natalie laughed. Both of them. Together. Who would have thought?

"Looks like a bonding moment to me," Brig murmured, then raised his voice to be heard above the TV. "Thomas, Natalie, if you're willing to watch Laila for half an hour, I'm going out for some fresh air."

"Of course we will," Natalie said. "Thomas and I have it covered."

"Molly's coming with me." When Brig caught her hand, Pop's look could have ignited the wood stacked in the fireplace. And Brig stopped.

"You have something to say, Thomas?"

Pop's eyes were all but bugging from his head. In that moment their recent truce was about to blow up. "I said what I had to say the first morning after you got here. You heard me then and the night we fixed the sink. Same message now."

His warnings must be playing like an old tape in Brig's head. "I'm keeping my hands to myself," he said, then drew Molly from the room to get their coats on.

Outside, they breathed in cold air and began walking. There might still be one last snowstorm or two, but right now a sunset display of red and orange and pink tinged with lavender glowed across the horizon. Darkness would descend before they had rounded the block.

"Those two are funny," Brig said, still holding Molly's hand. She felt it warm and strong around her smaller one, another painful reminder that she would miss him—and of course, Laila—when they left. "He likes her but is afraid to show it."

Molly gaped at him in the growing dusk. "Are you kidding?"

"Well, we know she likes him. And she took good care of him at the rummage sale when he tried to do too much. He might be grateful for that."

Molly mulled that over. "I have seen Pop give Natalie a look or two. And then there's

Ann," she said. At Brig's curiosity, she added, "She's having dinner with Jeff tonight. That's why she couldn't come to my impromptu party." Molly was still trying to process that.

"Good for her. Good for them, too," Brig said with a smile.

"Jeff must be a miracle worker."

"Maybe he has magical powers—like Natalie."

"Don't hold your breath about that." Molly sighed. "I'm glad Pop has had Laila to focus on, even temporarily," she couldn't help adding, "but I don't know what he'll do when she's not here."

She didn't mention Brig. Despite her dad's earlier warning glare, most of the time now he seemed to accept Brig's presence in their home.

Brig said, "Know what I think?" He and Molly turned the corner. "I think Thomas and Natalie are not so different."

"But Natalie's talkier and much more sociable than Pop. She's bubbly and he's like a clam sometimes."

"Two sides of the same coin," Brig insisted, swinging Molly's hand as they walked along the street. The sun had slid below the horizon, and lights had begun to come on here and there in the houses.

"Really?" Molly said. "You think they're—"

"Lonely," they both said at once.

For long moments they walked without speaking, her hand still tucked into his as if it belonged there, and Molly indulged herself in the fantasy that she and Brig had never parted. Instead, they had married and Laila was their child and they owned a house on this very street near Pop.

To make the all too pleasurable fantasy vanish, she asked Brig about his family.

"I talked to Mom. She said to tell you how much they appreciated all your help in Indiana. My grandmother's doing okay in rehab, but she's not happy there. At least she's walking now." He paused. "My mother claims they could be home within the next few weeks— once they spring Grandma Collier from rehab and talk her into moving to Liberty."

"Could they take Laila after all, then?"

"We didn't get that far. I doubt it," he said. "That wouldn't happen soon enough—and doesn't change their obligation to my grandmother. My dad's pretty hard-nosed about her selling her house. He'll want to do that first.

Which means even longer until they're likely to get home."

Molly didn't know what to say to that. Brig was probably right, which didn't help the situation with Laila.

Brig, too, was lost in thoughts. "You know something?" he finally said. By then they were on the front sidewalk again at Molly's house. "I lied to your father."

"About what?" Pop wouldn't care to hear that, just when he had begun to like, even trust, Brig again. Except with Molly.

"Keeping my hands off you," Brig said, and their relaxing walk around the block vanished like Molly's fantasy. In the near darkness he spoke even more softly. "I don't want to, Molly. I want—very badly right now—to kiss you."

She withdrew her hand from his.

"To be honest," he said, "I've never stopped wanting to."

Focused on his words, she failed to notice that Brig had pulled her off the path into the shelter of the big sycamore tree by the front porch. Surprised by his movement and her own lack of resistance, Molly gazed at him, trying to read his expression. In the soft glow of light from the living room, she could barely make out his eyes, so dark and…dear. The years hadn't changed that. *If I loved you,* she thought, *again.* But Molly knew she wouldn't dare do that.

She voiced the reminder. "So much has happened since you left, Brig. For both of us," she added. "We were finished long ago," she said to save herself. "There's nothing—"

"There's *something,*" he insisted. "Ever since Indiana at least."

Molly couldn't deny that. "But those were a few days out of time," she murmured. "Nothing more. I can't go back—"

The rest was never said. As Molly stood there, unmoving, he clasped her shoulders to draw her closer, and then Brig's mouth was on hers and Molly was in his arms. The warmth of his lips, the oh-too-familiar way he kissed, sent a wave of yearning through her even stronger than that night in the snow. Without even thinking, Molly kissed him back.

"We're already there," Brig whispered against her mouth.

CHAPTER FOURTEEN

THE LITTLE INN not far from her apartment was too cozy for Ann's comfort tonight. She had never felt this jumpy in her life and, considering her life since the accident, that was saying something. Asking Jeff out was the most idiotic thing she'd ever done and by far the most impulsive.

Sitting across from him in her favorite restaurant in Liberty, which wasn't saying much because there were only two in town other than fast food chains, threatened to shred the last of her nerves.

Jeff looked manly and handsome, as he always did, but too formal in dark dress pants and a white shirt with a well-fitted blazer.

"No tie," he told her when he caught her looking. "I hope that was okay for here. I'm not into suits."

They both seemed to babble in between awkward bouts of silence.

She tried again to keep up her end of the

stilted conversation. "Who's staying with Ernie?"

He named one of the aides from Little Darlings. "She helps me out now and then. She wanted to know who I was seeing tonight, but I didn't tell." He paused. "I wasn't sure if you wanted that to be common knowledge, and I figured the news would spread through the center fast, then all of Liberty." Jeff fiddled with his knife and fork. "Is it a secret?"

"One meal," Ann murmured. "A third meal, I mean. That's no reason to reserve the church for a wedding." *Oh, stupid.* Why had she said that?

Saving her from an explanation that would only make things worse, their waiter delivered their drinks. Jeff waited until he was gone.

"Ann, I'm coming out of my skin here. I'm about to break out in a sweat," he admitted. "Not about some wedding. You wouldn't believe the grilling I got from Ernie before I left to pick you up. I escaped before he guessed the truth, but it was a near miss." He took another sip of his drink. "Full disclosure? I'm nervous. I haven't had a date in over five years, and that was with my then fiancée, now ex-wife, who we're not going to talk about tonight."

"I haven't gone out with anyone since…" She didn't remember when. Soon after the accident, she'd met a few times with other classmates, who often ended up just wanting to know the gory details or even to censure her for what she'd done. And once she'd had dinner like this with a man from the gym she used to belong to, but that had been as uncomfortable as now with Jeff.

Which reminded her of her promise to come clean, the very reason for their date and, probably, her nerves.

"Maybe we should go," she said, not meeting his gaze. "I can't believe I asked you out. Put you on the spot like this." *And myself.*

If she kept her mouth shut, maybe they could at least be friends.

Across from her, Jeff was still playing with his knife. He clinked it against his water glass, producing a loud chime. He laid the knife down, then put a finger to Ann's chin, forcing her to look up at him.

"Why don't we start over? We've already ordered, and in spite of the heebie-jeebies I'm feeling, I'm hungry."

"So am I," Ann murmured. A little.

"I've heard this inn has good food," he said. "I hear a lot of things in my line of work— kind of like being a hairdresser." Jeff half smiled. "People confide all sorts of stuff."

Especially under pressure, she thought.

"They were right. The food here is good."

After that, they both started to relax. Ann's chicken marsala was delicious, and Jeff had no trouble digging into his steak. She didn't have to tell him anything if she didn't choose to. Ann even ordered dessert, a crème brûlée to share.

Then they were done, walking to the parking lot, and Jeff was opening the door to his own car, not the sheriff's department cruiser. He concentrated on his driving, a pop radio station softly playing to cover the silence, but all the way back to her apartment Ann worried again.

Could she tell him after all about the accident and hope he wouldn't see her as a monster? If she told him, would he run off, revolted, after dumping her at her door? Or, if she didn't talk, would he kiss her good-night? Which pretty much laid waste the friendship theory.

His closeness in the car overwhelmed Ann. She could smell his aftershave, something subtle and mildly spicy. Her onetime boyfriend, the guy she had thought she loved then, the man whose life she had ruined, had always laid the scent on too thick. If she passed someone and smelled that same brand, she felt dizzy. Now she was light-headed, but not for the same reason.

All too soon Jeff pulled into the parking space in front of her apartment building where he'd met her that night with Ernie. He kept the engine running because it was chilly outside, but Ann shivered anyway. The look in his eyes had grown serious, probing.

"Time's up," he said, as if he'd been anticipating this moment all night. "You promised to tell me something."

Ann's stomach clenched. She'd hoped he hadn't heard her that day. Hoped she might escape after all, chicken out with a quick good-night. But Jeff wasn't letting her.

Ann faced him, her back pressed against the passenger door. She swallowed twice before she could speak.

"When I was eighteen," she began, her throat tightening with each word, "I went to a party with a boy I was dating. He had, well, way too much fun—"

"Drinking. He was over the legal limit," Jeff guessed.

He sat against the opposite door, his long legs stretched out for comfort, or maybe to put Ann at ease. His casual posture didn't fool her. He would extract the whole truth from her now if he had to wait all night.

"Probably," she said, clearly surprising him. "But that wasn't all. I was drinking, too. Everything was fine until he and his friends began roughhousing. At first it was just pushing and shoving, a few insults tossed around the way guys do to be funny. But then things turned ugly. Someone didn't like what was said and threw a punch. Robert waded in, and all at once they were fighting seriously. It was a real brawl."

"Did anyone get hurt?"

Ann paused. "Robert had his back to some stairs. When another guy slammed into him, Robert went flying backward. He managed to break his fall but hurt his ankle. His right one."

Jeff understood. "His driving foot."

Ann nodded. "He was in a lot of pain, and the ankle was already swelling. I was afraid he'd broken it, and I wanted to phone his father to pick us up, but we were driving his

car that night, and Robert begged me not to."
She waited a minute before going on. "I didn't
want to call Pop, either," she added with a
sigh. "He didn't care for Robert, and at the
time of course I thought he was the one."

"At eighteen we're all sure."

So far, so good, Ann thought. Jeff wasn't
being critical.

She took a breath. "I considered phoning
Molly. I even tried. But she and Brigham Collier were still engaged then, and they'd gone
to some big dance at the Cincinnatian Hotel
downtown. She had her phone turned off."
Ann paused. "I didn't know what else to do
except..."

She trailed off and stared into the distance.
"Let me guess." Jeff pulled her back to the
topic she had hoped to avoid, and Ann realized she'd been woolgathering, stalling. "You
offered to drive."

Ann shut her eyes at the memory. "The
worst decision I ever made. Robert didn't
want me to—I guess the pain had sobered
him up—and he kept saying I shouldn't get
behind the wheel. But I insisted. I just wanted
to get him to the E.R."

"Tell me what happened."

"I decided to call his parents from there.

The route took us along unfamiliar roads. It was dark and raining by then, and there were no streetlights." She stopped, her breath coming faster as the scene replayed itself in her mind. "I was already having a hard time seeing." Ann's senses seemed to become more acute as she relived the horror with every word. "Then…while I was navigating a curve, pain must have overcome Robert, and woozy, he slumped against me, knocking me off balance."

"You lost control."

"That shouldn't have been a surprise. I'd only had my license for a few months. Pop didn't believe in his girls driving at sixteen. Without much experience I never came out of that curve. We veered off the road, then plowed into a high brick wall on someone's property."

Jeff waited a few seconds before asking, "Injuries?"

"Robert." Ann could still hear him, pinned into the damaged passenger seat, crying for help. "His side of the car had caved in, crushing him. The paramedics, the police, whoever had to cut him out."

"The Jaws of Life," he murmured.

She began to shake. So did her voice. "His

back was broken in the crash. He'll never walk again. His parents still blame me—as they should. You can imagine that was the end of our romance." The end of most everything.

She risked a glance at Jeff—and froze. His face held the exact expression she had most dreaded after telling him the truth. For a long moment he simply stared at her, shaking his head a little, and Ann thought, *I was wrong to tell him*. No wonder Jeff's face showed the horror he must feel.

"Ann—" he began, but nothing more emerged except a soft curse.

Well, she wouldn't have to worry about his interest in her again or how much she had come to like him.

She flung open her door and ran out into the night, toward her building and the safety of her apartment, without looking back.

MOLLY FELT AS though she was about to reach some point of no return.

A few days after Brig had kissed her under the sycamore tree in her father's yard, she was still reeling from the sensation. *We're already there,* he had said, but nothing could have served as a better reminder that he and

Laila would soon be gone from her life than today's meeting with Sean Denton's cousin.

In the living room Molly faced her with a weak smile. As she'd promised, she wouldn't think beyond helping Brig now to assess the dark-haired, thirtyish woman who sat across from her. For lack of anything else to say, Molly asked, "How was your drive?"

"Not bad." Susan Denton Frasier lived north of Columbus, an hour or so away.

Leaving Molly to invent small talk, Brig had gone upstairs to get the baby, whose schedule finally seemed more regular than not. She'd actually napped this afternoon and had slept almost straight through the night before. Brig was taking a long time to return, and Molly wondered if he was dragging his heels, but he finally reappeared.

"Sorry, she needed a diaper change—and I decided to try her newest outfit for the occasion. Meet Laila Denton."

Susan's face broke into a wide smile. "Isn't she lovely."

"We think so," Brig murmured, including Molly.

"May I?" Susan moved slowly so as not to startle the baby. She peered into Laila's dark eyes and the baby smiled, her gaze darting from Susan's face to her hair, which apparently fascinated Laila.

The little girl was wearing the pale pink-and-white romper with white tights that Molly and Brig had bought her in Indiana. She had a little pink-striped matching hair bow—Molly's addition to the ensemble.

Molly didn't know whether to hope this interview turned out well or not. On one hand, an agreement to care for Laila, at least until Brig could make more permanent plans, would relieve his growing tensions. On the other, a good result meant Molly would lose Laila almost immediately.

"She has Sean's smile," Susan said. "It lights her whole face, too."

"You said you were close to him," Brig stated.

"As kids, sure. We were like siblings. He was an only child, as you probably know, and my brother and I were the other two of our, well, triplets, you might say." Her wistful smile faded. "Sean didn't have the best home life after his mother died, so mine took over when she could. We spent a lot of time running around those Kentucky hills, fishing in the creek and swimming in the lake... I was shocked to learn of Sean's death. So young," she said, "and just when he'd gotten this little one." Susan paused. "You spoke to his father."

"Briefly, yes."

"I can imagine." After Brig explained the call, Susan looked at the ceiling. "He's a hard man. Not well at this point, as you know. My uncle never showed Sean much love, that's for sure. Even when he was younger and still healthy. He didn't like having us kids around, either. His house wouldn't have been a good place for this baby, even if he had been willing to take her. Still, he passed along my number to you. That's something."

When Brig offered to let her hold the baby, Susan didn't hesitate. It was as if she could touch Sean again. She gently scooped up Laila, and let her grasp her finger. When Susan looked up, tears glinted in her eyes. "I have two boys and a girl myself. My daughter would love to have a baby in the house...."

Molly's stomach clenched. She sensed a *but* in there somewhere.

Susan shook her head. "I wish my husband could see her. He's great with kids. He would have come with me today, but he lost his job last week and is scrambling to find another. With five mouths to feed, we'll run through our savings in no time." She paused again. "I've been working when the children are in school, but I'll be asking—begging is more like it—for extra hours as soon as I get back." She added, "I'm in HR, which is ironic now when I can't fill this job for you."

"I don't want to place a burden on you, Susan—but you understand my position. If there's any way you could—"

She glanced from Brig to Molly to Brig again. "I hope I haven't misled you, or given you false hope, but I wanted so badly to meet Laila. I'm terribly sorry. As much as I'd like to—for Sean's sake, as well—we can't help you."

Molly saw how pale Brig had become. He stared down at Laila, still in Susan's arms, with a despairing darkness in his eyes. "What about your brother?"

Susan shook her head. "He's not like Sean's father, but my brother has made some poor choices in his life. He's in a bad place right now. I could give you his number, but really, you wouldn't be doing Laila any favors. Besides, I doubt he'd respond much better than my uncle, even though I know he loved Sean."

"Are there other relatives? Someone else who would—"

Susan flinched. "No, my uncle, my brother and I are the last of our family."

"I see."

She frowned. "What other plans can you make for the baby, then?"

Brig let out a sigh. "I don't know."

When Susan kissed Laila softly on her hair, right beside her pink-striped bow, Molly spoke for the first time, her take on Susan's suitability as a caregiver no longer needed.

"Would you like to visit a while longer, Susan? It's still early. You could play with Laila—it's her best time of day—and even stay for dinner. I'm making a meat loaf." She forced a smile. "My dad considers it my specialty. You're more than welcome to join us."

After all, Susan was Laila's second cousin, and Laila was obviously a welcome member of the Denton family, even if Susan couldn't give her a foster home.

Susan handed Laila back to Brig. "I would love to. But with three kids…I'd better go. Otherwise I'd be even more tempted to 'kidnap' Laila. The traffic through Columbus won't be any picnic. If I start now…"

"Come back anytime. You're always welcome."

"Thank you." She didn't seem to remember that Brig wouldn't be here much longer, and he stayed silent and didn't remind her. He was standing in the middle of the living room, holding Laila a little too close, as if afraid she might get away. The baby was smiling—a contrast that worsened the moment. Molly could guess at the lump in Brig's throat. Which matched hers.

She'd been grabbing at straws by asking Susan to stay. Brig had had his answer. Molly could imagine him thinking, *What am I going to do about Laila?*

If she didn't miss her guess, with a deadline looming, his clock was ticking with a vengeance.

CHAPTER FIFTEEN

ALMOST LATE FOR work, Molly poured fresh coffee into a travel mug—an odd item for her to have, considering she rarely went anywhere—and started for the back door. Fortunately, her morning commute—across the yard—was even shorter than Ann's.

Just before she left, she glanced out the kitchen window and spied her father coming from Natalie Brewster's house across the street. Scowling, Pop slapped a rolled-up newspaper against his thigh. A minute later he steamed into the kitchen.

The headline in the local paper he was holding referred to tonight's vote at the zoning commission meeting. Accompanying the lead story was Natalie Brewster's picture.

"Have you seen this?" Pop asked.

She tried not to panic. "No. I'm sure you hurried across the street as soon as you picked it up from the mailbox."

"Well, someone had to set her straight.

How can she say no tonight to your proposal? It's not as if Little Darlings impinges on her property. She won't have kids running through her yard, stomping on those pink peonies she's so fond of. What's the big deal about some new swings and a sliding board behind a good-looking fence?"

Molly's heart sank. "She's not the only person in this neighborhood who objects. Does the article say all that?" she asked.

If so, in a few hours her worst fears would come true. Little Darlings would not be permitted to expand the center.

He looked away. "No, but I thought I should let her know there's no harm in saying yes."

Her mouth fell open. "You tried to sway Natalie's vote?" She waved the travel mug in the air. "Pop, you didn't."

"It was a friendly discussion," he insisted. "She even offered me tea."

"You don't drink tea."

"She made me coffee," he said. "Only thing is that gave her time to form her argument— and kept me at her kitchen table twice as long as I meant to stay there."

"Oh, Pop."

"Did you think I'd just let that meeting

happen tonight without speaking up for my daughter? After I saw this article?"

Molly gave up. She wouldn't influence the vote if she could, though she had no doubt Natalie would speak her mind, perhaps swaying the others on the commission. And this morning, Molly had different things on her mind.

For one, she'd had another rash of absences at the center because the flu showed no sign of letting up. Then she had Brig to worry about. And Laila.

"I have to get to work. I'll talk to you about this later."

"Nothing more to say," he told her with a guilty look.

At least she'd gotten her point across. "I never thought I'd hear myself say this—but, *please,* stay in the house today."

Molly had her hand on the doorknob to leave, but she stopped again. Brig had come down the stairs with a far more solemn look on his face than Pop had right now. Molly had rarely seen Brig in the past several days. He'd spent most of his time trying to find child care for Laila after Susan Denton's visit.

Now he was holding his still-open cell phone. "My orders," he murmured. "The whole situation just exploded in my face. I'd hoped for more time, but I'm due on base in three days."

Thomas made a sound of obvious distress.

"So soon? I mean, I know this Middle East thing has been going on—"

"Not there," Brig said. "A different trouble spot, it turns out. Not that I couldn't end up in two places before I get leave again." He glanced at Molly. "And that's all I can tell you about that." He blew out a breath. "Sorry. I know it wasn't the most tactful way to make the announcement."

Molly dared to ask, "And Laila?"

Her father's face threatened to crumple. He must be as sad to know Laila would soon be leaving their house as Molly was, but Brig squared his shoulders.

"Right after we saw Susan, I called a local nanny agency. I'm meeting with them later today. Keep your fingers crossed."

HER WORDS WITH Pop and then Brig's unwelcome, if expected, news set the tone for the rest of her day. Molly had to try hard not to give in to a black mood.

At Little Darlings she had no sooner stepped inside than she heard a commotion in the hallway. She looked toward the rooms at the far end—and saw Benjamin Crandall locked by Ernie Barlow in a wrestling hold on the floor. Molly couldn't make out their words, but the little fellows appeared angry enough to fight to the death.

"Boys!" She raced down the hall, intending to seize one of them by the arm and haul them apart. "Benjamin, stop!"

But before she could get there, Ernie was straddling Benjy. As Molly skidded to a stop, to her amazement, Jeff's little boy pulled back his arm, fist cocked, and delivered a solid blow to Benjamin's nose. Blood streamed down his face in an instant, then down his neck and onto his white polo shirt.

Ernie's face was beet-red. His eyes flashed. Neither boy had uttered a syllable. Theirs had been a silent struggle until the dull sound of flesh meeting bone.

"There!" Ernie said. "Don't ever hit me again."

"Ernie." Molly grabbed his arm before he could deliver another rounder. She dragged him off Benjamin just as Ann came out of the nursery.

"What's going on?"

"The four-year-old version of WWE—

world wrestling," Molly said, "or, more accurately, cage fighting."

Ann bent over Benjy, who had blood running through his fingers as he tried to cover his bleeding nose. "I didn't hear a thing."

"I think stealth was the plan," she murmured. "Ernie, I'm very disappointed in you. You know the rule here—if there's a problem with another child, you come to me or Miss Ann. I've told Benjamin the same thing. I'll have to speak to your father."

Ann was mopping Benjy's nose with the clean rag she'd been carrying. Each morning she prepared items for the day's crafts, among them play dough and crayons, and she'd probably been mixing tempura paint for today when she finally heard the scramble in the hall.

Ernie's chin set. "My daddy told me to," he said.

"Seriously?"

"He did, Molly." Ann helped Benjy to his feet. The other boy was crying now, which pretty well guaranteed that Debbie Crandall would be giving Molly an earful. "The last time the kids tangled, the time Ernie had stitches, Jeff advised him to deck Benjy the next time."

"Who started this?" Molly asked, her gaze darting between them.

"Benjy," Ernie said, the spots of color on his cheeks turning darker.

"No! Miss Molly, it was him." Benjamin pointed a finger.

"All right, Ernie. Come with me."

He tried to hold back. "Am I in trouble?"

"Yes. Whatever you were told, I doubt your dad will be happy about this."

"He will, too," Ernie said, chin in the air.

Molly had never seen him like this, but she refused to get into an argument with a four-year-old. She took Ernie's hand in hers and marched him down the hall to her office. "Ann," she called back. "You'll see to Benjy?"

"Under control," she said.

Molly was stunned by what had happened. It was true, as she'd told Debbie Crandall, that some of the boys tended to fight, usually territorial arguments over toys, but to see Ernie become the aggressor shook her opinion of him. She'd been wrong to see him as a paragon of behavior.

"Sit in that chair," she said, "the one in front of my desk. I'm going to phone your dad—and he'll have to come get you. You're 'suspended' for the day, Ernie. You'll have plenty of time to think over what you did and why it's not a good idea to let it happen again. Do you understand?"

Molly got no answer. Her back to him, she finished washing her hands at the sink in the half bath adjacent to her office. When she at last turned around and came out, she met with another surprise.

Ernie sat slumped in the cushy armchair across from her desk, his eyes red rimmed and bleary, his cheeks still red. For the first time since she'd met him, he failed to give Molly a smile. He knew he was in trouble, of course, but...

She touched a practiced hand to his forehead, which felt as hot as a bonfire. She wanted to blame that on his recent battle with Benjamin, but she knew better. Ernie was obviously the latest victim of the flu.

And her mood softened. "You're not feeling well, are you?"

He shook his head, then winced. One of the first signs of the current flu strain was headache.

"Would you like a book to look at until your daddy gets here?"

Ernie nodded. "I would like a book. Please."

By the time Molly retrieved his favorite story, Ernie was asleep in the chair. Molly covered him with a light blanket, then closed her office door and went down the hall to the nursery.

She beckoned to Ann, who had taken Benjamin back to his teacher. Molly could see him curled in a beanbag chair with an ice pack on his face.

"Could you sit with Ernie in my office? He's going home sick this morning."

Ann groaned. "Not him, too? You sure he's not overheated from the boys' fist fight?"

"Positive. How many cases have we seen? This year's vaccine doesn't appear to have any effect on this strain. I'd appreciate your help. Just be sure to sanitize your hands before you go in—and when you're ready to go back to the nursery."

"As if I didn't know," Ann murmured, but she didn't refuse.

Molly couldn't keep from teasing her sister a little. She needed a light moment.

"Say hi to Sheriff Barlow for me," she said, noting a now-familiar look on Ann's face as soon as she mentioned the name. Then Molly sailed down the hall to greet Debbie Crandall, who had just stepped into the center.

Benjy's teacher had phoned her, and Debbie worked nearby, so she was able to get there right away.

Molly could tell by the look on the woman's face that their conversation wouldn't be easy. This time she didn't blame her. She steered Benjamin's mother into a small anteroom by the front door and attempted to ease into the subject.

"I'm sorry for these cramped quarters, but my office is filling in for a nurse's station we don't have right now. The whole center has been fighting off this flu bug."

Debbie frowned. "I hope Benjy doesn't catch it," she said, looking around the room, "but I'm more concerned right now about his nose. Where is he? I hope it isn't broken. Where was his teacher when Ernie attacked him?"

"She was nearby, but it all happened so fast. I'm not sure who started it," Molly said. "They each claim the other did, but that's always the case." She cleared her throat. "Debbie, I'm terribly sorry."

Debbie's face tightened. "But you think this was Benjamin's fault? Again?"

"No, it appears he was this morning's victim. I saw for myself. Ernie Barlow punched Benjy while holding him down."

For a moment Debbie seemed both alarmed and satisfied. Then she said, "I need to see my son. Now."

"Of course."

Debbie followed Molly into the hall. "I'll let you know if my husband and I decide Benjy would be happier—and safer—at Playtime rather than here."

She swept down the hall and headed for the four-year-olds' room. Gazing after her, Molly had a sense of utter failure. She fought an inner urge to throw a chair.

The way today was going, tonight should be interesting.

ERNIE WAS HER weak spot.

In Molly's office, Ann smoothed a hand across his forehead. He was burning up. Considering her normal duties in the nursery, she shouldn't be here for fear of carrying the bug to one of the babies. She should go home as soon as Ernie left. Yet she hadn't thought to say no when Molly had asked for her help.

All she could think of was giving Ernie whatever comfort she could. Never mind his fight with Benjamin Crandall—or the lecture he would deserve from his father. Right now her whole being seemed to hurt for him.

Well, no. That wasn't all. She kept remembering the night he and Jeff had brought takeout food to her apartment and how nice it had been to talk with Jeff while Ernie watched a movie in the other room. How good it felt to have them in her home instead of spending another night by herself. What she should remember was the look of total horror on Jeff's face after she'd told him about her accident.

Ernie opened his eyes halfway. "I'm sick, Miss Ann."

"I know, sweetheart."

"My body hurts."

"That's part of this nasty flu," she said with a smile meant to reassure him. "You'll feel better after you rest at home for a few days." She noted the scraped knuckles on his hand and, with a wince, thought he'd probably feel those, too, along with all the aches from the flu. Maybe he would learn his lesson.

"Will you come to see me?" he asked groggily.

"Well, I'll…" She didn't know how to answer.

Jeff wouldn't want her to visit, but before she could make some excuse, she heard the main door open, then familiar footsteps in the hall.

His face a mask of worry, Jeff breezed into Molly's office, already holding Ernie's parka from the coatroom. He barely glanced at Ann, who tried to blend into the furniture. If he did notice her, she would catch that look of revulsion on his face and hate herself all over again.

"Hey, chief." The sound of Jeff's voice roused Ernie. "Not feeling so hot?"

Ernie smothered a cough in the crook of his arm. "I want to go home."

"That's why I'm here." He glanced over his shoulder, and his blue gaze homed in on Ann. "Thanks for watching him," he said mildly.

Ann knew that tone. It went with the look he had given her the day Brig Collier had tried to get into his parents' house.

"You're welcome. Molly told you about his fight?"

But Jeff only said, "Yes," and then, "I'll talk to him later."

"I took his temperature. It's pretty high."

"I've already called his pediatrician. Come on, Ernie." He held out the jacket. "Put this on and we'll be home in no time."

"Can I ride in the police car?"

"I brought it just for you." Jeff had been on

duty when the center phoned him, but instead of being annoyed, he was making his son feel special with this occasional treat of a ride in the police cruiser, and Ann's spirit twisted a little more inside. She almost missed him calling her Annie.

Ernie struggled into the coat. "Miss Ann's going to come visit me."

"We'll see." He lifted Ernie into his arms. As he passed her, Jeff leaned close so she could hear his lowered tone. "Or maybe you're afraid," he said with a short pause before he finished, "of picking up this virus."

"I'm not afraid," she said, although she was suddenly shaking again.

"Ann Walker, you're the most frightened woman I've ever met."

He happened to be right.

Which must be the least horrible thing he thought about her.

Ever since the night she'd told him about the accident, she'd been trembling over that look in Jeff Barlow's eyes.

Terrified of losing him.

Hey, Collier. News flash: All you-know-what has broken loose. Your phone is about to ring off the hook. Team's ready to go. The fuse is lit. Get back here, buddy, or you'll miss the train. We need you! Hugs to the little lady. Who's the lucky person who gets to keep her? H.

HENDERSON'S LATEST MESSAGE—wordy for him—had arrived minutes before Brig received his new orders. His team was waiting for him. He had missed them, and he was champing at the bit to get back into the action. But he was also in mourning—and not only at the prospect of leaving Laila behind. Assuming he could find a nanny for her to stay with Laila next door.

The obvious pain on Thomas's face that morning had shaken him, along with Molly's too-quiet acceptance of the news about the now-unlikely expansion of her center. He knew that whatever gains he had made with Molly while he was here, he was about to lose again. After he'd kissed her by the sycamore tree, no way would she forgive him for leaving Liberty, and her, this time.

Well, the least he could do was show Molly some support tonight.

He was already pulling into the community center parking lot. From the light spilling out the windows, and the murmur of voices he could hear as he climbed out of the car, he knew the six o'clock meeting was in progress. He could imagine Molly's nerves at facing the zoning commission, including Natalie Brewster.

As Brig entered the room, Natalie was speaking. He saw Thomas in the front row and joined him, taking the aisle seat and earning a quick nod from the older man. Ann sat on her father's other side, looking tense. And there was Molly beside her, her hands knotted in her lap and a pallor on her face that alarmed him. Was she about to faint?

MOLLY'S STOMACH CHURNED AGAIN.

"…and there is the overall issue of noise," Natalie was saying over the old microphone, which emitted shrill squawks every few words. Tonight she wore an acid-yellow pantsuit. Gold rings glittered on her hands, and larger shapes adorned her ears. Molly thought they looked to be hummingbirds. "Day after day, children playing on those swings—and a rock climbing wall, I understand—shrieking and shouting… The impact on many of our older residents could be just too much to live with."

From their seats several other neighbors echoed their agreement, and someone clapped. After each comment Natalie spoke again. Who knew until recently that Little Darlings was so unpopular in the residential area?

"Natalie, your time is up," the moderator informed her. "That's it for our commission members. We need to hear—briefly—from any other citizens who have views before we take the vote. I will now open the meeting for responses from anyone who wishes to speak to this proposal."

Molly's stomach churned even more.

With a huff, Natalie sat down at the table. Now the owner of a service station in town got up. He lived on Molly's street, too, but, to her relief, had no objection to the center's expansion. His twins had attended Little Darlings before they went to kindergarten, and he had nothing but praise for how the center was run. The noise never bothered him.

After a few more pros and cons were presented, Molly watched a woman approach the microphone. It was Ashley Jones's mother.

Melissa cleared her throat. "I'm here tonight not because I live on the same street where Little Darlings is located. I don't. But I'm at the center every day. My daughter has been going there since she was born." Melissa swallowed. "And I have many friends here who've told me just how much their 'older' children have learned at Little Darlings. It's a great facility—never mind the noise of children playing—and I see no reason that you shouldn't grant the zoning exemption to expand it."

"Thank you for your input," the chairman stated.

Melissa held the mike. "I haven't finished. When Ashley was born, I was the most insecure new mom you could find. But Molly gave me confidence." Melissa sent her a smile. "She's not only a good director for the center, a hard worker and an asset to this community. She is a kind and generous person who deserves nothing less than your full support—and her day care center does, too."

A smattering of applause broke out.

"Thank you," Molly mouthed to Melissa, and got a thumbs-up in return.

All the encouragement tonight was far more than she had expected.

Still, it wasn't enough. Molly didn't care for public speaking any more than she had writing her proposal, but this was her business, her future on the line. If she'd managed to make her presentation at the last meeting, she could defend it now. She stuck a hand in the air, then approached the balky microphone.

"Good evening. I want to thank everyone for coming out tonight—and for being so interested in our community. I appreciate all the comments, both for and against the expansion of my day care here in Liberty. But as flattered as I am by every one of the endorsements—" she glanced at Melissa "—this really isn't about me. It's about Little Darlings—and whether building onto my current place of business would be a benefit or a detriment to this area."

Molly paused to clear her throat before she went on. "I understand all your concerns about the noise. Children don't think about how loud their voices might sound to others. They're too busy having fun. I want them to be able to do that—but not at the expense of others. So I will do everything I can to ensure that noise is not a problem. For our new playground, as one example, we'll be using recycled rubber tires for the base, which should absorb much of the sound. I'll be talking to my architect, but I believe we can relocate the new climbing wall—certain to be a popular fixture—behind the present carriage house building to further muffle noise."

She paused, glancing around to see that everyone was still paying attention. "I and my staff will do anything else we can to minimize sound. I can't guarantee it will always be quiet on the street, but I feel Little Darlings definitely does more good than harm. I hope you'll agree. And, please, if you have any other issues, don't hesitate to let me know."

Molly was about to sit down when she had one last thought.

"Oh, and by the way—on evenings and weekends when most residents are home, the center is closed. The neighborhood will be peaceful. Little Darlings is a part of this community and we strive to be good citizens. Thank you."

When she sat down, Molly saw Debbie Crandall sitting across the aisle with her husband, both of them frowning. Oh, no. What if she got up and spoke about this morning's fight in the hall? Between his parents, Benjamin was kicking the chair in front of him, his nose now swollen like a prizefighter's. Debbie started to rise, but to Molly's surprise, Benjy stopped her.

"I like Miss Molly," he said, his voice

overly loud in the now-still room. "She tells me to be good whenever I'm bad."

"Anyone else?" the chairman asked to scattered laughter.

Debbie gasped and sat down hard in her seat without approaching the microphone. Her husband blinked.

A few more people spoke, none of them as eloquent as Benjamin. Then it was time for the vote. Molly had done her best.

When the voice vote began, she shifted in her seat. She felt breathless, light-headed. The expansion was critical. If she didn't get approval to build, Playtime, which Debbie Crandall had referred to that morning, would benefit instead of Little Darlings. Benjamin wouldn't be Molly's only lost child.

When the result of the vote was announced, the chairman's words buzzed in her ears but their meaning didn't register.

At last the meeting was adjourned. A few cheers filled the room, and a couple of boos protested the vote. Molly sat there, feeling dazed.

As the gavel came down, Pop was on his feet. So was Ann, and before Molly could rise, Brig was drawing her up into a hug.

"I knew you could do it!" her father said with a beaming smile.

Molly was stunned. She couldn't appreciate the warmth of Brig's embrace or the wide smile on Ann's face. "We won?"

"You won," Brig said. "Let's celebrate!"

Pop didn't seem to like Brig's suggestion, but Brig wouldn't take no for an answer. After a brief embrace with Molly, Ann claimed she needed to get home. She was never comfortable being even this far from her apartment or the center. Pop, she said, would drive her home in Molly's car.

All Molly could think was, at least she would have her expansion now to sustain her. When Brig left and Laila was no longer a part of her life.

CHAPTER SIXTEEN

"LET'S DRIVE INTO Cincinnati," Brig said. He'd left Laila at home with one of Molly's aides as a babysitter, and he seemed determined to celebrate, but for Molly her victory still seemed unreal, even strangely hollow. "Are you hungry?"

"Starving," she had to admit. "I couldn't eat a bite before the meeting."

"I'm glad you were approved. That must be a load off your mind."

"I'll have to be more than careful about noise, but with the new playground and extra space inside the center, I can take on more kids, offer more to them."

"Your kids," he murmured.

Molly used that phrase all the time, as Debbie Crandall had once pointed out, but tonight the phrase made her smile. "My kids," she agreed. Still, it was the image of Laila that flashed through her mind. What if the little girl and Brig didn't have to leave? What if he and Molly were right for each other after all?

She resisted the urge to ask where Laila would stay when he left. The mission was uppermost in his mind now. Her reverie came to an abrupt halt when she realized they had entered the city's Hyde Park neighborhood.

"Isn't this where you used to live?" Brig asked.

"Yes." The charming square lined with shops, the quiet residential streets that surrounded it, always reminded her of Andrew. "We had a house here." Molly pointed at the nearby intersection. "That right turn, two blocks down, then one block left. But there's nothing to see," she said.

"Isn't the house still there?"

"Yes, but…" Molly couldn't go on.

"You'd rather not see it," Brig said.

BRIG WAS STILL scolding himself when he steered Molly into the restaurant on the town square less than a mile from her former home. Why had he wanted to revisit her past? Simple curiosity on his part since they were in the vicinity, or the need to know where she had lived after she had married another man?

He was almost glad she'd resisted. That proposed visit had been for him, not her.

"Teller's is one of my favorite places to eat," she said after they sat down at their table. "I love this room best."

The small but cozy space was adjacent to the crowded bar and downstairs from the rooftop dining area that she'd told him was popular in summer. Brig liked this room, too.

"Great idea," he said, "to open this old bank as a restaurant. The granite facade is cool but using this vault for dining space is even better."

The room boasted its original huge tumbler lock on the thick steel door, which stood open. They ordered wine—one glass for Molly, to celebrate—and Brig picked a craft beer he'd wanted to try. If he hadn't just done something stupid again by suggesting Molly see her former home, this might have seemed like a date.

Their first, he thought, in eight years. And, probably, their last.

While they ate, Brig tried his best to keep the conversation light. He toasted Molly's success with the zoning commission. They talked about her revised plans, even touched on their trip to Indiana and the fun they'd had with his parents in the snow, the Parcheesi game with his grandmother. Brig avoided any mention of his imminent return to duty, until Molly finally asked about the baby.

"The nanny agency I've contacted is sending someone," he said. "The woman looks really good on paper, but we'll see." He ran a finger down the label on his bottle. "If she doesn't work out, I won't have time now to interview anyone else. And once I get to base, my time won't be my own. I'll be in full mission mode. The team's already turning up the heat."

"Then you'd leave Laila next door?" With her eyes downcast, and as if she'd just realized the nanny would be local, Molly finished her wine. "Maybe this candidate will be perfect. Maybe your mission—wherever it is—won't last long."

"You won't believe this, but at this minute I wish I didn't have to go," he said, realizing that was true for the first time.

As always, Molly was practical. She reminded him in a brittle, accusatory tone, "But you do. You wouldn't give up a job you're good at."

"Am I?" he said, having doubts, not for the first time.

Brig abandoned all pretense of eating and shoved his plate away. First Molly, he thought, and his boneheaded decision to leave her eight years ago. A decision that had changed the course of both their lives. And then years later…

"I keep thinking about Sean," he said. "I should have stopped him that day. Made him stay on base. Instead, I gave him permission to leave."

Molly didn't look up. "If he'd stayed on base, he wouldn't have seen Zada."

"He would have at least been here for Laila. She would've had a father."

"Brig, not to diminish Sean's loss, but she has a father now."

Which didn't help enough.

A heavy silence fell.

Molly had pushed aside her plate, too. Clearly, they were done. But Brig hadn't finished spilling his guts.

"He's still gone, Molly. And here I am, all but trying to give this baby away like a bunch of old clothes so I can go back to the team. What does that make me?" He met her gaze. "You already know. I did the same thing to you years ago—as your sister recently pointed out. You called me—my guys—patriots once.

But am I really?" He saw the distress in her eyes yet couldn't stop himself. "Or am I just some guy running away from the kind of life other men have?"

No one said a word on the way home.

Well, it was home for Molly, but Brig had no real home except an apartment or condo or whatever in the D.C. area. He probably wasn't there much except between assignments, and Molly envisioned a barren space with Spartan furnishings. Talk about lonely.

She didn't look forward to the next two days. She didn't know how to say goodbye to Laila—if she had to—or, again, to Brig.

He pulled the car into the driveway and cut the engine.

Molly grasped the door handle but didn't get out, and Brig simply looked at her in the dark, in the quiet. This might be the last time they would be alone, and she felt the undercurrent of tension, even greater than at dinner tonight or that night in the snow when the world, even with his parents there, had seemed to consist only of the two of them.

"I want you to know how much I appreciate everything you've done for Laila," he said. "For me."

Just what she needed. A tight little prelimi
nary speech of goodbye.

"What better place was there? Pop and
had room in the house. We all felt...awkward
at first, for obvious reasons, but we adjusted
This leave provided you time to rest and ge
your bearings." She added, "And to grieve for
Sean and Zada."

"I'll carry the memory of everything with
me—our trip, the blizzard..."

"The snow angels," she murmured.

"Yes, the snow angels." His voice had
turned low and thick. He was looking straight
into her soul, and she could see what he
wanted in his eyes. "Brig, don't..."

But he had put his arms around her and
drawn her close, and he held on tight. He buried his face in her hair, as he'd done in the
kitchen one night, and Molly felt him tremble
a little, this big, strong warrior with an even
bigger heart.

Molly couldn't help herself then. She lifted
her mouth to his, and at the same time Brig
moved even closer, and they kissed. "Oh,
Molly."

Within seconds he took the kiss deeper,
changing the angle, the pressure of his lips
on hers, soft and hard, then gentle again, light

and teasing and then desperate. And like that night on the walk nearby, under the sycamore tree, Molly felt the warm waves of desire flow through her like a tide. When he pulled back, he brushed one last kiss at each corner of her mouth.

"I wish…" he began with a sigh but didn't go on.

Molly laid a light but shaky hand over his mouth and tried to smile. In that moment she felt like begging.

Please, don't go. Stay this time.

ONCE SHE GOT home from the zoning commission meeting, Ann couldn't sit still. She hadn't felt like being part of a celebration tonight, even for Molly. She was too worried about Ernie.

Holding a small package, she took another deep breath, then rang Jeff's front doorbell again. No one had answered the first time, and for a moment she considered turning around and leaving. She'd already lost her nerve. What was it Jeff had said?

You're the most frightened woman I've ever met.

Add crazy to that, she thought now. And it was after ten o'clock, much too late to pay a visit, but the time wasn't what she meant. Why had she come here after baring her soul to Jeff? And knowing he wouldn't want her here?

When the door opened, she was already turning to go.

"Well, well." He loomed in the doorway of the one-story frame house he shared with Ernie. "Did you walk all the way over?"

Ann winced at the gibe. She had taken a cab. "No, but…how is Ernie?"

"I just put him to bed." Jeff opened the door wider. "That's why I didn't answer earlier." His steady gaze met hers. "Come on in. I assume you're here to see him. Better hurry before he falls asleep again."

"Is his fever down?"

"Halfway. He doesn't ache as much, so he's resting better."

Keeping up the small talk, he led her through a neat but modest living room and down a short hall to the room at the end. On the way Ann glanced into a larger room on the opposite side where a king-size bed proclaimed it the master bedroom—Jeff's room. Her face heated at the thought of him lying there with someone.

With her package tucked under one arm,

Ann stepped into Ernie's room. He was under a light blanket, his face barely visible in his makeshift nest. The fever flagged his cheeks, and his eyes, without their usual spark, opened slowly, his lids heavy. Her heart turned over.

"Hey, Ernie."

He sounded drowsy. "Miss Ann! You came to see me? This is where I live."

"Yes, sweetheart," she said, "I know."

Ernie drifted off to sleep while she was thinking what to say next.

Jeff shifted beside her. She turned, startled to find him so close, and held out the package. "I brought this for him. It's nothing big—but when he's feeling more like himself, it might help to pass the time."

"Thanks." He paused. "Anything else we can do for you?"

Ann knew she deserved that cool tone.

"No, I should have called first. Or dropped by tomorrow."

She headed for the living room as if the house was on fire. Jeff followed right behind her.

"Go ahead," he said. "Run off again the way you did the other night. Like some criminal in a stolen car, bailing out and forcing me to chase her all over Liberty."

Ann's shoulders slumped. Humiliation ran through her like water down a hill.

"Fine. You've caught me. What can I say?" She hadn't forgotten their date at the inn, how good it had felt to be with him until she'd told him the truth about herself. "You know what I did—the people I hurt, not only that boy, physically, but my parents and Molly, who must have been so ashamed—" The rest came on a sob that rose in her chest out of nowhere. "I saw exactly what you think of me, so you don't need to rub it in—"

Blinded by tears, she aimed for the door.

Before Ann could grasp the knob, Jeff slapped his palm against the wood panel just above her head. With his other hand, he turned her to face him. "You saw what, *exactly?*"

"Disgust. Revulsion." And horror.

His eyes widened. "Is that what you think it was?"

"And shock," she said. "I've seen it before."

She couldn't seem to get hold of herself. She should have stayed in her apartment, in the careful world she had fashioned for herself where no one could hurt her, where she would never harm anyone else.

He studied her face. And then shocked *her.*

"I didn't feel revulsion or disgust. You want to know what I felt?" His eyes searched hers. "Shock, yes—a natural reaction—but I saw a young girl—just eighteen then—involved in a horrific accident she can't ever forget. How could you forget, Ann? I saw a woman who still blames herself for crippling another human being." He took her shoulders in his hands. "You think I've never answered a call like that? When I was with Cincinnati P.D. it happened more times than I care to think about. Prom weekends were the worst. I've seen plenty of lives destroyed. I've seen sights you couldn't imagine in your worst nightmares—"

"But this was *mine!* My accident, my fault."

Jeff stared at the carpet between them, as if searching for the right words. He lifted his eyes to hers again.

"You know, I have a theory. In my experience—which has been considerable, as I said—an accident rarely happens, if ever, for one reason." He hesitated again before going on. "So maybe it's raining one night and the road is unfamiliar, dark and narrow with winding curves. Let's say somebody whose license is practically new, whose experience is limited, who's had one drink too many—makes a bad choice to drive someone else's car. You with me so far?"

She nodded, her eyes still on his.

"Then let's throw something else in here. Maybe the tires on that car have lost their tread. Or the windshield wiper blades do little except to smear the glass. Sound familiar? Or," he said, "the brake pads are worn." His voice gentled. "Two, three, even four things come together at the same instant. A confluence of factors," he said.

Ann could hear her own breathing. She looked away and felt the too-rapid thump of her heart through her whole body.

"But if I could undo it," she murmured. "If I could go back and not hurt—"

"You can't. You're responsible—in the end." After another moment he said, "You think I haven't wished the same about my marriage? I didn't want Ernie to grow up without his mom. But I made that decision." He waited until Ann's gaze met his again. "So did your boyfriend that night when he got into that fight—which isn't uncommon at parties like that. He was—we all are—responsible for the consequences of our actions."

Jeff wasn't like the other men she'd known. He wasn't like anyone else.

"But you've never made a mistake like I did."

"Ann. You think I'm a saint?" he asked.

"I know you're not." She half smiled. "You told Ernie to hit Benjamin Crandall. And so he did."

He raised an eyebrow. "True, and I shouldn't have. I've talked to him about that. It won't happen again." Jeff paused, then said, "You want to know where I messed up? It wasn't only Kay who killed our marriage. I was at fault, too. It always takes more than one. At the time I was trying to prove myself with Cincinnati P.D., working extra time, bringing the job home with me." He shook his head before going on. "You think I'm a good dad? I never saw Ernie take his first step. Never heard him say his first word or his first sentence. Half the time I didn't see him on any given day. I arrived home late, he was asleep. He got up early, I was either gone or trying to catch up on rest, dead to the world—and I almost lost him." He finished,

"To be honest, I wasn't the best husband or father in those days by a long shot."

"But if you could, would you go back to your marriage? Try to work it out?"

"No," he said. "I've made big changes in my life and I hope Kay has, too."

Ann had to ask. "Do you hear from her… from Kay?"

"Not much. She has Ernie every other Christmas, a good chunk of time in the summer. I hope that doesn't confuse him, but sometimes I wonder. For instance, that fight with the Crandall kid. Maybe Ernie's damaged and I don't see it."

She half smiled. Spending so much time at Little Darlings had given her a perspective on children at least. "Maybe he's a normal four-year-old boy who loves his father—and listened to him."

"Yeah," Jeff said, "that's the better theory, isn't it?" He hesitated. "Ann, what I'm saying is to take what happened years ago as the turning point. Use it. Accept it, then follow a different path in life for yourself."

She wanted to thank him for his understanding, but she didn't know how. It wasn't as if she could forgive herself, not yet, maybe not ever, but maybe she'd also had long enough to punish herself.

"Which brings me to us," Jeff finally said, startling her anew.

Us. The word went through her like a siren song, like a gift she didn't deserve. It had been so long since she'd allowed herself to even consider a real relationship. She barely knew how to start.

Ann took a first step and watched Jeff's eyes darken. When he didn't back away but kept staring at her with that open, welcoming look—or was it another challenge, a dare?—she moved closer yet.

He began to smile, and chancing it, Ann looped her arms around his neck. She drew his head down until their lips were almost touching. It was she who closed the last distance between them.

After a few lovely moments, he said, "Why don't we do this right?"

"What?" she murmured.

"The courtship thing. Sounds old-fashioned, doesn't it, but why not? Dating. Seeing each other. Whatever."

Ann didn't need to answer. She guessed he already knew. She initiated the second kiss, then a third. When at last she began to pull away, her heart still pounding, Jeff traced a shivery line with his finger along her throat.

"No good?" he asked, his eyes still warm, his tone teasing.

"Way too good," she answered.

Way too good.

CHAPTER SEVENTEEN

MOLLY'S PULSE POUNDED like a drum. Was this a good idea or not?

The morning after the zoning commission meeting and her dinner with Brig, she drove back into the city. In the two years since her husband's death, she had been there no more than twice. Now, as if it had a mind of its own, her car was rolling onto her former street in Hyde Park, to the house she and Andrew had shared on a big corner lot with twin maple trees in the front yard.

And there it was, to her surprise, looking smaller than she remembered. Molly pulled over at the curb. She'd panicked last night at the very thought of coming here, and had been relieved when Brig hadn't pushed her. This was something she should have done long ago, something she needed to do on her own.

Revisit the memories.

She found herself smiling. The old Tudor

had been a wreck when she and Andrew had first seen it. The chimney had leaned like the Tower of Pisa, with chunks of mortar missing here and there. The first thing they'd done after falling in love with the crumbling wreck—and its vastly reduced price—had been to fix and repoint that chimney.

Molly had been twenty-five then, Andrew twenty-nine, and they had had practically no money. Pop had lent them part of the down payment.

She studied the front facade. In this house her marriage had flourished—until her miscarriage. She would never forget how their relationship had tumbled downhill after that, and then on that last morning...

Her smile faded. She and Andrew had argued the entire time they were getting ready for work. They'd even snarled at each other as they got into their cars...and one half of their couple had never come home.

Molly felt a chill run down her spine. The last thing she'd said to him had been in anger. *Maybe we should get a divorce.*

Did Andrew know she hadn't meant that? Yet at the time, she had.

Lost in memory, Molly gazed at the house. A red tricycle lay abandoned on the front walk. A collapsible stroller leaned against the first porch step. Obviously children lived here now, other people's children. The house didn't belong to her.

But, oh, that first night... She blinked at the memory.

After the closing on their home, the fire Andrew had made without first opening the flue, the smoke that threatened to drive them out and ruin their romantic evening, until they'd flung open all the windows, then collapsed on the living room floor, laughing at their naïveté as first-time owners, and made love on the carpet in the one place in the world that was theirs...and always would be.

Molly straightened in her seat. Now this house belonged to other people in another marriage with another family. Her past was finally the past.

She wouldn't need to come here again.

ON THAT SAME day, his last in Liberty, Brig studied the young woman across from him in Thomas Walker's living room. As he'd told Molly, her credentials were impeccable, but she was no Susan Denton. She hadn't smiled or said much since he'd opened the front door. The first sight of this nanny candidate had sent Thomas to his room with clear sorrow in his eyes. That this woman and Laila would be staying next door if Brig hired her hadn't seemed to register with Thomas.

As for Molly, Brig hadn't seen her since she'd left this morning. Obviously she didn't want to be part of this interview.

Laila sat kicking her legs in her swing, the music playing "Row, Row, Row Your Boat." The hems of her miniature jeans stopped above her ankles. She would need new clothes again soon. Remembering his shopping trip with Molly in Indiana, Brig wondered who would buy them when he wasn't around. This woman—Patti—perhaps. But she looked so young.

"She's small for her age," Patti said at last, studying the baby.

"Laila was born in a war zone. In an impoverished country. She'll catch up," he said, then tried a smile. "She's small but mighty."

When Patti didn't respond, Brig went on. "You can check with her pediatrician," he said. "Laila is doing everything any other baby her age does. She's eating solid food now—cereal and fruit. She's up-to-date on all her inoculations," he added, as if to prove

Patti needn't fear catching some dire disease. "Maybe you'd like to hold her."

He wanted to see if the baby took to her. However this went, he still had to leave to-morrow. Yet he couldn't hire someone who wasn't good for Laila. Brig watched her lift Laila from the swing. The baby's legs locked, and she flailed her arms as if she were falling. Then she let out a howl of protest.

"Most babies love me," Patti said, shifting her hold to make Laila feel more secure. "I wonder if she's as nervous as I am right now. I'm sorry, Mr. Collier—but I really want this job. I live in town with my parents, but I'd like to be more independent. I've had lots of experience as a babysitter and a nanny, too. Last year I worked for a professor and his wife in Cincinnati taking care of their three boys. The baby was about Laila's age. We did fine."

That was the most Brig had heard her say, and he felt himself relax a bit. "Your creden-tials are very impressive. I'm on edge my-self," he admitted. "It's critical that I find the right person for Laila, and I don't have much time left in which to do it."

She actually smiled then. "The right per-son's very important. And the right kind of care." Tears sparkled in her eyes. "Have you heard? In the orphanages in some foreign countries, the children are left in their cribs all the time."

His mouth tightened. "As you can see, Laila isn't."

Patti jiggled her gently and looked into Laila's eyes. "There now, you're fine. Pretty girl. We'll have lots of fun together."

Brig handed Laila a toy. The brightly colored ball with a noisemaker inside was Laila's current favorite. She had learned to grasp and shake it, the activity providing endless fun for her.

In another minute Laila was gurgling with delight. Brig could tell she liked Patti. Thank God, this was going better now for everyone. But just to make sure... "Laila has been feeding on demand from the beginning," he said. "Over time she has established her own schedule, not without effort on everybody's part, I admit, but we let her take the lead for now."

"We? I didn't realize there was a Mrs. Collier."

Molly came far too easily to mind. Together, they had made a pretty good team, too, just like his unit. "There isn't. Other people have been helping out. But with my situation changing—"

"I can start tomorrow if you'd like."

Brig let out a breath. "That would be... great. Exactly what we need."

"I'll take really good care of her," Patti assured him.

He took the baby from Patti and walked Patti to the door. In the end she'd passed every test. She had all the warmth and interest of Susan Denton. All he needed was to check her references, let her tour his parents' house, then buy supplies before he left. And yet...

"I'll give you a call," he said. "I'll let you know."

THAT EVENING MOLLY wandered into the kitchen and stopped. Brig stood at the sink with the baby draped across his shoulder, Laila looking boneless but secure, the image of the two of them reflected in the darkened window glass. He was washing something with one hand while protectively cupping the baby's head with the other. The contrast between tall, muscular Brig and tiny, delicate Laila made her want to weep. In that moment his tenderness made him more of a man to Molly than any military mission ever could.

She would miss them both. A serious understatement if ever there was one.

But if Laila stayed next door with a nanny, at least Molly could see her now and then. And Pop could offer to take her for walks in the stroller she and Brig had bought at the rummage sale.

She cleared her throat. "How did the interview go today?"

Brig made a sound she couldn't quite interpret. She watched him rinse out the bottle, then carefully measure formula into a clean one. His shoulders looked tense.

"Perfect. She seems perfect, like you said."

A man of few words, she thought, like Pop when his feelings were raw and he didn't want Molly to see that. She didn't feel reassured.

Brig screwed the cap and nipple onto the bottle. Laila was beginning to fuss, perhaps having sensed dinner was on the way. He poured more milk into a small bowl, then stuck the bowl in the microwave. Molly waited the few seconds until the timer chimed.

"You've come a long way, soldier," she

said, remembering his first night here and hoping now to ease his downcast mood.

He didn't respond. A dark pall seemed to hang over the entire house tonight. Pop had even muted the news on TV, as if to keep from reminding Brig of where he was going tomorrow.

"You're a master at diapering, feeding, changing," she went on, unable to stop herself, "and no one gives a better bath, mister."

"Molly, quit." He turned at last with the bowl in one hand, the other still cupping Laila's dark head. The baby was decked out in her yellow sleeper with the white lambs on it.

"The girl was great," Brig said after a moment. "I've checked her references and the agency's website reviews, all of them glowing."

Yet something was wrong. "Maybe they don't post the other kind."

He held her gaze, his blue eyes looking like purple pansies. He sifted rice cereal flakes into the warm milk in the bowl. Laila followed his every motion, her dark eyes bright.

"I need to pack," he said abruptly.

And her pulse lurched. Even with a nanny nearby, tonight might be Molly's last chance to hold the baby, to be with her in this house.

"Why don't you go upstairs," she said. "Do whatever you need to. I'll feed Laila. She can stay in my room until you're done."

He passed the baby to Molly but didn't meet her eyes. "I'll make it short."

"Take all the time you need. I'm not going anywhere."

The words rang all too true. This time—like eight years ago—she would stay behind.

IN HER ROOM Molly rocked Laila and listened to the sounds of Brig packing across the hall. Maybe she should stay in bed tomorrow until he left. Molly couldn't imagine saying that final goodbye.

"Aren't you the one," she crooned to Laila in her arms. "You ate all your cereal, yes, you did. You drank every last bit of your milk, too. If you're not careful, little girl, you're going to need Weight Watchers. Yes, you are."

Molly laid her cheek against the baby's hair and swallowed.

She ached with the loss that hadn't happened yet. Even with Laila next door for a time, Molly wouldn't really be close to her. The nanny would take over. How could she let Laila go?

As if she had any choice.

How could she let Brig…

No choice at all there, she thought, even after the kisses she and Brig had shared the other night. How silly she had been, letting herself get used to having Brig and Laila in the house, teaching Brig to care for her, listening at night for Laila's cries, feeling as if she and Pop were part of a new family when clearly they weren't. Once Brig was gone, her father would slip back into his routine of staying inside, seeing few people, leaning on Molly.

"Oh, Laila." She smoothed her cheek against the baby's head. She picked up first one tiny hand, then the other to kiss each. Her tummy full, Laila was nearly asleep, impossibly thick, dark lashes shuttering her eyes. Molly didn't realize she was crying until she heard Brig's voice.

"Molly. Hey," he said, leaning one shoulder against the door frame. Pale light streamed into the room from the hall, but his face was in shadow.

"This isn't turning out to be the best night." Molly dabbed at her tears. "Really, I'm not the type to blubber…I don't know why I am."

Laila hiccupped in her sleep, making both

Molly and Brig laugh when there was little to laugh at.

Brig came into the room. He hunkered down in front of her and the baby, smoothing Laila's hair, his touch brushing Molly's hand.

"There's no easy way to do this, is there?" His voice sounded husky.

Brig tried to ease the baby from her arms, but Molly couldn't let go.

"Not yet," she said. "I don't mind holding her while she sleeps. Once tomorrow comes and you leave and Laila is next door..."

"I do have one other idea."

Molly wasn't sure she wanted to hear it. But no, this wasn't about the nanny he would hire. She could tell by the look in his eyes how different this idea was, and her earlier fantasy flooded back. But, no, he wouldn't. Would he? He wasn't quite down on his knees, but his posture reminded her of another time when Brig had asked her to marry him in just this way. Would he say those words again now? Her pulse began to race.

"Brig, is this a proposal? For Laila's sake?" She wasn't expecting that, especially since it would be for the wrong reason. Yet he hadn't seemed that enthusiastic about the nanny today. "I mean, I realize that could

be the 'something' you need for Laila…"
Molly could hardly say the words. "But that
wouldn't work for me."

Brig appeared stricken. "No, Molly. I didn't
mean that. I thought maybe…" He took a long
look at her, as if seeing her disappointment,
her embarrassment. Molly Darling, the two-
time loser. The woman he'd left at the altar.
He tried again. "I thought… I'd hoped… But
no," he said. "I can't ask. Forget I said anything."

Molly could guess what he'd been about
to say instead.

In a perfect world, she'd once told him, *Pop
and I would take Laila.*

In a perfect world Brig would give up his
military career.

Wishing she could offer herself but knowing she couldn't, she gazed down at the sleeping baby in her arms. She couldn't blame
Brig for trying—he needed someone for the
baby—yet she did blame him. All over again.
When push came to shove, Brig would always
choose black ops, even over Laila. How foolish she had been to believe things could be
different, that this time *he* was different.

Pop and I will watch her, she almost said.
There's a day care program right in our

backyard. A crib across the hall. All her things are here.

Maybe this solution had been in Molly's mind all along, softening her resolve until she actually thought—believed—he was again asking her to marry him. If she said yes about Laila for the next few weeks or months until Brig's latest mission ended, if she offered to keep the baby here, she could pretend that Laila was hers.

Molly's eventually broken heart—one more time—would wait a little longer.

But what good would that do Molly?

With Brig and the baby, she had come to almost believe in having everything she'd always wanted after all.

At the last instant she couldn't say the words. She couldn't take the risk.

BRIG TOSSED THE last of his clothes into the bag and zipped it shut. There. He was ready. As ready as he could be now.

Strange, but in the past weeks he'd come to feel at home here, even with his parents gone and in what he might at one time have called enemy territory. Now he and Thomas were, if not actually friends, at least civil and could treat each other with respect. As for Molly…

He ran once more through his options for Laila. There was nothing wrong with Patti, who would make a fantastic nanny. After their rocky beginning, once they got past the nerves on both sides, he'd had to change his opinion of her. Yet her very rightness for the job troubled him. *Perfect,* Molly had said, and Brig had echoed the words tonight. Yet something kept nagging at him.

And then there was the mess he'd made, all over again, with Molly. He could still see her in her room across the hall, and the way he'd stumbled through his clumsy request for her help—and Molly had assumed he was proposing.

Brig sat down on the bed with his laptop. He scanned his emails one last time, but nothing from the team scrolled into view. He would see them soon anyway. After he'd read their older messages again, hoping they would bring a smile, he started to shut down the computer. It was time to pack that, too.

But just before closing the email program, he stopped. And stared at several of the messages from Henderson.

In that instant Brig knew what to do about Laila, and that what he was doing was right. If Molly couldn't keep the baby—and he understood why not, especially after she'd taken his words the wrong way—he might have another solution. He hoped.

He didn't know why he didn't feel better about that.

Right, but not better.

He still had to tell Molly.

In the morning.

ANN DIDN'T KNOW what to expect from tonight. She had already bitten one fingernail to the quick waiting for Jeff to pick her up.

The courtship thing. Dating. Whatever.

Their last date hadn't turned out well, but tonight there would be no confessions on her part. She still couldn't believe he'd been more concerned about the accident's effect on her than about her guilt. Not that he'd let her off the hook. He'd held her accountable, and himself, too, for his marriage.

When the doorbell finally rang, she jumped a foot, then ran to answer.

"You look great," Jeff said, his gaze skimming over her.

So did he. He'd had his hair cut and appeared freshly shaven. He also appeared, to Ann, much paler than normal. Ashen, in fact.

"You ready?" Her heart rate jumped when

Jeff guided her to his car with a strong hand at her elbow. "I thought we'd take in a movie. The eight o'clock show. Okay with you?"

She smiled. "Is it a comedy?"

"Romantic," he said. "What else?"

The movie was hysterical. She and Jeff both laughed until their sides hurt. In the end the couple onscreen vowed eternal love. Ann, though, couldn't imagine her life working out to such perfection.

In the car Jeff made a confession of his own. He wasn't that hungry. If Ann didn't mind, could they stop for a late-night meal at a fast-food restaurant instead of the inn?

"Do they have fries?"

"I'm sure they do."

"Do they have a Big Mac with my name on it?"

"Definitely."

Over her burger and his salad, the lightest thing on the menu, they talked about Ernie. "You should see him," Jeff said. "He's so eager to get back to Little Darlings I almost have to tie him down in bed for a nap. He's off the wall."

"He should stay out, though, until he's completely well."

Jeff pushed his salad aside and gazed at her. "You like Ernie."

Ann grinned. "Who wouldn't?"

"And what about his father?"

Despite their easy conversation and the laughs they'd shared during the movie, Jeff still looked gray. Ann had seen that shade too often of late. He insisted he was fine, put their trash in the nearby bin, then walked her out to his car. He paused there, looking at her again, his eyes searching.

"We've done better tonight," she said. "No sad tales of mine to relate."

"True, but I've been meaning to ask, Ann." He hesitated. "What happened to Robert, your boyfriend, after that accident?"

"He's done well, actually," she admitted. "He finished college, got his degree in computer technology—a job he can do from home much of the time. He also has a van totally equipped so he can drive himself wherever he wants to go."

"That doesn't bother him? Getting behind the wheel after that accident?"

"I don't think so. No."

"Which leaves you with the real handicap."

Jeff was right. That fact always hovered over her, a constant reminder of hurt on very side and of her guilt. Her brother-in-law's death and, before that, her mother's had only added to the ever-present sense of loss.

"Ann, the accident happened years ago. This is now," Jeff reminded her.

He held the car door for Ann, but by now his face looked white instead of ashen. "Are you all right?" she asked.

He sagged against the open door. "No, to be honest. I'm not."

Ann touched his forehead. "You're as hot as Ernie was. You have fever, Jeff. You should have canceled our date."

"Are you kidding?" He smiled, but it didn't reach his eyes. "I was like a kid at a carnival. I wouldn't have missed tonight for anything." He paused. "I shouldn't have exposed you to this flu, however."

"I've been exposed a hundred times. I have a good immune system."

He passed one hand over his eyes. "My head is pounding. I'm hot one minute, cold the next." Ann saw him shiver. She could see how bad he felt. Under the parking lot lights, he now looked green and his teeth were chattering.

Ann's pulse began to throb. She sat for a

moment, having an intense conversation with
herself. *You know how to drive, don't you?*

Yes, but I'd rather call a cab. And then she
thought, *Why expose someone else? Waste the
money?* Her mind tumbled over the words.
know. But I can't....

This was a test. And she was failing.

Her pulse skipped a beat. For another sec
ond she wondered if Jeff was doing this be
cause he was truly ill or to torture her.

But he was clearly shaking now. He closed
his bleary eyes, forcing Ann to make the de
cision on her own.

Yet Jeff would never risk Ernie's future i
he didn't trust her. He wouldn't let Ann take
the wheel of his car in control of his own life

"Call it an errand of mercy," she said under
her breath as she left her seat. "Jeff, get in
On my side." As soon as he was settled, she
scrambled around the car. He was asleep in
the passenger seat before she turned the igni
tion key. Ann was essentially alone.

"Jeff," she said weakly, but he didn't an
swer. She sat there, engine running, for a full
five minutes before she found the courage to
slip the car into gear. She repositioned the
side and rearview mirrors with all the con
centration of a first-time student in a drivers'

education course. Or during the community service hours she'd spent in class to improve her driving skills after the accident. Her heart thundered loudly enough to be heard in the silent car.

Breathing fast and light, she eased off the brake.

What if she missed a curve again...what if she hurt Jeff and, thus, Ernie?

She had hurt someone she loved once already.

The realization stunned her.

Still, after nine long years, she didn't need to be afraid.

Her growing smile warring with her worry about Jeff and the flu, Ann pressed the accelerator and drove him home.

CHAPTER EIGHTEEN

"I DID IT!"

The next morning Ann all but danced through the back door and into the kitchen. Still yawning, Molly gazed at her blankly. She hadn't slept last night. Brig was upstairs now with the baby, and Molly was trying not to think that he would leave within the hour. What arrangement had he made for Laila? She hoped he'd hired the nanny who had sounded so perfect.

"Did what?" she asked.

"I drove!" Ann hugged her, nearly cutting off Molly's air supply. "I drove Jeff all the way home. I didn't make one mistake." She paused. "All I could think of was getting him in bed."

Pop strolled into the room. "Getting who in bed?"

Molly groaned. "He caught Ernie's flu," she guessed.

"With a vengeance. Poor guy," Ann said.

"Jeff Barlow," she told Pop, still smiling. "I stayed the night at his house."

His frown deepened.

"Not the way you think, Pop." Her face flushed, Ann helped herself to a cup of coffee. "I sat up with him and checked on Ernie, too. This morning Jeff's temperature was down a little, so I decided I could come to work."

"Huh." Pop didn't appear convinced that the night had been innocent. But when he'd talked to Molly before about Jeff and Ann, Pop had seemed to approve of a relationship between her sister and the sheriff's deputy. He'd pushed more for it than Molly had ever thought to do.

He studied Ann's face now as if searching for cracks in her story. In Molly's view, Ann driving Jeff home last night had required true courage.

"You drove?" he said at last.

"I'm so glad you took that chance," Molly said.

From upstairs she could hear the rumble of Brig's voice, most likely as he talked nonsense to the baby the way they all did. Time was running out. If he didn't hurry, he might miss his plane.

After last night's standoff, the idea seemed all too tempting. Maybe he could take a later flight, stay a few hours longer, allow Molly to store up the memory of his voice and the love in his eyes whenever he looked at…Laila.

But she'd had her chance. And lost it.

If she were inclined to jealousy, she might envy Ann now.

Molly turned away, unable to hide the sorrow she felt, even if it was of her own doing.

"Silly," she said.

Pop turned. "What is?"

"Daydreaming."

Needing some distraction, Molly glanced out the kitchen window. From here she could just see Natalie Brewster walking down her porch steps to examine her peonies, probably hoping to see the first new sprouts that would herald spring.

Ann followed her gaze. "Pop, there's your friend."

He leaned to see around her. "Not my friend," he said, "after that zoning commission vote," but in a weaker tone than usual, and Molly's ears perked up.

"Natalie didn't change her view about Little Darlings' expansion, but other members of the commission did. The important thing is, work will start soon." After Brig was gone. Molly wasn't quite looking forward to the new building as much as she'd expected to.

In an expansive mood this morning, Ann said, "Pop, why don't you ask Natalie to join us for dinner some night? Molly and I will cook."

"Don't you girls start matchmaking. She'd drag me into all of her committees if she could."

"Worthwhile projects," Molly said, remembering her talk with Brig one night. "Consider this, Pop. For Natalie, maybe they're another escape from that big house she lives in alone." She paused. "Like you."

"I'm not alone. You're here."

Molly sighed. Overhead she heard footsteps on the spare room floor. Brig would be down soon. And out the door. After last night, maybe that was best.

She tried once more. "I had hoped the rummage sale might change *your* mind. Wasn't it good to be around other people then?"

"If you mean Natalie Brewster, I'll give you that. A man doesn't mind being taken care of now and then."

"Exactly. It's not good, Pop, to stay indoors as much as you do. What would be the harm in picking out a few activities to keep you involved in the community? Like Bess and Joe Collier? Since you retired, you've spent way too much time on your own. Ann and I are at Little Darlings all day. Being busy yourself could be a good thing."

"Winter isn't my best time," he said, his gaze not meeting hers. "Just what I need—to step outside, slip on the ice and break my hip on my way to some meeting. Then you'd have an invalid on your hands. Like Joe's mother."

"You're in good shape. Mrs. Collier is getting better every day. And winter's almost over."

Ann was peering out the window again. "Natalie just looked this way. I almost feel sorry for her, Pop."

He groaned. "No need to feel sorry for her, believe me." But then, to Molly's relief, he mulled that over. "Okay, so she does have some redeeming qualities. She did raise a lot of money with that rummage sale."

Ann chimed in. "And Molly told me what a good time you had together when you watched the Cavs play—and babysat Laila. I'm sorry I missed seeing that."

With a quick shake of his head, presumably at his daughters' not-so-soft sell, he took a quick peek at the house across the street. "Maybe you're both right, then, and she's not that bad."

Stunned, Molly and Ann exchanged silent high fives.

Neither of them dared to say anything more.

Pop shrugged into his coat. His mouth twitched with a smile he couldn't suppress, and his eyes twinkled. Molly should have known he'd given in too easily.

"You girls think you're so smart, pushing your dad at a woman he doesn't seem to want. But for your information, I can make my own friends." He paused, then said with a laugh, "I'd already planned to ask Natalie out. And you two can kindly close your mouths. They're hanging open."

After a long moment he ambled across the kitchen and through the dining room to the front door, leaving them still gaping after him.

"Guess I'd better head her off," he said, his posture that of a doomed man, although Molly knew now that was mainly a pose. "I can teach her a thing or two about those peonies this spring. And she makes a mean cup of coffee," he added. "We'll see how it goes."

As soon as the door closed behind him, Molly and Ann danced in place.

"He was tweaking us!" Molly said.

"I know, but I can't believe it. For how long?"

Molly said, "I thought he just needed a little shove."

"I guess not. As he said, he did this on his own."

They sat at the table to drink their coffee, and after a few moments, Molly returned to their earlier topic.

"Now, let's hear more about Jeff...."

"I think I love him," Ann murmured without hesitation.

Molly got up to hug her.

And Ann said with a grin, "He and Ernie are quite a package deal."

For the first time in a long while, Molly saw true happiness on her sister's face and fresh hope for the future. Molly prayed that her own unhappiness this morning didn't show and dampen Ann's better mood.

Ann gave her a thoughtful look. "And you?"

"Me?" She shrugged but couldn't hide the sadness inside after all. "You know. I'll be okay. I've been there before—and don't I sound like a real case?"

Ann gazed at her for another long moment. "He still makes your motor run, doesn't he?" She went on without waiting for Molly's answer. "Don't even try to say no. I can see for myself. And I warned him not to do wrong by you again. Yet I saw that look in his eyes at the rummage sale. I see how he is with Laila." She paused. "If I can change, then why not Brig? Jeff keeps telling me a lot of years have gone by. And he's right."

"Please don't tell me to think about that. I have."

"Maybe you should *do* something instead," Ann said.

Molly glanced at the ceiling. They could both hear Brig now, crossing into the hall and starting down the stairs. What a morning this was turning out to be. First Ann. Then Pop. With luck, their isolated lifestyles would be changing for the better. That left only Molly. After Brig left, she would be the one alone.

"Maybe we've all been hiding out," she said just as Brig hit the last step.

MOLLY COULDN'T BEAR THIS.

Tall and straight, he walked into the kitchen

with the baby in the crook of one arm. His eyes showed a combination of emotions: unhappiness at leaving, she wanted to think. *Believe it or not, I wish I didn't have to go.* Yet she could see that underlying excitement, the eagerness to get back into battle once more. Molly had seen that look the day he left eight years ago.

She wasn't going to change him. As if after last night she needed another reminder of her own foolishness.

He passed Laila to her. Beside her, Ann bent to kiss the baby. Then to Molly's surprise, she went up on her tiptoes to kiss Brig on the cheek.

"You're all right, Brig. At least I'm leaning that way. You hurry with that mission of yours. Come back safe." She paused. "Come back," Ann said.

Molly's eyes were already misting over, even when she knew how pointless tears would be.

"See you at the office, big sister," Ann murmured, squeezing Molly's shoulder before she headed out the back door, obviously intent upon leaving them alone. "I plan to enjoy these last few days of relative peace before the place is filled with dust and the whine of saws, the *rat-a-tat-tat* of nail guns." At the door she looked back at Molly. "Remember what you just said."

After that there was silence. Molly couldn't seem to break it. She tried not to even look at Laila in her arms, as she had avoided doing on her first night in this house, but after a moment she couldn't resist. This morning Laila looked especially adorable in a pink-and-white top, pink tights and little white baby shoes, her first pair, although she was months away from really needing them to walk. Brig had brushed her dark hair, somehow managing to keep her still enough to form a tiny ponytail wrapped with a pink-and-green ribbon.

Molly almost smiled at the vision of Brig playing hairdresser, wrestling with a minuscule elastic and a squirmy Laila at the same time. As if he sensed her thought, he did smile.

"It wasn't easy," he said, "but I wanted to take extra time with her this morning before we travel."

At the word *we,* she flinched. She felt as if someone had jumped out of the bushes and punched her in the stomach.

"You're taking her with you?" Molly could

barely breathe. "What about the nanny you were going to hire?"

Brig looked away. "Last night, after we talked, I realized what was bothering me. I can't leave Laila with Patti this suddenly, trust her without really knowing her, even as good for the job as she seems." He hesitated. "Then in the middle of the night I remembered one of the posts the team had sent while I was here. You know they love Laila— a bunch of tough guys who melt every time they see her—and, well, there it was right in front of me. 'We would all adopt her, if we could.'"

"Oh," Molly said, surprised that the word actually came out. Her throat had closed. "I see." Yet she didn't. Surely the group adopting Laila wasn't an option.

Brig didn't appear to hear the tightness in her voice or see the sorrow that must show on her face. But then, he wasn't listening to her or looking at her.

"And I realized all over again that we're a family in our own way. We don't leave anyone behind. When someone gets wounded or…killed, like Sean, we take over to help his wife, his kids." He couldn't seem to meet Molly's eyes. "I called base, and after some back and forth, I now have three offers—two from guys who had quit the team this year, the other from a wife whose husband will be going with me on the mission."

Her heart rate was running wild. "That's... wonderful, Brig." No, it wasn't. Not from Molly's standpoint. He had found the solution for Laila, for now, and because Molly wouldn't take the risk last night, both Laila and Brig would be leaving now. She should have known he'd come up with something beyond the baby staying next door close to Molly, who had all but rejected her last night.

"Wouldn't you know?" he said. "Laila didn't move a muscle while I dressed her. She just stared at me. She must sense we're leaving."

Molly couldn't answer and Brig shifted. If he started one of those stiff speeches again, she would melt into a puddle on the floor.

"About the nanny," he said. "That was clumsy of me. I didn't know how to tell you, Molly." He paused. "Well. Guess we'd better take off. Today's our travel day and getting Laila settled before I report for duty tomorrow morning."

Across the street Pop and Natalie had gone inside to share coffee, tea and conversation.

The street looked empty—until Molly saw a cab roll up to the curb in front of the house, and her pulse lurched. Brig and Pop had returned his rental car yesterday. This was it.

Hadn't she known since he turned up at her Valentine's Day party that this would be the end of his surprise visit?

"Walk me out?" he said.

"Of course." Aching in every part of her being, she followed him through the house. But at the door Molly balked. Hiding her face, she kissed Laila and gave her back to him, her throat constricting. "I'm sorry, Brig, but no. I can't."

"We'll say goodbye here, then," he said and laid a gentle hand, his strong warrior's hand, against her cheek. As if she understood the moment, Laila stayed quiet in his arms, her dark gaze moving between them, searching. Molly yearned to touch her once more but didn't dare. If she did, she wouldn't be able to let go.

Goodbye. That one word sounded so final.

Instead of saying it, she touched Brig's forearm and made her own little speech. She might not get another chance. "Brig, before you go. I need to say something…. That years ago when you left, I told myself not to remember any of the good times we'd had. I vowed to put you out of my life—because that's what I thought you wanted." She felt hard muscle under her hand. "But I won't ever forget. And I want you to know…"

His voice was husky. "I'm forgiven?"

"You're forgiven." She gazed down at Laila. "I know it's difficult right now, but you were right to take her after Sean died, to bring her here. To rescue her," she added. "Because that's really what you did. Maybe…that was your greatest, and best, mission."

"Ah, Molly." Brig glanced toward the curb and the waiting cab. She sensed the driver must be a moment away from tapping the horn with impatience.

Brig didn't go on. Maybe there were no more words to say. Their oh-so-different lives would be lived again on opposite sides of the world, just as they had been for the past eight years.

She squared her shoulders. "If you don't go, you'll miss your flight. I'll worry about you," she murmured, "and…well, what Ann said."

Come back.

But would he ever? Brig was a confirmed risk taker. He always had been and Molly was not, last night being only the newest proof of that. Like Brig with his elite team, she had made her choice, too—to stay here in her own small corner of the world.

For another moment, very much in the present and one she wanted desperately to avoid, Brig looked at Molly.

"This is hard," he said. "Harder than ever."

Brig gazed deeply into Molly's eyes. He bent toward her, and she thought he would kiss her, but he straightened as if pulling himself together, as she was trying to do. Unable to speak, Molly leaned to kiss the baby once more but couldn't say a word either to Laila or Brig. He said, "Let's go, cupcake," and started down the porch steps.

Molly stood there.

And watched him go.

Her world, she thought, had suddenly become as narrow as Pop's.

SHE WAS STILL standing there, arms aching with emptiness, when Brig reached the front walk. Molly drank in every step he took, watched his strong back and his broad shoulders and the way he carried Laila effortlessly. At some earlier point he had put his duffel bag, her three suitcases and the baby's car seat by the curb.

Molly clenched her hands. What would it be like to have to leave like this? To pack most of your belongings in one military-issue bag and jet off halfway around the world into unspeakable danger? To deprivation and hardship with no clean water or hot food or a soft bed to sleep in? To have your very life hang in the balance every day? To fear—because only a fool wouldn't, that this time you might not come home again? To feel so utterly alone?

Lost in her own misery, she'd never considered that before. Not really.

Eight years ago, just like this, Brig had left her. He'd broken their engagement to follow his dream, and to become, yes, the man he was now.

How unfair she had been to blame him but not herself. To keep blaming him still this time for who he was then, instead of who he had become.

He loved Laila with all his heart. He had loved Sean and Zada, too. He grieved for them and had blamed himself. It was a heavy burden to carry.

Maybe years ago Brig had even felt as she did now, but she had simply stood there then, too, and, without fighting, let him leave. Did she face eight more years now, if not forever, alone and lonely?

Though Ann had seen it before she did, Molly had said the words.

Maybe we've all been hiding out.

Because Little Darlings was more than her means of earning a living—as much as Brig's elite unit was more than a paycheck to him. The center was also her refuge. Like Molly's cozy bedroom in Pop's house filled with the remnants of her marriage to Andrew. His shirt hanging in the closet, for example—until Molly, after her visit to the Hyde Park house, had finally packed it away with her memories.

What if her careful existence wasn't enough? And someday, even with the new expansion, Little Darlings wouldn't be, either? Then what would she do? Molly's restlessness wasn't that new. And in this moment, she knew why.

Yes, Andrew was gone and she had made her peace with that loss, but there were other kinds of loss, too. Other kinds of love. New and old.

She and Ann and Pop had hidden from the world together. But Molly wasn't doing her father any good by living with him, enabling him to keep to himself. And even Ann had her own apartment. Now her sister's future looked bright with Jeff and Ernie. Pop might find some kind of happiness, too, or at least companionship, with Natalie. But what about Molly? The happiness she had wished for them was genuine. But wasn't such happiness what Molly wanted for herself?

As Brig reached the middle of the walk, she heard Laila whimper. And in a flash, with Ann's words in mind, Molly knew what to do.

The important thing is not to waste the time you have.

Brig's grandmother Collier was a wise woman, Molly had thought during that hospital visit in Indiana, but she hadn't really gotten the message then. For anyone, for everyone, safety was nothing but an illusion.

Molly would never know if her marriage might have survived. She couldn't know with Brig, either. She had sent Andrew off that last morning, though, in anger, and she couldn't do the same now, in sorrow, with Brig.

If the future held more loss, perhaps it also held joy and love. Life. And part of that was taking this first ever, and most important, risk. For Molly it was more than time.

"Brig!" she called. "Wait!"

And on that glad cry Molly took off running.

As HE WALKED down the path to the waiting taxi, Brig's steps dragged.

The past few minutes had been the hardest he'd ever known. Harder than when Sean had died in the bombing at the hospital with Zada. Harder than his decision to accept guardianship of Laila and bring her to the States without knowing how to even change a diaper.

If Molly hadn't stepped in then...

But she had. She had.

The past weeks had turned him into someone else, someone better, he hoped. But what about now? And Molly. If only he had something else to offer her except long separations and uncertainty whether he would come back to her alive, in one piece, time after time.

Last night he'd almost begged her to take Laila—and Molly had imagined he was proposing again. She'd had that much faith in him, that much trust after what he'd done to her before.

Instead, because he hadn't said the right words, Brig remembered the humiliation and embarrassment in her eyes. After all her losses, she needed security, not a battle-hardened soldier whose every day was filled with risk, who was now carrying a baby dressed in pink to a waiting cab. A baby who was beginning to squall—as if she, too, didn't want to leave.

Maybe Laila was your best mission, Molly had said.

In the middle of the walk, he stopped. Even though the team had stepped up to help now, he owed Laila more than that. But above all, he owed Molly.

Someday you'll have to come home, Brigham, his grandmother had told him. *Don't wait until it's too late.*

He had nothing to offer Molly except his love. Why hadn't he seen it before? That was all she'd ever wanted from him.

At the same instant he turned with Laila screaming her head off, he heard Molly's voice call out.

"Brig! Wait!"

To his amazement, she was running toward him.

Brig tightened his hold on the baby and he ran, too. They met in the center of the walk, and with Laila between them—and a part of them—he hauled Molly into his arms.

"I can't leave you like this," he said hoarsely.

"I can't let you go like this. Not again." She spoke into the crook of his neck. "I'll care for Laila, Brig. It was crazy for me not to offer. Of course I will. There's no need to take her with you...your teammates will understand."

She drew away, already lifting—prying—the crying baby from his arms. A second later she rubbed her nose against Laila's tiny one and the baby stopped fretting. She looked up at Molly with clear recognition in her dark eyes. And smiled that perfect smile.

"You know what you're getting into here?" he said, his gaze turning serious. "If you take Laila, and something happens to me over there like it did Sean..."

She shook her head. "It can't. I won't let it."

He couldn't help but smile. She meant it, too. "But if it does..." He insisted she consider the possibility that had been weighing more and more on his mind lately. As she'd said, he was a father now. He had to make contingency plans.

"If something did happen...Laila would stay with me," Molly said. "I love her, Brig."

"Okay, then," he said on a wave of relief. "As soon as I get back to base, I'll have the proper documents added to my file."

But Molly hadn't finished. "One more thing…" She raised up to kiss him. "Brig, I do love you," she said. "I always have."

"Same here." He briefly closed his eyes. "I love you, too, Molly."

At that moment the door across the street opened and Thomas stepped out. He must have seen the cab. He jogged over to Brig, clapped him on the shoulder and said a few encouraging words that Brig, feeling dazed, frankly didn't comprehend. All he knew was that he had Thomas's acceptance after all. Thomas grinned as he plucked Laila from Molly's embrace, carried her back up the walk and went into the house. The door closed behind him. With no warning for Brig this time.

Alone with Molly, Brig took a shaken breath, knowing the words he was about to utter were the right ones. "So here's what we'll do."

Her eyes were glowing. "Orders, soldier?"

"I learned from the master—the admiral, my mother still calls him. She followed him all over the globe." He paused. "Could you do that, Molly?"

She appeared to think about that. "I'm not the best traveler, but I did fine on the trip to

Indiana. That's a start." She smiled. "I'm ever better at waiting."

"But you won't have to," he decided. For some time Brig had been pondering the end of his career in black ops. He had Laila to think of now, and pretty soon there'd be new recruits running up his back anyway, eager to take his place, and rightly so. And he had Molly to consider.

He would always take pride in his service—for the rest of his life he'd still be one of them. But several of his teammates had already retired to spend more time with their families. Why had it taken Brig so long to realize that his own priorities had changed, too?

"Listen," he told Molly as the cabbie blew his horn impatiently. "There's nothing I can do today about taking off. My team is waiting. Something's heating up on the Pakistan border—and to set your mind at ease about where I'll be, I've just leaked classified information." He smiled, only half joking. "But I've been thinking for a while now." He looked into her eyes. "I need to fulfill my obligation for another year, but when that ends, I'll move on to something…safer."

She stared at him. "You'd really 'hang it up'? Take a desk job?"

"No, I'd still want to do something physical. Like training other warriors." A sudden doubt crossed his mind. "Of course, you'd have to move, at least once—if you can leave Little Darlings."

Her smile grew, happiness in her eyes. "Brig, I've been thinking, too. Even after the commission approved the expansion for Little Darlings, it didn't feel quite right. Now I know why." She hesitated, as if mulling over what to say, then she went on in a stronger tone, "I've made a decision, too. I'm going to turn the nursery part of the business over to Ann. She's so good with the babies, and she's more than capable at managing our staff. But—and this is a concession to Natalie and the neighbors—I'm going to keep the center as it is. There'll be plenty of room for children from birth to age two who won't be outdoors to play that much. No noise," she murmured. "I'll split the business in half. Then a newer building for the preschoolers can go up on a less residential site. My architect and I can look for the right location here before I leave. I'll have the year, won't I?"

"No more than that," he said.

"I'm already thinking about another idea. What if I started a service near the base for soldiers who are deploying somewhere and have to leave their kids behind? A kind of clearinghouse where people take turns providing in-home care while other parents are gone?" She grinned. "I'll call it Away from Home."

"l like it. If you're willing to, we could buy a nice house in Virginia with plenty of outdoor space for Laila. Let her make all the noise she wants. After the wedding we'll get right on that and—"

Her eyes widened. "*This* is a proposal?"

Carpe diem, he thought. Seize the day. "This time a real one." He pulled Molly close to kiss her. In the background the cabbie honked the horn again, but Brig ignored him. "Will you marry me, Molly Darling?"

She didn't hesitate. "Yes. You know I will."

After another, longer kiss he drew away.

"Then that's settled, too. We're settled." He brushed a stray strand of hair from her cheek. "You and Laila start planning the wedding. I promise I'll be there."

"I'm counting on you."

Brig had been about to take a step toward the waiting taxi but stopped. A chill snaked down his spine. "That's what Sean said to me right before he went to the hospital."

And at long last, Brig forgave himself for he accident that had taken Sean Denton's life nd Zada's. Because in honoring his commitment to them and raising Laila with Molly, he vould honor his friends, too. He knew they vould have liked the woman he loved, liked ner as a mother for their child.

Here, in the hometown he'd left so many years ago, he had not only found care for Laila, but in Molly, he'd found care for himself.

Their hands linked, she walked him the rest of the way to the cab. The driver gave them a thumbs-up and grinned. Before he opened the door, Brig slowly released Molly.

"I'll be back," he said, holding her gaze with the promise.

"I'll be waiting." Molly closed the small distance between them—and the larger one of their past—to kiss him again. "I'd wait for you forever."

With her vow, his spirit lifted, but he'd taken enough risks in his life. She wouldn't need to wait long this time. He would do his best to make this mission the shortest, safest, of his career.

Brig climbed into the cab, remembering how he'd come to Liberty Courthouse weeks

ago with Laila in the pouring rain. This morn
ing the sun was peeking through the clouds
the temperature was milder than it had been
all winter and spring was in the air.

The cabbie tooted the horn before driving
off toward the airport, leaving Laila's car sea
and bags at the curb. Brig saw Molly waving
On his way to yet another foreign hole-in-the-
wall, he watched until, appearing smaller and
smaller in the rear window, she finally disappeared. Just for now.

Brig relaxed against the seat cushion, ready
for whatever one of his last missions might
hold.

Bring it on, he thought.

In his mind, in his heart, he had already
come home.

From his own internal war.

Home, at last, to Molly.

* * * * *

ARGER-PRINT BOOKS!

T 2 FREE
RGER-PRINT NOVELS *Love Inspired*
US 2 FREE
STERY GIFTS

rger-print novels are now available...